THE KEYS OF
ELECTRUM

GRANT HENNING
J.D. HENNING

THE KEYS OF ELECTRUM

A MODERN-DAY
MYSTERY
OF ANCIENT
EGYPT

TATE PUBLISHING & *Enterprises*

Published by Tate Publishing & Enterprises, LLC
127 E. Trade Center Terrace | Mustang, Oklahoma 73064 USA
1.888.361.9473 | www.tatepublishing.com

Tate Publishing is committed to excellence in the publishing industry. The company reflects the philosophy established by the founders, based on Psalm 68:11,
"The Lord gave the word and great was the company of those who published it."

Book design copyright © 2011 by Tate Publishing, LLC. All rights reserved.
Cover design by Amber Gulilat
Interior design by Stephanie Woloszyn

Published in the United States of America

ISBN: 978-1-61777-399-0
1. Fiction / Mystery & Detective / Historical   2. Fiction / Action & Adventure
11.03.22

DEDICATION

To Grant, the best friend, father, and coauthor a son could ever have. To my mother, Ruth, whose love has sustained us on so many incredible journeys and touched so many lives. To my wife, Angel, the very best part of my life's adventures; and to our children— Jonathan, Madison, and Naomi—who fill us with such joy.

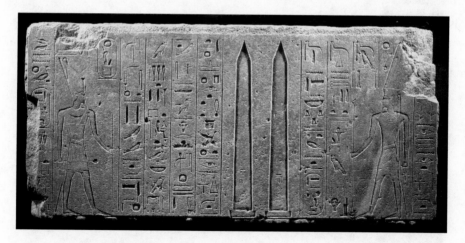

This stone tablet of Queen Hatshepsut (on left) presenting a pair of granite obelisk to god Amen-Ra (on right) was found inside of the 3rd Pylon of the Karnak Great Temple of Amun. The tablet is now kept on display in the Luxor Museum. The opening inscription reads, "I was sitting in the palace and I remembered the One who created me; my heart directed me to make for him two obelisks of electrum, that their pyramidions might mingle with the sky amid the august pillared hall between the great pylons of [Tuthmosis I]"

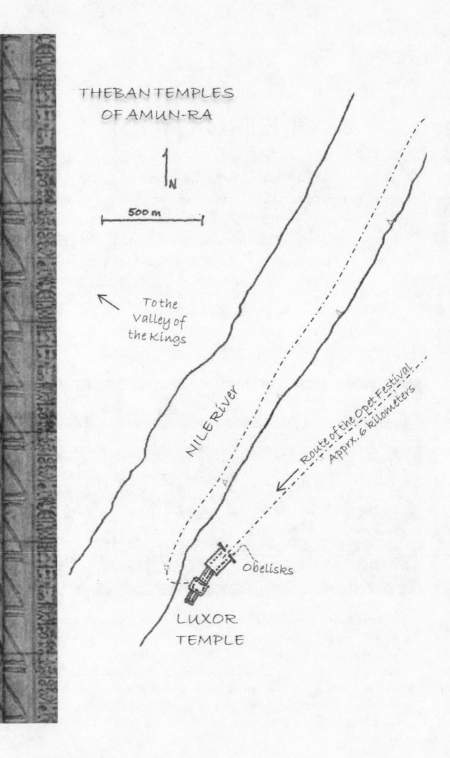

THEBAN TEMPLES
OF AMUN-RA

N

500 m

To the
Valley of
the Kings

NILE River

Route of the Opet Festival
Apprx. 6 kilometers

Obelisks

LUXOR
TEMPLE

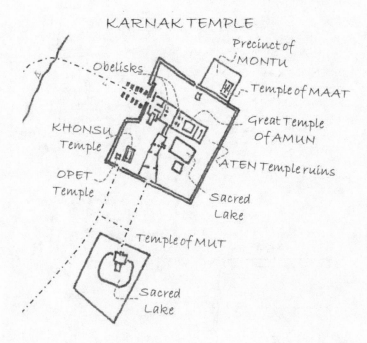

KARNAK TEMPLE

Obelisks

Precinct of
MONTU

Temple of MAAT

Great Temple
of AMUN

KHONSU
Temple

OPET
Temple

ATEN Temple ruins

Sacred
Lake

Temple of MUT

Sacred
Lake

Annotated Map of Luxor Temple, Thebes

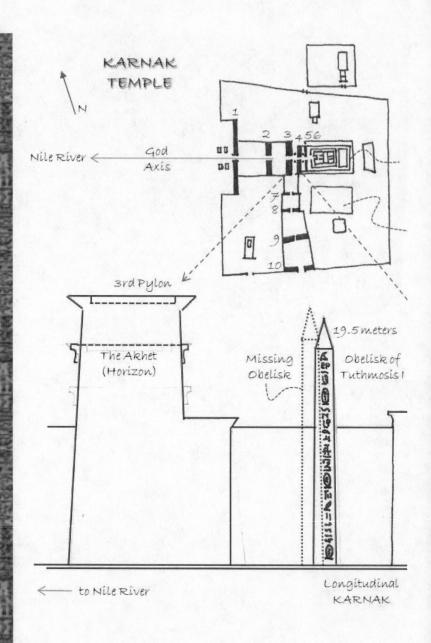

KARNAK
TEMPLE

N

Nile River ← God
            Axis

1

2   3 4 5 6

7
8

9

10

3rd Pylon

The Akhet
(Horizon)

Missing
Obelisk

19.5 meters

Obelisk of
Tuthmosis I

← to Nile River

Longitudinal
KARNAK

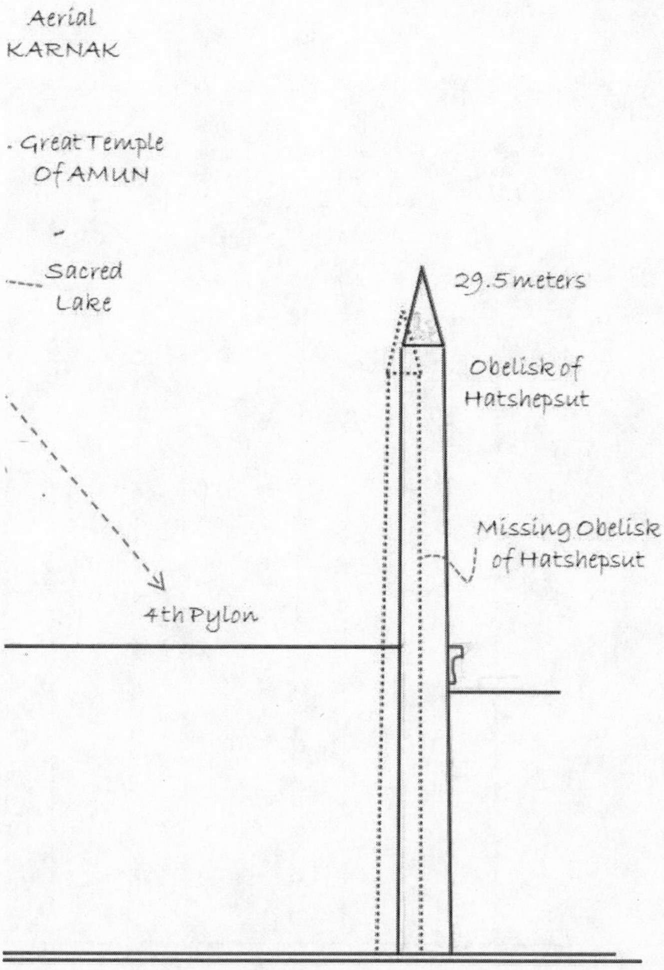

Aerial
KARNAK

. Great Temple
  Of AMUN

.

---- Sacred
     Lake

29.5 meters

Obelisk of
Hatshepsut

Missing Obelisk
of Hatshepsut

4th Pylon

Annotated Map of Karnak Temple, Thebes

ANCIENT EGYPTIAN OBELISKS
Still Standing

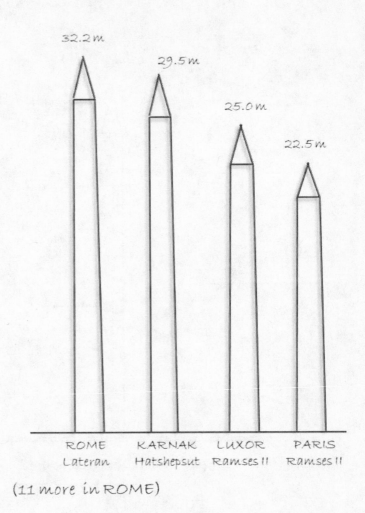

32.2 m

29.5 m

25.0 m

22.5 m

ROME
Lateran

KARNAK
Hatshepsut

LUXOR
Ramses II

PARIS
Ramses II

(11 more in ROME)

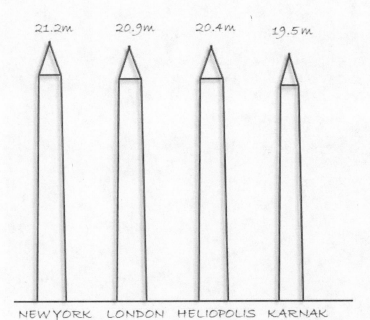

21.2m   20.9m   20.4m   19.5m

NEW YORK   LONDON   HELIOPOLIS   KARNAK
Tuthmosis III   Tuthmosis III   Sesostros I   Tuthmosis I

Annotated Drawing of London Obelisk,
Thames Embankment, with measurements dated June 27.

CHAPTER

1

THE HIGH PRIEST OF AMUN STOOD atop the great outer wall of Karnak, his fist crushing a papyrus scroll. Hemenhoreb stood motionless with a powerful gaze over his elaborate complex of temples, his lips tight and muscles tense, emboldened by the warm summer evening. Workers scrambled to complete the last etchings in the fading light. Priests milled about the vast courtyards. He had read the Pharaoh's decree dozens if not hundreds of times in disbelief. Under his breath, he cursed the messenger who delivered the scroll; the scribe who wrote it; and the young pharaoh who dared to challenge the gods and, even more, to challenge the priesthood of Amun. Hemenhoreb felt the anger welling up as he watched the great sun, Amun-Re, descend beyond the Nile in the western sky.

His fist tightened fiercely around the papyrus scroll as he whispered a vow. How could the Pharaoh abandon the blessed Amun? Why would he forsake this sacred temple ground in exchange for another? His mind closed on the brutal reality of the words of the scroll; and with such clarity as he had never felt before, he thought, *I will not be the last high priest of Amun.*

The adrenaline, the anger pulsing to a crescendo, the stately priest suddenly thrust his ornately decorated arms into the night sky and lifted his hands; with head tilted toward the heavens, Hemenhoreb repeated the vow to Amun-Re.

"Curse the pharaoh, and may Amun protect me so that I may do everything to preserve your dominion until my last breath."

In all his many years, Hemenhoreb had served the pharaohs well with his genius. Much of the glorious Karnak was constructed in his younger days under Amenhotep III by using his architectural mind, his passion for engineering perfection, and creativity worthy of the gods. His priests had overseen the construction, but it was he who had provided the vision and glorified both pharaohs and gods alike with his abilities. The known world marveled at Karnak, the Egyptian seat of religious power and prominence throughout the land. Now this decree, this heresy to worship only one god, the Aten, could not prevail. It would not prevail so long as the last high priest of Amun-Re had strength in his body and determination in his mind. In the last light of the setting sun, Hemenhoreb surveyed every shadow of the temple complexes, the sacred lake, festival halls, and centuries of tribute from Pharaohs long past extending impressively over hundreds of acres in the most detailed and elaborate sculptures of worship ever made.

Then he turned and descended the stairs on his way to the holy of holies to make unto Amun his greatest supplication. He dared not disturb Amun while he slipped peacefully below the western horizon into realm of Osiris, but his faithful Amun would understand that there could be no delay, that his very gate upon the earth was being threatened. He would address the high council of *hem-netjer* priests in the morning at their sunrise assembly; but tonight, he would call on the power of the gods for the greatest vision they could give him. Somehow, in his strength, he must resist the god-incarnate pharaoh. His mind racing, Hemenhoreb walked in a slow, regal pace across the darkening courtyard in utter contrast to the violent thoughts crashing in his mind.

I could poison the pharaoh. I could have him murdered. I could separate him from power. Yes, take away the power of his god. Take from him the authority of his god. Take away the treasure of his god.

Suddenly stopping before the temple of Ptah and examining the treasury quarters to the east, Hemenhoreb knew what he would do.

I will remove from Pharaoh the contents of the treasury, all the wealth of Thebes. And the wealth of Amun will never glorify another, he thought proudly. *I will protect all that is Amun's and crush the pharaoh.*

CHAPTER

2

MORE THAN 3,300 YEARS LATER in the same part of Egypt…

The hot Egyptian sun beat down on the gray-haired American as he slowly climbed the stairs with a heavy leather satchel in his hand. Flies buzzed around his face, and he could feel the day's sweat on his neck. Dr. Donald Romiel enjoyed the white, contemporary-style flat in Luxor that had been his home away from home intermittently these past three years; but the outside stairs to the second-story apartment were not getting any easier for his old legs to climb, and the summer heat made him strain for breath. The University of Cairo Archeology Department had provided the large flat for the visiting professor when he first began consulting on the Opet Festival project in Luxor. As he strained on the last few steps to the decorative, black-tiled landing that led to his door, he remembered the spectacular view of the Nile that the apartment offered and why each climb was always worth it after a long day in the dust. With his free hand, he fished his keys out of his dirty, brown vest, only to find the door slightly ajar.

The archeology professor moved slowly closer, looking carefully at the lock and listening for any sounds for concern. There was clear evidence of a forced entry, and Dr. Romiel considered his next move with caution. He peered through the narrow opening, scanning for movement, being careful not to touch the door while he quietly slipped his keys back into his pocket. For a few minutes, he waited in silence, thinking what he should do. The view through the cracked door was not enough to see beyond the foyer. Curiosity, as it often did, got the better of the professor; and pressing the door open slowly, he slipped into the apartment.

As his first view of the apartment struck him, time stopped and the professor felt sheer confusion as the blood rushed from his face. Everything in the apartment had been trashed. Dishes were strewn across the living room floor in shattered pieces. Cushions from the couch had been sliced, foam bits scattered about. The curtains had been pulled down, and a rod hung diagonally across the otherwise-picturesque, oversized window framing the spectacular view of the Nile. His small TV lay splintered on its face in the corner of the room, and strewn everywhere on top of the destroyed furniture were his clothes. Most terrifying of all was the horrific splattering of red paint throughout the otherwise-neutral-colored walls of the apartment. In the same red paint, written in plain English on the wall above the couch, the professor could read the large, frightening words from the front doorway: "Leave Egypt now or die."

Without a sound, he quickly backed away from the door, moving deftly across the landing with his leather satchel still gripped tightly in his hands. There could be no hesitating; the message was clear. This was the fiercest and final threat that he would endure. Professor Romiel had rehearsed his next step for several weeks. Ever since he had reported his suspicions to the ministry of the interior and his warnings had gone unheeded, he knew something was wrong. He was being watched, and even his closest Egyptian colleagues seemed to be avoiding him. Now he knew what he had to do. He was driven, not so much by fear as by determination, to see justice done and to avoid anything that might prevent him from doing what he knew he had to do. Summoning inward strength, he was down to the street in no time and, with hardly a break in his stride, had hailed a cab and jumped quickly into the back seat.

"Luxor Airport *imshee allatool!*" he shouted. "*Y'Allah imshee!*" the professor shouted again at the driver, his own hands trembling and his breath coming at shorter intervals. He did not look back. The taxi stopped within sight of the sign reading *DEPARTURES* in Arabic and English. Romiel handed the driver a large bill and did not wait for change. At the service desk of the tiny Luxor airport, he quickly confirmed his flight to Cairo and reserved standby passage to New York.

Once on the ground in Cairo, Professor Romiel looked carefully behind him to see if anyone was watching as he raced toward the gate to board American Airlines flight 115 bound for J.F. Kennedy Airport with a brief connecting stop in London. He was fortunate there had been a cancellation so that he could change planes from Luxor and get the only evening flight out from Cairo departing at 5:30 p.m. He was still clutching his only luggage: his leather briefcase filled with the documentation from his research project. No doubt there was information in this briefcase that had provoked someone to destroy his Luxor apartment so thoroughly. If he was right, his briefcase held the key to the greatest archeological treasure in all of history.

There was no time before his flight to communicate with his daughter in Yonkers; his sponsoring agency in New York City; or with Brad Beck, a close sailing friend and a former Coast Guard intelligence officer. He knew Brad would have some ideas about how to proceed with this situation. He would carefully plan the phone calls to his daughter and Brad in flight and place them in London while he was making his next flight connection to New York City. He would have to e-mail his sponsor, because he had no phone number for him. He thought he might also have enough time to complete his measurements of Cleopatra's Needle at the Victoria Embankment on the Thames in London.

Normally, Romiel dreaded the twenty-four-hour connecting flight to NYC; but this time he was grateful, because he needed the time to think. Who was behind this? Why were they after him? Why didn't the minister of interior's office staff take his suspicions seriously? What should he do now? He settled into his coach-class seat between two British tourists and carefully placed his locked leather briefcase under the seat in front of him. He felt exhausted, but he had no desire to sleep. He hoped the stewardess would soon appear with a hot cup of black coffee. He took a small pad of paper and a pen from his coat pocket and began a list of things to do. He could always think better with pen and paper in hand.

He had to put an end to this scheme before it was too late. This had to be the greatest archeological discovery in a hundred years, if not ever; and whom could he trust? Time was running out, and his fear was growing that the treasure was being stolen in plain sight.

CHAPTER

3

THE NEXT DAY IN A SUBURB OF NEW York City…

Bradford Beck arrived early. Finding an open stretch of curb in front of the Nyack Boat Club, he pulled his blue GMC Yukon snugly to the curb and jumped out. Sail bags filled his trunk, and one by one he lifted them to the sidewalk. The sun was just emerging above the trees in early morning twilight over the Hudson River. Hook Mountain rose prominently in the Western sky. Brad tethered his sunglasses around his neck, gathered up the long sail bags, and headed down the stairs around the boat club through the lush, overgrown garden, stepping quickly toward the delicious smell of bacon. Even at a quarter to seven, the wind was beginning to rustle the trees and the glow of the rising sun revealed not a cloud in the sky. Brad was charged up. This was going to be a perfect regatta weekend to finally win back the Ensign Cup.

As he reached the back deck of the boat club, the enticing smell of bacon was joined with the aroma of coffee and the sound of a sizzling grill in the sailors' kitchen. Brad passed around the club deck that was lined with a dozen high-backed, white rocking chairs and made his way into the sailors' lounge.

"Good morning, Brad," Hoshi sang out from behind the breakfast grill. "What'll it be this morning?"

As he greeted Hoshi, he chuckled. Where else in the world could a sailor be served breakfast by a Nobel Prize-contending organic chemist. A fine yachtsman, an early riser, a humble chemist twice in contention for the elusive Nobel prize, Dr. Hoshi Nabuya enjoyed the role of weekend breakfast chef; and there too he excelled.

"Thanks, Hoshi. I'd like an egg over easy, bacon on white, and some of that great coffee I smell."

Brad kneeled and stuffed a sail bag into the open lockers and checked his cell phone. As more sailors strolled sleepily into the lounge in search of food, Brad hit the speed dial for voice mail; and as he pressed the phone to his ear, a warm, familiar voice greeted him.

"Brad, hi. It's Professor Romiel, Don Romiel. I need your help."

The recorded voice turned distinctly fearful; and Brad stood up, listening with more intensity.

"I can't talk. I think I'm in danger. I'm on a flight from Cairo, and I will be in JFK on American Airlines flight one fifteen at eleven p.m. late Friday night. We have to meet."

The professor paused for a moment as airport noises filled the phone. A boarding announcement ended, and the professor wrapped up the call.

"Brad, please call me as soon as you can. I think you'll know what to do."

The message ended, and Brad followed the phone's methodical voice instructions to save the message for fourteen days.

Brad kicked himself for leaving his phone in the car after work Friday. "The professor is already here," he thought as he moved to an open plastic patio table and settled quickly into a white, plastic chair, his mind racing. Glancing at his Citizen sailing watch, he thought, *How long has it been since I talked to the professor? February? No, January. It must have been just after the boat club's annual roast the first week of January. That was five months ago! What kind of trouble could the demure retiring archeologist possibly have gotten into? Why would the professor need my help?*

Brad dialed the professor's number, pressed the phone to his ear, and concentrated on the rings. More sailors were making their way into the lounge, sail bags and oversized coffee mugs in hand.

"Brad, your bacon egg sandwich!" shouted Dr. Nabuya as he held up Brad's paper-wrapped breakfast sandwich and turned to take more food orders. Brad waved with his free hand and prepared to leave a voice message. Then he heard a click and then silence. He looked at the phone and saw he was connected but without voice mail instructions.

"Hello? Professor? Don, are you there? Can you hear me? It's Brad. Hello?"

Silence. Then a stern voice came on the line.

"What is your name?"

"Who is this?" Brad responded.

"This is the professor's assistant. What is your business with Dr. Romiel?"

Brad thought for a moment, puzzled by the terse exchange. "Where is the professor? Can I please speak to him? I'm returning his call."

"The professor cannot be disturbed right now. Would you like to leave him a message?"

"Can you tell me where he is? I need to meet with him. He said it was very important. What's your name?"

Suddenly, the call ended. Brad stared at his cell phone, confused by the voice of a stranger answering the professor's cell phone. *Did Don have an assistant? Who was that guy? Where is the professor? Is he all right? Something's wrong. The professor said he was in danger, and I didn't call him back in time.*

Brad felt a firm hand thump down on his right shoulder.

"Good morning, Skipper. How you doin' today?"

It was Foley Arnold, the lean, wiry foredeck trapeze artist of his crew and the most experienced sailor on Brad's team.

"Have you ordered breakfast yet?" Foley asked as he let go of Brad's shoulder with a friendly squeeze and flopped in the plastic chair next to the tall and perplexed-looking skipper.

Brad was always happy to see Foley. They had served together on the Coast Guard Cutter *Intrepid* and had shared many harrowing experiences. They had a lot of respect for each other, and their friendship went back more than a decade. Foley had gone on to serve as a deck officer on a buoy tender here on the Hudson. Now Foley was a private citizen and had become one of the finest graphic artists in the business. Brad had enlisted his help in designing several of the blade turbines they had been placing in the Hudson River in a new underwater experimental project to generate electricity for New York City. Brad's own experience as a Coast Guard diver was useful during the placement and inspection of the turbines.

Brad ignored the questions. Still holding the cell phone in his calloused hands, he said, "Listen, Foley," with heavy pause. "I think Don Romiel is in serious trouble. I just got a message from him, and it sounds like something bad is going down."

"Well, how bad? " Foley asked. "Is the professor hurt? Where is he?"

"That's just it. I don't know. I need to try to call him back and see if I can find him. He said he was flying in from Cairo and would arrive last night. I've got a bad feeling, a really bad feeling." Brad had that kind of intuition that could sense the favored side of the course long before the wind shifted and the fleet changed tacks. This time, it was not a winning feeling as ominous dread washed over him.

Most of the crews were in the lounge now, feeding on caffeine and protein for the long day ahead. Someone had dropped off Brad's breakfast sandwich and coffee at the table, and he began hungrily downing both as he thought through his options.

"I can't stay," he said. "I've got to do what I can to track down the professor and make sure he made it back all right. Tell the crew for me, Foley." Brad got to his feet. "Sails are right over there," he said, gesturing to the bags piled by the locker.

"Crew's here, Brad. Why don't you tell them yourself?" Foley waved over the three less-than-bright-eyed sailors coming in the door. Sarah Johnson, Billy Heckman, and Nigel Pearson made their way through the breakfast melee and gathered round the white, plastic table with questioning looks. They were casually clad like typical grad students looking for adventure to break the tedium of study during the week. Actually, Sarah and Billy were grad students at NYU, where Sarah studied archeology and had met Professor Romiel in the same department. Billy was a student of ancient history, and his interest in history was exceeded only by his interests in sailing and in Sarah. The professor had introduced them to the boat club on several weekend cruises. Nigel was a throw-off from an earlier generation. Originally from Britain, he was something of an anomaly, a wizened computer geek who now ran his own hedge fund. He was older and wealthier than anyone could guess by judging from his apparel and his jovial mood. His trading ventures had been so successful that he had been invited to become part owner of the boat club, where he and Hoshi often traded sailing stories. He loved sailing and hobnobbing with the younger generation and found this to be a therapeutic escape from the rigors of his trading activities.

"Guys, I'm sorry. I've got to run," Brad said apologetically.

"It seems Professor Romiel is in deep trouble," Foley piped in.

"Yes. Got a strange phone message from him. He said he was in danger and was leaving Cairo on the first plane out and should have arrived last night. I missed his call, haven't heard from him, and someone claiming to be his assistant answered his cell phone. Very strange. I've got to go find him, I'm sure you can manage without me just for today."

"That is weird," Sarah added. "He wasn't due back from his latest dig until September."

"Did he call any of you?" Brad asked quickly as he picked up his boat bag; pulled the zipper; and extracted a laminated chart of the race, bearing compass, grease pencil, and a few other items to pass along to the crew.

"No. Haven't heard from him in months," Billy stated with head shakes from Sarah and Nigel as well. "Sure enjoy sailing with him when he's in town but seems like he has been busier than ever this past year. Gosh. I really hope he's not in any serious trouble."

"Me too," Nigel added. "Anything we can do, Brad? What are you going to do?"

"I guess I should call his daughter, Allison, in Yonkers to see if she's heard from her father and then try to meet up with him as soon as I can." He zipped closed the bag after handing the selected items to Foley. "Here you are, Foley. You always wanted to skipper a regatta. Go win it. I'll call you guys as soon as I get in touch with Don."

With a few handshakes and a couple of half hugs with a bag in the way, Brad made his way out of the Nyack Boat Club just as swiftly as he had arrived.

CHAPTER

4

IN THE DARKNESS OF THE EARLY SUMMER
morning, Hemenhoreb convened the ten *hemnetjer* priests
of Amun to beseech the wisdom of the god. Gathered in a
small circle, some on wooden chairs inlaid with golden images, others standing near ornately colored walls, the elder
god-servant priests pressed in to hear the written proclamation of
Pharaoh as read from the papyrus scroll by a still tense and sleepless
Hemenhoreb. From the illumination of the torches, the tall, strong
features of the high priest reflected a godlike presence in a cramped
inner chamber of the Great Temple of Amun.

"I read to you now the decree of the Pharaoh Amenohpis IV,
and may Amun forgive the blasphemy of the words I speak in this
his temple.

"'My Lord has appointed me to be the overseer of the great city
of God and all its resplendent monuments and treasures. Let me
join myself to those who are holy and perfect in the divine other
world, and let me appear with them to behold your beauties in the
evening. I lift my hands to you in adoration where you, the Living
One, dwell. You are the Eternal Creator and are adored at your
setting in heaven. I have given my heart to you without wavering,
oh you who are the mightiest of all. So let it be known god is One
and Akhenaten is his appointed one of all mankind in which he

CHAPTER 5

BRAD RACED EAST ALONG HIGHWAY 87 across the Hudson River and then turned south toward Yonkers. He still had Allison and Don's home phone number on his cell phone directory. He remembered Allison as an attractive and intelligent young research librarian who lived alone with her father after her mother's death from cancer. After a quick call, he was even more puzzled to learn that the professor had phoned her from London the day before and had told her of his unexpected departure from Cairo, but he had never appeared that night as promised. He had said he would arrive home late Friday night and that he would explain everything then. He had told her not to worry, but the tone in his voice had the opposite of the intended effect. The most disconcerting news was that the professor had never arrived home, and Allison was beside herself.

"Please come quickly," she said.

As Brad turned his old Yukon SUV into the lane where the professor's house was situated overlooking the Hudson, he was surprised to see two police cars parked near the gate. He drove straight up the driveway and parked near the front door. A tall, middle-aged man in his fifties, wearing a wrinkled, brown sports coat, answered the door and peered at Brad curiously.

"I'm here to see Allison. What's going on? Where's Allison?" Brad asked.

"I'm afraid there's been an accident," the man said. "I'm Lieutenant Davis, homicide division. Miss Romiel is in the living room."

As they walked together toward the living room, the officer asked, "Who are you? What's your relationship to Professor Romiel?"

"I'm Brad Beck, a friend of the family," Brad replied as they rounded the corner into the spacious living room. There, seated on a sofa, was Allison, gazing down at the floor with moist eyes, her long, brown hair matted on her shoulders. Around her were two uniformed policemen and one female social worker.

Allison looked up immediately at Brad. "Oh Brad," she blurted out, "my Father's dead!"

The shock was apparent on Brad's face as his worst fears were confirmed. "I'm so sorry, Allison," Brad murmured as he moved toward her. "What happened?"

"It was apparently a mugging," Lieutenant Davis volunteered. "We found his body this morning in Central Park. He was stabbed. He had no wallet or identification beyond this business card that we found in his shirt pocket," he said, holding out Professor Romiel's NYU business card. "We contacted his university department, and they directed us here to his home. We have a few questions, and we'll need someone to come with us to identify the body."

"What was he doing in Central Park?" Brad asked. "He was on his way home from JFK."

"That's just what I was about to ask you," replied Lieutenant Davis. "The coroner placed the time of death at around midnight last night. No one seems to have any idea why he would visit the park at that hour, especially after a long trip from abroad. His body was found next to the large obelisk near the center of the park."

"I know Professor Romiel was doing research related to ancient Egyptian temples, but I can't imagine why he visited the park at that hour," Brad shared.

"Well, Miss Romiel, do you feel up to accompanying us to identify your father's body?" the lieutenant asked.

Allison sobbed softly as she reached in her nearby purse for something to wipe her eyes. Still dazed, she murmured, "Okay, I'll come."

Brad had already made up his mind to accompany Allison. And he had a few unanswered questions of his own. Besides, he still felt a twinge of guilt for missing the professor's call. If only he had met him at the airport, this might not have happened.

As the two of them sat somberly together in the backseat of the police car, Brad turned and asked, "Allison, exactly what did your father say in his phone message to you?"

"Well," Allison replied thoughtfully, "he seemed obviously worried about something. He said he'd left a phone message with you and had notified his sponsor by e-mail. Then he told me not to worry, that he would be home soon and would explain everything."

"Anything else? Try to remember. This could be important."

Allison furrowed her brows in concentration. "Not that I can— Oh! I forgot that he said he was planning to mail an important package to you from the airport. Oh, Brad, I can't believe this could happen to my dad. This is the worst day of my life."

Brad gave her a consoling hug. "I know, Allison. We'll find out what's going on. I promise we'll get to the bottom of this." Brad was convinced that Allison would find consolation in her strong faith to weather this storm, just has she had done in the case of her mother. "Just one more thing, Allison. What was your father doing in Egypt? I mean, what was the nature of his work and who was he working for?"

"I don't know exactly. His field was Egyptology, you know. Whenever a major research grant came through, he would take a leave from his classes at NYU and go off on some dig for weeks at a time. He would always keep in touch by phone or e-mail, but he seldom said anything about his work. He did ask me frequently to find references to early Egyptian archeological and historical publications. I saved all of his e-mails. I think his sponsor this time was some museum in the city."

CHAPTER 6

ALLISON AND BRAD WENT TO-gether with Lieutenant Davis to a basement room of the city morgue where they pulled the corpse out from the wall on a sliding drawer. Brad felt thankful under the circumstances that the attendant knew which drawer held the professor's body so they had no need to look in any other drawers. The attendant deftly unzipped the plastic body bag, and Allison sobbed softly as they recognized the pale, bearded face of the professor.

After the identification of the body and the relevant paperwork, Brad accompanied Allison back to her home. He felt a growing sense of protectiveness toward this attractive young lady. He could only imagine her feelings at the loss of her father. He learned she had an older sister in New Jersey married to an attorney. She would help Allison with the funeral arrangements. Allison was already on the phone with her sister as Brad excused himself and went out the door toward his parked car. He knew she needed to speak with her sister privately, and he needed some time alone to think about his next step.

Who was that guy who answered Professor Romiel's cell phone? Why would he have possession of his phone anyway? Brad knew that Nigel had the technical ability to run a GPS trace on the cell phone. It was now after noon, and the regatta would be over. He would call Nigel and tell him what had happened. Also, Brad needed to retrieve the package that Allison said her father had posted for him at the airport; unfortunately, that would not be delivered until Monday at the earliest. But perhaps that would give him time to visit the actual crime scene to see if some detail had been overlooked. Clearly the police were treating the professor's murder as a routine mugging and robbery, and certainly there were plenty of those in New York City; but something told Brad that this was much more than a simple mugging. He climbed into his car, took out his cell phone, and dialed up Nigel.

"Hey, Nigel! Are you still at the club?"

Nigel sounded exuberant. "Yeah. We won the first day of the regatta. Billy and Sarah went off to celebrate. Foley's still here with me. Did you find the professor?"

"Yes. I'm afraid so. It's not good. Allison and I just identified his body at the city morgue. The police think it was a mugging in Central Park. His cell phone was missing, so I need you to run a GPS trace on the phone."

"Good heavens! Of course. Give me the number, and I'll do whatever I can. How's Allison taking it?"

"Very poorly, I'm afraid." Brad gave Nigel the professor's cell phone number and asked him to put Foley on the line.

"What's up, Brad?" Foley asked impatiently.

"Well, it's a long story. Pretty awful. The professor was killed last night in Central Park. The police have written it off as a random mugging, but I'm sure there's more to it than that. How soon can you meet me here at the professor's home so we can go together to Central Park? I can fill you in on the way."

"I'll leave right away," Foley replied.

CHAPTER 7

BRAD AND FOLEY DECIDED TO PARK near the Van Cortlandt Park subway terminal and take the subway to the Eighty-First-Street exit on the west side of Central Park. They would walk from there to the obelisk that was located on the edge of the Great Lawn section near the center of the park. As they walked toward the subway entrance, Brad thought of the strange twists the day had brought so far and realized the day was still far from over. If all went well, they would still have several hours of daylight to examine the crime scene and decide their next step.

After they had flopped down tiredly in empty seats on the subway car, Brad turned to Foley and said, "There are several things here that just don't add up, Foley. For one thing, what was the professor doing in the park at midnight after a long flight from Cairo? And who was that guy with the professor's missing cell phone? I've tried to phone that number several times since, but there's never any answer. And the police lieutenant said something about the professor's body being found near an obelisk. Does the obelisk have something important to do with his work in Egypt?"

"You're right," Foley replied. "It doesn't make sense. The professor's just not the kind of guy to take unnecessary risks. Either he had some critical mission in the park or else..."

"Or else what?" Brad asked impatiently.

"Or else somebody kidnapped him at the airport and forced him to go there for a reason."

Finally, they reached the Eighty-First-Street stop, exited the subway car, and climbed the stairs two at a time to the open air above. As they reached the surface and turned into the park, Brad noticed a large sign advertising the Museum of Natural History. But he paid little attention at the time. Everything came as a jumbled mass into his consciousness along with the noise of automobile horns and the conversations of people sauntering or jogging in the park on a Saturday afternoon. Soon, they saw the obelisk appear through the trees.

Near the obelisk, a familiar, yellow-taped barrier had been erected to cordon off a small area. They saw two police officers removing the tape and packing equipment into a nearby police van.

As they approached the area, one of the officers turned and said, "Move on. This is a crime scene."

Brad explained that they were close friends of the victim and he had just come from the city morgue, where he had helped Lieutenant Davis identify the body. Now he needed more information.

The officer said, "All we know is that an officer on patrol found the body around two a.m. and called it in. It was a stabbing and a robbery. It happens here all the time. Usually these crimes are drug related."

"Was there anything unusual here at the scene?" Brad asked.

"Just the message the victim wrote in blood. Look over there. You can still see a little of it, but the crime scene people got their pictures and cleaned up most of it."

Brad and Foley peered over the tape at the capital letters A-T-O-N faintly visible in the fading afternoon light. Beside the letters, they could see an arrow pointed toward the obelisk. Clearly the professor was trying to send a message.

Brad decided to walk around the tape toward the obelisk in the direction the arrow was pointing. There was nothing special to be seen. At the base of the obelisk on one side of the pedestal, a bronze plate read, "This obelisk was erected first at Heliopolis, Egypt in 1600 B.C. It was removed to Alexandria in 12 B.C. by the Romans. Presented by the Khedive of Egypt to the city of New York. It was erected here on January 22, 1881 through the generosity of William H. Vanderbilt."

Brad pondered the reference to the generosity of William H. Vanderbilt. He recalled from somewhere that the original designer of Central Park, Frederick Law Olmstead, was also the principle architect of the gardens and grounds of Vanderbilt's estate near Ashville, North Carolina. As Brad puzzled over the scene, wondering what a massive ancient piece of stone had to do with the professor's death, his cell phone rang. It was Nigel.

"You're not going to believe this," Nigel said. "Didn't you guys say you were going together to Central Park? Well, our trace on the cell phone said it is located in the vicinity of a museum on the west side of the Park."

"Wow! That *is* interesting. Is there anything more we can do to narrow down the signal?"

"Oh sure. We could pinpoint it easily." Nigel chuckled. "But I'd need one of those hand scanners the sig ops teams are using at the NSA. Know how to get one?"

"Not at the moment, but can you track it if it moves?"

"Brad, don't worry. I'm back in my trading center with all of my electronic equipment. I'll keep an eye on it and keep you posted. With the network I have access to, I'm accurate only to about a quarter of a mile. But if it starts moving, I'll know. Have you found anything yet?"

"Well, only that the professor wrote the word *ATON* in blood on the ground and drew an arrow that seems to be pointing to an

Egyptian obelisk a few feet away from where he was found last night. Any idea what he might be trying to tell us?"

"No clue, my friend. I'd ask Allison and see what she knows about that, but I'd bet it's linked to Don's project down in Luxor."

"Thanks, Nigel."

Brad hung up and stuffed the cell phone into his pocket as he turned to Foley with a puzzled look and gestured through the trees in a westerly direction, back toward where they had entered the park.

"Nigel picked up the professor's phone signal, and it's coming from over there in the direction of the museum. I think we've seen all there is to see here for now. Let's go back there and check out the museum."

CHAPTER

8

AS THEY WALKED TOGETHER BACK toward the museum and the subway entrance, Brad tried to piece together in his mind what he knew about the American Museum of Natural History, located on the west side of Central Park.

"Foley, have you ever been to this museum before?" Brad asked.

"Never."

Brad could see the puzzled expression on Foley's face and anticipated his next question. "I have only ever visited the museum once, in the summer of two thousand and seven, when they had hosted an exhibit of gold artifacts from around the world. I remember distinctly that some of those gold artifacts were from ancient Egypt and were on loan to the museum from the Egyptian government. I read also that at one point in history most of the gold amassed by civilization was kept in Egypt, much of it mined from the eastern desert between the Nile River and the Red Sea or taken as spoil from surrounding nations."

They approached the main entrance to the museum from the park side. They could see a sign near the entrance stating that the museum hours of operation were from 9:00 a.m. to 5:45 p.m. daily. Unfortunately, it was now 5:30 p.m. and there would not be time to make a thorough examination of the museum. They decided instead to get a brochure and briefly check the museum layout. The park entrance was actually on the second floor of the museum. The subway entrance was on the lower level, so they proceeded down the stairs to the first floor. Brad stopped briefly at an information desk to pick up a brochure.

Acting on intuition, Brad asked the female attendant at the information desk if she had ever heard of an archeologist named Dr. Donald Romiel. Her eyes flashed with instant recognition.

"You mean the distinguished American Egyptologist? Of course I've heard of him. He often visits here and has served as a consultant on Egyptian history and ancient artifacts. Right now, I believe he is collaborating with Dr. Donald Medford of the University of Pennsylvania on the Akhenaten Temple project in Egypt. Why do you ask?"

Brad dodged her question but followed his own with another. "Whom might he have worked with here that I could speak with to learn more about his work?"

The attendant replied, "You might try Dr. Gunther on the fourth floor. He's the deputy curator, and he has worked with Dr. Romiel. But I think he's gone for the day."

Brad smiled and thanked her profusely. He was sure from her demeanor that she had not yet learned of the event that had transpired in the park the night before. Together, he and Foley turned and went up the stairs to the fourth floor. There, they found a hallway with a suite of offices. They continued down the hallway until they came at last to a door with a nameplate on the outside that read *Dr. Daniel Gunther, Deputy Curator*. Brad tried the door only to discover that it was locked. Suddenly, a security guard appeared as if from nowhere with an intercom device in his left hand.

"This wing is off limits to the public," he said. "And the museum is now closed. What are you doing here?"

Brad responded, "Our business is with Dr. Gunther, but he appears to be gone for the day. We'll come back another time."

"See that you make an appointment with Dr. Gunther's secretary," the guard volunteered tersely as Brad and Foley turned and began to retrace their steps.

As they made their descent and reached the first floor, they could see that most of the museum visitors had already left and the few who remained were in the process of exiting the building. Brad noticed a small sign beside a passageway on the first floor with the words *Security Office*. In the hallway beside the sign was another security guard with an intercom phone to his ear, who seemed to be eyeing them suspiciously. It was just one more detail that registered in his trained mind as they began their way down the stairs to the subway entrance on the lower level. He knew they had gathered all the information they could get here for the present. They needed to assemble what they had discovered and determine a plan of action.

One detail that Brad and Foley had missed in their visit to the park and the museum was the tall stranger who had boarded the same subway car on the return trip and had quietly taken a seat two rows behind them. If they had noticed, they might have observed that the stranger was wearing a wired earpiece connected to a pen-sized amplified shotgun microphone discretely recording every word they said.

CHAPTER

9

I T WAS AFTER 6:00 P.M. WHEN BRAD AND
Foley finally emerged from the Van Cortlandt Park subway
terminal and proceeded together on foot toward Brad's
parked car. Once again, Brad took out his cell phone for a
brief call. This time he needed to speak with Allison.

"Yes?"

"Allison, it's Brad. Foley and I are on our way back from Central
Park. How are you holding up?"

"Thanks for your call. I'm still numb, I guess. My sister, Jill,
is helping with the business and funeral arrangements. I still can't
believe all that's happened. Did you learn anything at the park?"

"Well, maybe. That's what I need to talk with you about. You
mentioned that you helped your father with his library research.
Did anything ever come up with reference to the obelisk in Central
Park or the American Museum of Natural History? And what
about the name A-T-O-N? Do you know anyone by that name?
Your father wrote out those letters as he was dying."

"I do know that Dad has worked with that museum in the past.
I'll run a search on the obelisk and on Aton. I'm pretty sure that's an
Egyptian sun god. I can even run a trace on Dad's e-mail messages
to see if the terms *obelisk* or *Aton* come up. Meanwhile, I'll bet you
two haven't had dinner yet. Look, why don't you and Foley stop by

for something to eat on your way home? It's no trouble because our housekeeper is here for the weekend. I can have the information for you by the time you get here."

"That sounds like a winning proposition," Brad responded as they got into his car. "We need to stop by your place anyway to pick up Foley's car on the way."

Although it had been nearly five months since the last time Brad had had dinner with the professor and his daughter, he still savored that visit. He needed little convincing. Foley phoned his wife, Susan, and explained what had happened, asking her to hold off on dinner.

As they drove off purposefully from their parking space, they failed to notice that same tall observer from the subway write down the number of Brad's license plate from a vantage point in the shadows behind a large tree.

CHAPTER

10

AFTER BRAD AND FOLEY HAD
hungrily devoured dinner and the housekeeper
had cleared the dining room table, Allison
brought out some papers she had printed out that
were related to their inquiry. She spread them out
on the table.

"First of all," she said, "here are some things I found concerning
that obelisk. I found this *New York Times* article dated July twenty-
first, eighteen eighty. That was the year the obelisk arrived from
Egypt."

Brad picked up the article and read several excerpts aloud.

"'From ancient Egypt, dead and dusty Egypt, to the raw, lusty,
noisy land which we call the United States of America, how vast
the stride! There is almost nothing tangible that is older than the
obelisk. There is nothing much younger than New York. The ex-
tremes have met.'

"'The obelisk was the finger which pointed to the sun. But it
never pointed upward in solitary state. Two of these striking and
impressive monoliths ever appeared together.'"

And there was another portion about where to put the obelisk:
"'Then there are those who think that this granite monolith, which
soared above the horizontal lines of the Temple of the Sun, should

be shaded in the bosky dells of the Central Park, and a nice background of verdure should be given to relieve the severe lines of the sun-pointing finger, on which lately poured the white light of an Egyptian sun. At best, the obelisk is out of due keeping.'"

Allison interrupted, "As the article says, there were two companion obelisks. They were known as Cleopatra's Needles because she relocated them from the Temple of the Sun in Heliopolis, near present-day Cairo, to Alexandria, Egypt in twelve BC. The New York obelisk arrived here two years after the sister obelisk was taken from Egypt to London, arriving there on September twelfth, eighteen seventy-eight."

Allison had learned that the New York obelisk was raised in Central Park in January 1881 amid the cheers of more than ten thousand spectators. At that time, before the skyscrapers were built, it was one of the tallest structures in the city.

Brad and Foley were dazzled by Allison's easy grasp of historical trivia. But then, she was a librarian who worked in a public library right there in Yonkers. Brad recalled that she had once shared that there were more public libraries in America than there were McDonald's outlets. But she went on to point out sadly that people eat more hamburgers than they read books. However, what moved him most about her and filled him with a kind of puzzled awe was a certain profound depth of insight and maturity for such a young lady. For example, Brad found it hard to understand how she was able now to maintain such composure and serenity on what was arguably the most devastating day of her life. Clearly, there was more to Allison than was apparent on the surface. She was also evidently deeply grateful for their continuing interest that justice would be done in the case of her father.

"What did you find out about *Aton*?" Brad asked.

"Well, according to Wikipedia, the online encyclopedia, Aten/ Aton are the interchangeable names of the ancient Egyptian mythological deity represented by the sun disk," Allison replied. "I have heard these names many times. Among other things, my father was an expert on the period of Akhenaten, the pharaoh who introduced monotheistic sun worship to Egypt. However, Dad always used the expression A-t-e-n in all of his research and writing, never A-t-o-n. There is an A-t-e-n that also stands for the Association for Theological Education in Nepal, but that is certainly not relevant in this case."

"No, it was clearly a letter *O* and not an *E*," Brad answered. "And I doubt very much that your father would change the spelling he had used throughout his career without some special reason. He could have been trying to send us a special message that he didn't want to fall into the wrong hands."

Foley suggested, "Or maybe it's just as simple as the fact that he knew there was no difference between *Aten* and *Aton* and he just didn't have the strength to write out an *E* instead of an *O*. Or maybe even his killer was some guy named Anthony."

"Maybe so," Brad said. "I hope the package he mailed me sheds some light on this when it arrives on Monday."

Together, they spoke of their plans for the next few days. Brad and Foley had committed themselves for the final day of the sailing regatta that would begin early the next morning. They realized there was nothing more that they could do until the package arrived at Brad's condo on Monday. Meanwhile, Nigel would be monitoring any movement of the missing cell phone. They would see him on Sunday as well. The funeral and a memorial service had been set for Wednesday, when many of Professor Romiel's university colleagues would attend.

Allison would, as her custom was, attend her small church on Sunday. There, she knew she had a small support group of friends who would provide meaningful consolation at this difficult time. Brad and Foley had witnessed a lot of death. They could tell of times during their Coast Guard days when they had fished the bodies of scores of Haitian refugees out of the Caribbean. They were, therefore, especially attentive to Allison as she sought to deal with this dark trial that had now come to her personally. They had learned that much of life was spent in finding the meaning of suffering and death.

"You know, I'll miss Dad terribly," Allison shared, "but I have to believe his death was for some purpose. I mean, we're not just insects who come and go on this planet with no purpose. My father used to tell me that all things work together for good for those who love God and are called according to His purpose. And though darkness and evil appear to have taken him away from me, I have to believe that there is still light and goodness in this world that can dispel all darkness and overcome evil."

Brad was still pondering her words as he glanced at his watch and saw that it was approaching 9:00 p.m. He and Foley excused themselves, took leave of Allison, and headed home for the possibility of early sleep in preparation for the regatta they had committed themselves to complete on Sunday.

As they went out the door, Brad turned and said, "Just one more thing, Allison. Could you please run a search on the names of Dr. Daniel Gunther, Deputy Curator of the American Museum of Natural History; and on Dr. David Medford, an archeologist from the University of Pennsylvania? They told us at the museum that these are men who had been working recently with your father."

CHAPTER

11

SUNDAY MORNING WAS A LOT LIKE Saturday morning. The wind was right, and there was no rain. The only clouds were those that surrounded the untimely death of the professor. Brad was once again the first one of his crew to the yacht club. He was grateful again for the hot breakfast and especially for the fact that Hoshi knew how to brew coffee so black it seemed that his spoon would stand straight up in the cup. As he opened the locker that held their gear from yesterday, he was gratified to hear the *clip clop* sound of Billy and Sarah's sandals entering the locker room.

"Hey, Skipper. How'd it go yesterday?" Billy asked.

"Yeah. We heard about the professor. That is just so sad," Sarah chimed in.

"Well, grab a bite of breakfast and I'll tell you what I know when Nigel and Foley get here," Brad answered.

Within five minutes, Nigel and Foley had arrived, ordered breakfast, and joined them at the same table.

"Look, guys," Brad began, "you all know pretty much as much as we know. The professor was murdered in Central Park near the obelisk around midnight Friday night on his way home from the airport. The police are convinced it was a random mugging, but Foley and I are not so sure. He left a message in blood at the scene.

He wrote out *Aton* with an arrow pointed at the obelisk. His daughter, Allison, informed us that it might refer to the ancient Egyptian sun god but that her father always spelled it A-t-e-n instead of *A-t-o-n*. So we have no idea what that message means. Allison said he also mailed a package to me from the airport that probably won't arrive until tomorrow."

And Foley added, "Yeah, and his cell phone was missing. But Nigel here has traced it to an area on the west side of the park where the American Museum of Natural History is located. By the way, Nigel, are you still monitoring that signal?"

"We have a dedicated screen on it in my trading center, and my staff workers are watching it now as they gear up for Asian currency trading this evening. So far, the signal is intermittent but hasn't moved. I'm only sorry we can't locate it more precisely with our network. I can't even say for certain that it is in the museum or just somewhere nearby. Tomorrow is triple-witching day—you know, options expiration and all that—so I'll be busier than a one-legged chicken hopping on a hot brick all day, but someone will always be watching it."

"Wow! You sound really busy." Billy laughed as he tried to picture a one-legged chicken hopping on a hot brick. "You sound like you're pressed for time, like one of those Egyptian mummies." Billy couldn't resist his own opportunity to lighten the conversation with a weak attempt at humor.

Brad quickly changed the subject. "Well, it seems there is not much more to do until that package arrives and until Allison finishes checking on a couple of the professor's associates; not much more, that is, than to race hard and beat the other boats today! By the way, I heard you guys did okay without me yesterday. What was that all about?"

"We're pretty hot stuff! Hardly need a skipper with this crew!" Sarah interjected.

"We'll see about that after you finish eating and we load up the boat," Brad responded with a smirk.

CHAPTER

12

BRAD KNEW IT HAD BEEN A GOOD
sailing day as he surveyed the sunburned faces, chapped
lips, and calloused hands of his crew.

As they strolled contentedly up the pier toward
the boat club, Brad said, "We learned that the professor's funeral and memorial service are scheduled for sometime on
Wednesday. I can provide more details later for any of you who
might be free to attend."

Billy volunteered, "Sarah and I will likely be attending with
some of the professors and students from NYU who knew him.
We can find out the exact time and place from the administrative
assistant in his department."

"While you're at it," Brad said, "why don't you inquire in the
department about his sponsoring agency? Try to get all the details
you can about who was paying for his work, what the scope of his
work was, and how much he was being paid to do it."

"We're on it," Sarah responded.

After handshakes and hugs all around, the five of them parted
once again. Brad climbed into his four-wheel-drive Yukon and
pointed it toward home. As he parked in his condo parking space
and made his way toward his front door, the first thing he noticed
was that the blinds in his front window were pulled shut. He always

left them open in the daytime so that his Areca palm tree would get plenty of light. He looked around and saw no sign of cars or people, and he soon found that his front door was still locked just as he had left it.

But when he turned his key and opened the door, he was shocked by the scene that presented itself. His carpet had been partially rolled up. His books had been flipped open and thrown from their shelves to the floor. All of the pictures were down from the walls, most of them ripped or with broken frames. His office file cabinet had been pried open and was lying on its side, with most of the files strewn all over the floor. Even his houseplants had been tipped out of their pots, and the potting soil was in heaps around the house. Every drawer had been opened and tipped, with the contents scattered everywhere. The sofas and mattresses and pillows had been slit with a knife and were lying chaotically around.

Brad could tell that someone had made a thorough search of every inch of his condo. But he still could not find anything missing. His bank records seemed to be intact. Then he noticed that his handgun was missing from its case in the drawer where he had left it beside his concealed weapon permit. Also, he was unable to find his passport.

He knew he should report this break-in to the police. Perhaps they could identify the culprits. At least for insurance purposes, a report would be necessary. Brad dialed 911.

"Hello. My name is Brad Beck. There's been a break-in at my condo at four twenty Monroe Park Avenue. Please send someone. And also alert Lieutenant Davis of New York Homicide Division. I think this break-in might be related to a murder case he is working on."

After a few moments, a squad car arrived with siren blaring. Two officers jumped out and rushed to the front door. Brad had anticipated their coming, so the door was open. One of the officers whistled his shock as he looked around the room.

The other officer asked, "Are you the party who called in the break-in?"

"Yeah. I'm Brad Beck. Any word from Lieutenant Davis?"

"Well, they notified Homicide Division. It's Sunday night, and Lieutenant Davis is out. And the controller said they couldn't see how a routine break-in could have anything to do with the mugging in Central Park that Davis was working. Is anything missing here?"

"So far, I can't see anything missing but my passport and my registered handgun. It was a standard model, nine millimeter Glock seventeen. That and any sense of security and safety I might have had are gone. I don't see any sign of forced entry. They must've had a key to get in," Brad said.

"I think we'd better call in the forensic team to get prints. Don't touch anything. They'll want your prints too for comparison," the officer said.

"Are you sure nothing else is missing?" the other officer asked as he continued to look around the room.

"That's all I can tell so far," Brad answered. "I guess I need to wait for forensics to finish up before I can start to clean up this mess. I didn't feel like spring cleaning tonight anyway."

Brad took out his cell phone and dialed Foley's number. "Hey, buddy," he said. "Have you and Susan got a spare bed for a homeless guy?"

"Sure. What's up?" Foley asked.

"There's been a break-in at my condo. The police will be checking for prints. The place is a mess. I need to camp out somewhere else tonight."

"Sure. Our guest room is waiting. I'll leave the light on for you. Do you think it has anything to do with the business with the professor?" Foley asked.

"You bet I do," Brad said heatedly. "They took my gun and my passport. One consolation, though. I don't think they got what they were after—the package the professor sent. That must be still on the way."

After the forensic team had arrived and fingerprinted Brad, he gathered up a few valuables and some clothes and toiletries and headed for the door. He could tell by their thorough manner that their investigation could take hours. "Here's my cell phone number in case you have any questions. Please lock up in here when you're done," he said and then added sarcastically, "not that it makes much difference."

He placed his overnight bag in the backseat of his Yukon, along with the few possessions he had collected, and headed off in the direction of Foley's house. Foley lived, along with his young wife, Susan, in the same neighborhood, less than a mile from Brad's condo. Brad had been best man at their wedding; and now that Foley was a full-time graphics consultant on Brad's Hudson River turbine project, they were often together at work. It seemed that Foley and Susan were always trying to find a woman for him—not that he minded that much, but their efforts had met with little success so far. Brad drove up the driveway and parked beside Foley's car, his headlights announcing his arrival. Foley came out and greeted him on the porch steps.

Susan called out from inside, "Have you eaten? I can warm up some leftovers."

Brad thanked her, and the three of them found seats in the living room. Brad could hear the coffee percolating in the next room. They didn't need to ask him about that.

Catching his breath, Brad began, "I think someone is aware of our interest in the professor. They probably spotted us in the park. Or maybe they forced the professor to tell them about the package he had mailed. In any case, we'll need to be especially careful from this point. Whoever it is, they were able to enter my condo through the locked front door in broad daylight. And they certainly didn't care about my learning that they had been there."

"I hate to say it, buddy," Foley interrupted, "but if they've been through your financial records and if they got your gun and passport, you could be in for a world of hurt."

"I've thought of that," Brad responded. "I made sure it got into the police report. And first thing tomorrow I need to cancel credit cards and notify the state department to get my passport replaced. I should also replace my pistol and keep it with me."

"I'd start on the credit cards right now. Tonight," Foley suggested.

Brad agreed and added, "Look, Foley. Given what's happened, I really can't show up for work tomorrow. Will you fill in for me and take charge of the turbine current monitoring? You know the process as well as I do, and you know all of the team and their individual assignments. I might be out for several days."

"Sure, Brad. I can handle it. Is there anything else I can do?"

"I'll know more tomorrow after I've seen the professor's package."

Acting on premonition, Brad took out his cell phone and dialed Allison's number.

"Hi, Allison. It's Brad. Everything okay?"

"Everything's fine, Brad."

"Listen, Allison. I had a break-in at my condo today. I think it might have something to do with your father. Frankly, I'm concerned about your being alone there."

"Well, I do have a housekeeper here on weekends. But she has a family and can't stay during the week," Allison said.

"What are the chances of your moving in with your sister?" Brad asked.

"I could probably call her tomorrow and set it up if you think it's necessary," Allison replied.

"No. I think you should go tonight," Brad insisted.

"That serious?" Allison responded more soberly.

"Until we know what's going on here, we can't afford to take any chances."

"Okay. I'll pack some things and be on my way," Allison said. "By the way, I did an Internet search on those two associates of my father's, as you asked. There was nothing special to report. They both had research publications in the area of ancient Egyptian archeology. They both had interests in the same period of Akhenaten that my father was studying."

CHAPTER

13

THE NEXT MORNING, AFTER A QUICK breakfast, Brad took leave of Foley and Susan. He had a list of things that needed his attention. He knew that the mail delivery would not be until sometime between 11:00 a.m. and noon. That would give him time to go to the federal building and start the passport replacement process. Then he would return to the same gun shop where he had bought his Glock and replace his weapon. He remembered to bring his concealed weapon permit with him this time. He also enrolled in an identity theft prevention program he had seen advertised just in case.

At about 10:30 a.m., he returned to his condo to await the delivery of the mail. As he entered the front door, he could see that nothing had changed. His condo had been thoroughly trashed, and most of his possessions were still scattered about on the floor where the police had left them.

He sighed. "Might as well start picking up," he muttered, walking into the kitchen to grab a trash bag.

At least he would make a pathway through the mess as he awaited mail delivery. He started with his books and a few articles of clothing. Forty-five minutes later, he had replaced most of the desk drawers and was reassembling the files in his file cabinet when his doorbell rang. He reached for his gun on an empty bookshelf near the front door and peered out through the peephole in his front door. He could see the mailman holding a large manila envelope. Brad pocketed his gun and opened the door.

"Here's a package for Brad Beck. It was too big to fit in the mail slot. Whoa! What happened here?" the postman asked as he stared past Brad at the remaining chaos in the condo.

Brad glared at the postman and accepted the envelope, quickly shutting and relocking the door.

Brad turned and walked impatiently through a passageway he had made in the debris toward a seat he had arranged on his damaged sofa. When he turned the envelope over in his hands, he could see that the professor had used his own Yonkers home address as the return address. He had generously overpaid the postage cost, using stamps he probably got from a machine.

Brad carefully tore open the envelope using a small key on his key chain. Inside, he could see a handwritten note and a kind of journal or log book. The note was in Professor Romiel's handwriting.

Brad,

I'm in danger. Guard this journal with your life. It's what they're after.
I'll explain it when I see you.

Don Romiel

Brad then opened the journal to see what the valuable information might be. He could see that it was a loose-leaf ring binder with a lot of drawings, dates, and numbers. The first few pages appeared to consist of maps or schematics of large temples. He could see that the first was labeled, "Temple of the Sun, Heliopolis." The second drawing was entitled, "Karnak Temple, Thebes." A third indicated, "Luxor Temple, Thebes." The entries appeared to be in chronological order of the professor's activity, with separate dates atop each page. There were many drawings of obelisks with measurements under each one. Thumbing through the journal to the last few pages, he could see one page labeled, "Festival of Opet, Route," and he began reading some of the handwriting.

"The sun disk rises above the horizontal of the walls. Do all the obelisks extend above this horizon? Maybe that is the answer. List of obelisks to measure."

The page listed a string of data preceded by names of obelisks, locations, and pharaohs.

One of the obelisk entries caught Brad's eye: "Cleopatra's Needle, London, Thames River Victoria Embankment." He remembered the old newspaper article Allison had read to him. He looked at the meaningless numbers that followed and thought they had to be important.

Judging from the date of the entry, June 27, Brad realized that the professor must have made this entry during his stopover in London en route to New York from Cairo. The final page with any writing had only the title, "New York Obelisk, Central Park." There were no entries on this page. Presumably, the professor had intended to make entries during his visit to New York.

Brad still could not understand the significance of the journal. Most of the entries made no sense to him, and he had no idea what information was here that was worth killing for. As he puzzled over this new development, he considered what he should do now. He knew that Foley, with his graphic arts skill, might be able to interpret the drawings. Nigel, being a former resident of London, might know more about the London obelisk. Sarah was an archeology student who had made two earlier field trips to Egypt. She might be able to interpret some of the archeological terms in the journal. And Allison might know more about exactly what her father was doing. He decided to waste no time and go immediately to his job site to confer with Foley.

As a precaution, Brad took out the pages with temple and Opet maps and the last two pages with information on the obelisks. He folded them neatly and put them inside his jacket pocket. Then he checked his pistol in its shoulder holster and made his way to the front door. Once outside, he turned to lock the front door with his key. Suddenly, he felt a powerful blow to the back of his head. Then everything went black.

CHAPTER

14

BACK AT THE KARNAK TEMPLE COMPLEX in the year 1342 BC...

The sound of crude hammers and chisels striking granite began to echo across the enormous expanse of the Karnak temple complex as the glorious rising sun god, Amun, began to break the horizon from his recurring cycle in the underworld with Osiris. The cool morning air and dark night sky slowly yielded to the emerging light of the deified sun disk. By the time the stately high priest, Hemenhoreb, adjourned the meeting at the arrival of dawn, the elder priests were of one mind.

"For the glory of Amun," Hemenhoreb proclaimed as sternly as he had hundreds of times ceremoniously but with more sincerity than he had ever felt before. He had a certain sense that his last days serving Amun would be full of the greatest danger and suffering he could ever imagine and with more resolve than ever he turned his gaze to the elders.

"For the glory of Amun, the lord of the universe," they replied in chorus with all the determination of decades of devotion to Amun.

Their lives had been poured into the masterpieces of priestly engineering constructed now for generations throughout the vast temple complex. Then they dispersed to their respective temple duties for cleansing and the daily sunrise rituals, intensely unified in the grandest scheme they had ever masterminded. Each was keenly aware that any compromise would cast every devoted servant of Amun into the ruthless hands of the most powerful army under the sun and completely at the mercy of their heretical young pharaoh.

Hemenhoreb walked his separate way from the meeting of elders and made his way from the inner chamber down the southern corridor of the great temple and out toward the grand outer courts in the direction of the Nile River. As he passed westward through the enormous fifth pylon towering into the open sky, he stopped to gaze upon Hatchepsut's twin obelisks dedicated to Amun more than a hundred years before. His quiet rebellion against the pharaoh was underway, and the weight of struggle that lay ahead felt at this moment as heavy as either one of these three-hundred-and-twenty-ton monolithic granite obelisks.

The rising sun was already reflecting off the perfectly plated electrum that covered the pink granite ben-ben stone, the pyramidian of the obelisk. As he gazed upward, Hemenhoreb could see rays of the sun reflecting through the dust particles that rose more than ninety feet above the temple floor. His mind wandered briefly to his boyhood days when he had seen the flash of the sun shooting off the obelisks of Karnak from miles away in the morning hours and even many times as the sun set.

"*Ubenek em Ben-ben*" he whispered as he had been taught to say in his youth. "Amun, you shine at the tip of the obelisk."

His heart swelled again with pride as his thoughts returned to his responsibilities as the high priest of Karnak, the highest servant of the gods. He vowed again under his breath that he would not be the last priest of Amun. The plan was set, and the servants of Amun could not fail. He continued his long walk through the fourth pylon, moving in the direction of the Nile, all the while reciting from memory a few verses to Amun written by Queen Hatchepsut that still adorned the two greatest obelisks ever constructed.

"She made as her monument for her father Amun…two great obelisks of enduring granite from the south, their upper parts being of electrum of the best of all lands, seen on the two sides of the river. Their rays flood the two lands when the sun disk rises between them at its appearance on the horizon of heaven. I have done this with a loving heart for my father, Amun, after I entered unto his secret image on the First Occasion of the Jubilee…I know that Karnak is the horizon of heaven upon earth, the august ascent of the First Occasion, the sacred eye of the lord of the universe."

Then, turning left off the main temple axis and moving in a southerly direction past the two obelisks dedicated to Tuthmose I, he lifted his gaze beyond the next rows of pylons. From there, his tired eyes could see the newly constructed temple of Khonsu in the distant southwest corner of the enormous Karnak complex. Dwarfed by other temples in Thebes, this one dedicated to Khonsu stretched nearly fifty meters long and fifteen meters wide and was perfectly situated next to the Opet temple where the extravagant annual festivals of Opet commenced.

"This is the place," he whispered as his thoughts raced. "Where could there be a better place to begin the demise of the heretic than from his father's last project of worship to the triad gods?"

Khonsu comprised the third god of the Karnak triad deity, the only son of the gods Amun and Mut. Symbolized by the moon, the meaning held even more significance to Hemenhoreb as the great sun disk was now being seized by the wicked pharaoh.

"By the light of the moon shall we defend the sun," he muttered as he regained his pace in the direction of the temple.

Another great vision was coming together, and he ignored the gesticulations of the scribes and artists, the foremen and the laborers, and even the wab priests dutifully at work managing the detailed elements of the inscriptions, moving briskly onward with plans that would forever alter a great empire and leave a mystery for mankind.

CHAPTER

15

IN A HOSPITAL IN PRESENT-DAY NEW YORK...
"Where am I?" Brad mumbled as he struggled to regain consciousness. He thought he could detect a faint smell of formaldehyde, and the light seemed much too bright as he slowly forced his eyes open to take in his surroundings.

"City hospital," the voice came back. "You were hit in the back of the head. Some jogger found you sprawled out on your front steps and called for an ambulance. If you weren't such a hard-headed guy, the doctor said you'd be dead by now."

The voice sounded strangely familiar, and then Brad started to make out Foley's smiling face.

A softer voice on the other side of his hospital bed said, "Brad, you suffered a concussion from a powerful blow to the back of your head. You've been in a coma for three days. We're so relieved you decided to rejoin us."

Straining to turn his head, Brad could just make out Allison's smiling face. As he slowly regained consciousness, the events of the past few days began to register.

"My clothes! Where're my clothes?" Brad gasped.

"Don't worry, pal," Foley replied. "Your things are right there in the drawer beside your bed. But they won't let you out for a day or two."

"Where's the journal?" Brad continued.

"What journal?" Foley responded. "All you had on you were your clothes, your wallet, your keys, your gun, and some papers you had folded up in your jacket pocket."

"Then they got the journal!" Brad reflected somberly.

"Who're they?" Foley asked.

"The same ones who killed Professor Romiel. It was his journal they wanted all the time." Brad felt a dull throbbing at the back of his head and reached up to feel a thick bandage. He felt a wave of nausea as he slumped back on his pillow. "They must've known the journal was in the mail to me and were watching my condo. Thankfully, they didn't get everything they wanted. Show me the papers that were in my jacket."

Allison opened the drawer in the stand beside Brad's hospital bed. She carefully drew out the three pages of the notebook that had been folded in Brad's jacket pocket. Instantly, she recognized her father's handwriting.

"These pages must have been part of my father's journal," she gasped. "It's too bad I don't know enough about his work to tell you exactly what they mean," she added as she clutched the pages.

"Three days! You said I've been here for…for three days?" Brad stammered with shock as he continued to collect his senses. "Then they've had three days to analyze the data in your father's journal! What else has been happening?"

"Well, yesterday, my father's funeral and memorial service were held at the funeral home and at his NYU department. A lot of his colleagues were there from NYU and many other academic institutions. Jill and her husband went with me. I've moved in with them," Allison responded solemnly. "It was gratifying to see the large turnout but so sad to realize the occasion. My father was a good man. All he wanted to do was to explore history as a way of helping us understand who we are and our pathway to civilization. Anyone who could do this to him would have to be truly evil. I still can't believe this has happened," she added, still overwhelmed with waves of emotion.

"Billy and Sarah were there," Foley said. "They said they had information about the professor's sponsors. Oh, and Lieutenant Davis of the homicide division came by here and said the police will want to interview you now that you're conscious."

"What about the cell phone? Has Nigel found out anything?" Brad asked.

"No. I'm afraid we've drawn a blank there. Nigel says he can only trace the location when the phone is activated, and it has gone dead. There's no longer any signal," Foley responded.

"Look," Brad concluded. "I've got to get out of here as soon as possible and meet with Billy and Sarah. We've got to figure out what's so important about the journal. And we've got to bring Nigel in on this. I'm afraid our adversaries are way ahead of us. They might even still be monitoring our movements. For sure they would like to get their hands on these four pages of the journal."

"Hold on, partner!" Foley replied. "They won't let you out of here without a physician's approval, and he won't even be making his rounds until this evening. Besides, Lieutenant Davis wants us to call him now that you're conscious. He'll want to ask you some questions. Billy and Sarah are in class now anyway, and Nigel is busy trading equities or commodities or whatever. I can set up a meeting with them for tomorrow."

"You're probably right, Foley," Brad said. "Right now my head feels like it was hit by a truck. And you'd better take charge of these journal pages. Make some backup copies. They could provide the key to the whole matter."

After some conversation about progress at work and a brief call to Lieutenant Davis, Foley and Allison took leave of Brad and promised to return for him as soon as he was released. That evening, a young intern on duty signed off on Brad and said he thought it would be safe for him to leave the hospital in the morning.

CHAPTER

16

I T WAS 9:00 A.M. FRIDAY WHEN FOLEY parked his late model SUV in the hospital emergency parking lot and proceeded on foot between two rows of cars through the large automatic doorway to the reception desk. He was not particularly surprised to see Brad fully dressed and seated in the lobby. The only clues that Brad had been a patient there were the bandage still on his head and the fact that he was a little slower than usual to rise and greet his friend.

"Hey, pal. Had your coffee?" Foley asked cheerfully.

"I sure did," Brad responded. "But hospital coffee is not half strong enough."

As they proceeded out through the automatic doorway toward Foley's car, Foley asked, "Did Lieutenant Davis come by last night?"

"He did," Brad replied. "But the meeting was not very productive. I didn't see my assailant, so I could contribute nothing for identification. Beyond that, Lieutenant Davis is still not convinced there was any connection between the random killing of Professor Romiel and what happened to me. When I told him about the cell phone, he concluded that it must have been lost somewhere in the bushes in the park and the battery had gone dead. I didn't feel comfortable about sharing details regarding the journal yet. Where are we meeting with the others?"

"Nigel suggested we meet at his trading center not far from the boat club. He said it was protected against electronic snooping. After what happened to you, he seemed paranoid about security. He said we should not share any more details on the phone either," Foley answered wryly.

"He's probably right about that," Brad said. "That could explain how they knew my address so soon after our visit to the park and the museum. And it would explain how they knew about the journal. Whoever is behind all this is well funded, technologically sophisticated, and has international reach."

Foley wound his SUV around some back streets behind the Nyack Boat Club and drove up a hill to a gated entrance sheltered from view by several large elm trees. He got out of his SUV and punched a coded signal into the keypad beside the gate. The large steel gate swung slowly open. As he drove through the gate, he could see in his rearview mirror that the gate was closing automatically. A few minutes later they arrived at a paved parking area in front of a large stone building surrounded by a vast expanse of well-maintained lawns and gardens and a closed-in forested area. There were other vehicles, and Brad recognized Sarah's beige Honda Civic.

As they proceeded up the pathway to the large front door, Brad asked, "Do you have the journal pages?"

"I do," Foley replied. "And I made two copies, but I haven't given any out yet."

There was a large brass knocker on the door that did double duty as a knocker and doorbell. The door opened, and Nigel greeted them with his most charming British accent.

"Hello there! Welcome back to the land of the living. I see you have adopted a new headdress. The latest fashion, perhaps?"

"I'm starting a new fashion," Brad replied. "It's one that I'd like to present to whoever gave me this knot on the back of my head."

"Well, we'll see about that. Come on in and meet the crew," Nigel responded warmly.

They proceeded up a large, circular staircase and past a long row of computer monitors. Two traders waved in greeting as they went by and entered a large conference room on the opposite side of the room with the computers. There was a large mahogany table and heavy, leather-covered chairs around the table. There was a plethora of charts and graphs and a large, white eraser board surrounding them on the walls. Brad recognized Billy, Sarah, and Allison as Nigel pulled shut the sound-proofed door to the conference room.

"Choose your poison," Nigel said as he motioned toward a large decanter and coffee urn on the bar at one side of the room.

"I'll try some of that coffee that smells so good and appears to be such a hit with the others," Brad volunteered as he reached for a large, white coffee mug.

After they had all taken seats and Foley had taken out copies of the journal pages, Brad proceeded.

"Thank you all for gathering here on short notice. I wish we could have met sooner, but they tell me I've been out of commission for a few days. We seem to have entered a kind of war here, one not of our own choosing, and we've already lost the first few battles. We don't even know who the enemy is, and we have no idea what we're up against or what the odds of success might be. I've called for this meeting because I desperately need your help. Can I count on you?"

Billy spoke for the others when he said, "We're all in this with you. The professor was our friend too."

Looking around the table, Brad could see their nods of agreement. "This is no sailing regatta, guys. We're talking life and death here," Brad continued. "Whoever we're up against will stop at nothing, and no doubt they are powerful and smart and—"

"What we're up against is evil personified," Allison interrupted. "My father was onto something important that they wanted. If we can find out what that was, perhaps we can find out who they are."

"Yes," Brad continued. "And that's precisely why I need your help. Billy, Sarah, did you find out anything about the professor's sponsor and what his assignment was in Egypt?"

Billy motioned to Sarah to begin.

"We sure did. We learned that Professor Romiel was given a million-dollar grant to provide information on the period of the reign of Pharaoh Akhenaten. Specifically, he was to uncover information related to the economy of Egypt during the transition from polytheism to monotheistic sun worship. He was assigned three excavation sites: the Heliopolis Temple of the Sun, the Temple of Karnak, and another site near Luxor. The Heliopolis site was the original site of the obelisk in Central Park, although it dates back to the origin of sun worship at a period much earlier than the reign of Akhenaten. The large amount of the grant was not unusual because the university typically requires about eighty percent of all such grants as university overhead, which left only about two hundred thousand to cover travel and other expenses related to securing permissions, and Professor Romiel's personal compensation was just commensurate with his university salary."

Billy interrupted, "None of that was unusual. What was unusual was the fact that the sponsor remained anonymous and the funds came through the American Museum of Natural History as an intermediary."

"Yes, and one other unusual fact," Sarah continued. "The professor was required to report to the sponsor on a weekly basis. Normally, such reports are not filed until the project is completed or unless some unique discovery is made."

"Is there any way we can find out who that confidential sponsor is now that the professor is deceased and the project is terminated?" Brad asked.

"The museum probably has that information, but we're not sure how to access it ourselves," Billy responded.

"How about getting access to the professor's weekly progress reports?"

"Well, I have his e-mail address and password. If he made his reports by e-mail, maybe we can run some kind of trace on all of his messages," Allison said.

"Leave that to me," Nigel volunteered. "My staff is particularly adept at acquiring personal e-mail messages. That information is to be kept between us, of course."

"Of course," everyone chimed in with knowing glances.

Foley spoke up. "I would not be surprised to learn that the deputy curator of the museum, Gunther or whatever his name is, has had some hand in this. We learned that he has had some sort of working relationship with Professor Romiel in his Egyptian expeditions."

"Gunther? I know him," Sarah interrupted, glancing at Billy. "As a graduate student in archeology, I was asked, along with several other classmates, to make two brief field trips to Egypt to serve as interns. Gunther was in on our orientation session."

"Yes, and he came to the memorial service on Wednesday," Billy added.

"Well, maybe you two can tease some information out of him about the confidential sponsor, but be very careful and don't give out any information. We don't know who we're dealing with here," Brad suggested.

Foley added, "We have one other piece of vital information. Brad here was able to rescue four pages from the professor's journal before they mugged him and made off with it. I made copies for your confidential inspection. Allison has already seen this, and she confirmed that the handwriting is her father's. But she was unable to shed any light on the meaning of the pages. We thought you archeologists and numbers people might know something about it."

"Let's have a look-see," Nigel said as he took a copy and passed another to Billy and Sarah.

Brad and Foley glanced down together at the original.

"Well, I do recognize this drawing of Cleopatra's obelisk at the Thames Embankment in London," Nigel offered. "I have visited it several times. I supposed these numbers underneath are measurements of some kind. We could verify that easily by checking them out at the scene."

"Measuring obelisks! How exciting!" Billy interjected. "Did you know that America was discovered by measuring obelisks?"

"Oh be serious, Billy! We've got a lot to cover here!" Foley remarked.

"Foley, I am being serious. This is completely true. I learned about it just last semester. Listen, there was this Greek librarian in Alexandria, Egypt, in the third century BC named Eratosthenes. Someone told him that at noon on the longest day, the summer solstice, there were no shadows cast in Syene. Syene, or modern-day Aswan, was the southernmost Greek outpost in Egypt, about five hundred stadia south of Alexandria, approximately five hundred statute miles away and was located approximately on the Tropic of Cancer. He measured an obelisk in Alexandria, its height and the length of its shadow at noon on the longest day. Then he traveled south to Syene and found that, indeed, there were no shadows from vertical objects at that same precise time. Back in Alexandria, he applied the Pythagorean Theorem to his measurements of the obelisk. He found that the angle of the shadow was seven degrees and twelve minutes or approximately one fiftieth of the three hundred and sixty degrees of a circle. He reasoned, therefore, that the earth was round. And multiplying the five hundred stadia by fifty, he estimated that its circumference was approximately twenty-five thousand stadia or twenty-five thousand miles. Only its true circumference is actually about twenty-four thousand eight hundred and sixty miles at the equator. Still, when this information was passed down to Columbus, it provided enough justification for him to get funding for his attempt to reach India by sailing westward."

Sarah added, "The amazing irony here is that Eratosthenes might even have used the obelisk in Central Park to make his calculations, except that it had not been moved to Alexandria by Cleopatra until around twelve BC."

Allison couldn't resist adding, "I hope none of you have missed the point that it was a librarian who made the discovery of America possible."

Billy chimed in, "It seems to me that great things happen when risk-takers like Columbus take the time to study history."

"I admit that library science and history are fascinating subjects," Brad said more seriously. "But I doubt very much that Professor Romiel was trying to determine the circumference of the earth or discover America with his measurements. He must have had some other purpose."

"And whatever that purpose was," Foley added, "must have been worth a lot of money to Professor Romiel's sponsor."

"I recognize these other drawings," Sarah continued. "This is the Temple of the Sun in Heliopolis, and this is Karnak Temple near Luxor. This other one shows the route of the Opet Festival, where they carried the idols of the gods from Karnak to Luxor and then back down the Nile to Karnak again. These locations must have been significant to Professor Romiel."

Nigel re-entered the conversation at this point. "My friends, as a venture capitalist, I confess that I am beginning to smell a lot of money at play here. I am prepared to fund an expedition of our own. We might need to send our own team to Europe and to Egypt. Consider it an investment in justice."

"Okay," Brad summarized. "Things are beginning to come together here. We still need Billy and Sarah to ply Gunther about the anonymous sponsor. And, Nigel, we accept your offer to trace the professor's e-mail messages. And, of course, we probably could use your financial support. Allison, you said earlier that you had kept your father's messages to you. Would you please scan them for any possible clues? Foley and I need to finalize some things at our work site. How about we gather together here again tomorrow evening to compare notes? And be careful, all of you. Let's leave these pages of the journal here with Nigel. And no more critical information in our cell phone messages."

CHAPTER

17

I T WAS STILL A FEW MINUTES BEFORE noon on Friday when their meeting finally broke up, and they each went out of Nigel's trading center the same way they had entered. Once outside, Brad and Foley briefly discussed the possibility of arranging work responsibilities in such a way that they might be available to travel abroad if necessary. Then Foley had to part company to run an errand for Susan. Brad proceeded to his work site on the west side of the Hudson River to check on the engineering project. He stopped for fast food along the way to make up for the hospital breakfast and to give him time to see if he was being followed. Convinced no one was watching him, he left the restaurant using a door different from the one he had entered.

Nigel set about tracing Professor Romiel's e-mail messages using the account information Allison had supplied. He actually assigned one of his talented assistants to that project while he resumed his daily trading routine. Within a few moments, he was pouring over the latest unemployment statistics and contemplating a reshuffling of capital in several exchange-traded funds (ETFs) he liked to trade. He took a careful reading of Bollinger Bands and nine-day stochastics on major indices and began his trading in earnest.

Allison had taken several days leave from her work. She decided to drive by her home in Yonkers to retrieve some personal items on the way to her sister's home in North Jersey. Her notebook computer would be especially helpful as she sought to recover her father's e-mail messages. As she drove up the front driveway to her home and parked outside the doorway, she failed to notice a late-model, black Mercedes sedan parked several houses down the street.

Billy and Sarah went together in Sarah's Honda back toward their NYU department in the city with the intent of having lunch together and spending some time in the library gathering information about recent archeological work in the Akhenaten period.

On their way, Sarah commented, "You know, Billy, it's still early and we could even meet with Gunther this afternoon to ask about Professor Romiel's sponsor."

"What would we tell him? And we don't even have an appointment," Billy objected.

"Well, he knows I'm an archeology student. Maybe I could say that I'm seeking a sponsor for my own research and I need his help," Sarah responded.

"It sounds a little farfetched," Billy responded. "What kind of research are you supposed to be doing?"

"Well, I could say that I'm especially interested in the Akhenaten period and I was inspired by Professor Romiel's research," Sarah replied. "After all, I am interested in that period. And I certainly wouldn't mind another excuse to go back again to Egypt. And I could say that I remembered him from the internship orientation and thought he might be able to advise me."

"Well, okay. It might be worth a try, but you'd better do most of the talking. I'm sure you're a lot more convincing than I am," Billy responded hesitantly.

"Yes. Men always find me convincing," Sarah added coyly.

"C'mon. Let's just get it over with. But first let's have some lunch. I'm hungry enough to eat a horse," Billy added impatiently.

"There are some eating places right by the museum," Sarah responded.

"Yeah, and maybe Nigel will give us an expense account to cover the restaurant, parking, and museum costs," Billy added sarcastically.

"He just might do that," Sarah responded optimistically as she turned into a moderately priced parking facility near the museum.

Together, they went down the elevator to the street level, crossed the street, and found their way into a small Italian bistro within view of the museum. After Billy had unceremoniously wolfed down two calzones and a house salad, they proceeded up the street to the museum entrance. Once inside, they went first to a young lady at the information desk.

"Hi," Sarah began. "We're graduate students from NYU, and we would really like to speak with Dr. Daniel Gunther. We don't have an appointment, but he might remember me from an internship I did in Egypt last year."

"Hold on," the young lady replied. "I can check his schedule with his secretary. What were your names again?"

"Sarah Johnson and William Heckman," Sarah replied.

After a brief phone conversation, the information lady said, "Dr. Gunther will meet with you, but he has someone in his office right now. If you proceed to the fourth floor suite of offices, the receptionist will show you where you can wait."

Thanking her, Sarah and Billy proceeded to the fourth floor.

"Please have a seat," the receptionist said, smiling. "I'll call you when Dr. Gunther is free."

Billy and Sarah took cushioned seats against the wall at the head of the corridor of offices. Settling in there, they could not help but notice the security camera facing them from its swivel attachment near the ceiling across the hallway. After a few minutes, they noticed two burly men in dark suits with security badges on their coats. The four of them exchanged quick glances as the men passed by them on their way back into the museum. Presumably, these were the visitors to Dr. Gunther's office.

Within a moment, Dr. Gunther himself came out to meet them. Shaking hands affably, he said, "Welcome to the museum. I believe I remember you, young lady, from one of the internship orientations I conducted at NYU last year. Won't you please join me in my office?"

As they entered his office, Sarah said, "Yes, and we also saw you this week at the memorial service for Professor Romiel at NYU. That's what reminded us of your connection with Professor Romiel's work. You see, Professor Romiel was my mentor, and I hoped one day to follow in his steps as an archeologist in Egypt. As you might remember, I did take two internship trips to Luxor and Karnak. But now that he is gone, I have no one to guide me in this career."

"Yes. I remember you from the memorial service as well. That was an unfortunate business. Don was a distinguished scholar and a friend of longstanding. I'd be happy to help you any way I can," the deputy curator responded, appearing sincerely interested in her plight.

"Well, this is my situation," Sarah continued. "I want to continue my graduate research in the Akhenaten period. But as you know, archeologists are totally dependent on their sponsors. I need to find a sponsor to underwrite my research. We thought maybe you could connect us with the sponsor who was backing Professor Romiel, and we could submit some kind of proposal to that person."

"Well, actually, I can't do that," Gunther replied. "You see, that sponsor only agreed to support your professor on the basis of strict anonymity. Even Don did not know his sponsor. He could only file his reports to an e-mail address each week, according to the terms of the grant. Also, he had to sign a nondisclosure agreement promising not to share the details of his research. All I can tell you is that the sponsor is not an individual but a corporation. I'm assuming Don never discussed the details of his research with either of you."

"Of course not. We thought that now that Professor Romiel is deceased, his sponsor might be particularly responsive to Sarah's wish to continue his research," Billy finally contributed. "Maybe Sarah could give you some sort of proposal, which could pass on to the corporation in her behalf. Of course, she could use your help in drafting the proposal so that it addressed the exact scope of work that Professor Romiel was pursuing."

"That's actually an excellent suggestion, Mr. Heckman. Why don't you leave a contact number so I can check with the sponsor to see if there is any desire to pursue the work further? I can contact you in any event," Gunther offered.

"Thank you very much, Dr. Gunther. And thank you for your time. I'll wait for your call," Sarah gushed glowingly as they all stood. She handed Gunther her NYU research assistant business card, and they shook hands and parted amicably.

As Sarah and Billy retraced their steps through the corridor, past the receptionist, and down the stairway, Sarah said happily, "That was an excellent idea at the end, Billy, about continuing Professor Romiel's abandoned research. It just might work!"

"It might indeed. But it looks like we're still no closer to identifying the sponsor. Nigel will have to do that," Billy replied. "I'm also a little troubled by the fact that we gave out more information than we received."

"What do you mean?" Sarah asked.

"Well, Gunther now has our names and your complete address and phone number, but he refused to identify Professor Romiel's sponsor beyond just telling us that it was some corporation. He also knows now that you're interested in pursuing Professor Romiel's work. He also seemed particularly concerned that we not know the details of the professor's research."

There was still time for the two of them to cross the street to the parking facility where Sarah had left her car and return to the NYU library for a few hours of research into questions of concern that surfaced in the pages rescued from Professor Romiel's journal.

CHAPTER 18

IT WAS A RAINY SATURDAY EVENING at 7:30, just thirty minutes before the scheduled time to reconvene at Nigel's trading center. Brad had cleaned up his condo as well as he could, and it was now the responsibility of his homeowner's insurance to replace furnishings that had been destroyed. He had installed new dead bolt locks on his doors and had invested in a security alarm service as a measure to prevent any new break-ins. He now constantly felt an urge to be looking over his shoulder to see if anyone was watching or following him throughout the day. He still wished he had any clues regarding whom their adversaries were and what their motivation might be.

He decided to leave a few minutes early to gather news from Nigel and make a few notes in preparation for the meeting. As he climbed into his Yukon, he surveyed the neighborhood for anything suspicious. Backing down his driveway and into the street, he glanced in his rearview mirror to see if anyone was preparing to follow. On this dark, cloudy evening, the asphalt glistened with the fresh rain as he wound his way around the back streets to Nigel's front gate. The steel gate swung open automatically as he approached. Brad noticed the new security camera that was focused on his approach.

This time, the parking lot was almost empty as he parked and walked quickly toward Nigel's front door. Before he could knock, the door swung open.

"You're a bit early. I'm glad to see you lost your attractive head gear." Nigel said, noticing that Brad had removed the bandage from his head.

"Yes, and I seem to have lost some patience along the way as well. I thought I'd come early to see what you've discovered about the professor's sponsor. Any luck tracing those e-mail reports?"

"Well, yes and no," Nigel replied as the two of them ascended the stairway toward the conference room. "Getting into the professor's e-mail account was a piece of cake. We have a complete record of all of his e-mail messages over the past year. He was using encryption software, but we were able to break it down and decode all of his messages. We've printed them out for this evening's meeting. And we have the e-mail address where he was sending his reports. But tracing the location of that address has been a bit of a problem. We thought we had located the server in Taiwan, but that turned out to be a dummy server that led us to Brazil. From there, we got as far as Finland. But that is where the trail stops. Obviously the sponsor does not want anyone to locate and identify him. There's still one way we might find the location of the address, but that involves sending a tracer message. When they open our message, we can nail their location. But I didn't want to send the wrong message that would just alert them that we are onto them and give away our own location."

"You did right, Nigel," Brad said. "At our meeting tonight, we can discuss a way to respond if necessary. It's possible that Billy and Sarah got the information we need from the museum deputy curator. And maybe they've gathered some insights into the obelisk measurements. Anyway, it's great to know that at least we now have a hot line to the sponsor if we need it."

Brad took a seat at the conference room table and began leafing through the large folder of e-mail message copies that Nigel had placed in front of him. "Did you find any other clues in these messages?"

"I haven't had a chance to look through them yet. They're hot off the press," Nigel replied. "You can see that we've organized the messages chronologically into three categories: his correspondence with the sponsor, his correspondence with family, and his correspondence with colleagues and friends."

Brad was leafing his way through the sponsor correspondence section when he heard the sound of an alarm coming from a monitor within the conference room. Brad reached for the loaded Glock 17 inside his coat as a kind of involuntary response.

"No problem, Brad," Nigel commented, glancing up from a monitor with a grin. "It's just Billy and Sarah. Antonio will let them in. You see, I've added a little security of my own since our last meeting."

A few seconds later, Billy and Sarah ascended the stairway, passed by the trading monitors, and entered the conference room through the door that had been left ajar.

"Hi, Nigel, Brad. Who's the gigantic bouncer?" Billy asked.

"Oh, that's Antonio," Nigel responded cheerily. "He came with impeccable credentials."

As everyone migrated toward the bar with its welcoming coffee urn, Brad noticed his phone light up. "I think I have a phone call, but it's not coming through."

"You'll have to step outside the room and down the stairs," Nigel explained. "This floor is wired to block all wireless messages."

As Brad left the room and descended the stairway, he could see on his iPhone screen that Allison had left a message. Opening his message box, he heard the words, "Brad, if you're there, pick up, please. I'm being followed. I don't know what to do…"

Brad quickly pushed the call-back button and waited breathlessly for Allison to answer.

"Brad, is that you?"

"Allison, where are you? Are you still being followed?"

"They're right behind me," Allison answered nervously. "I'm north of Yonkers but not quite to the bridge turnoff. I tried to shake them. That's why I'm late to the meeting. They sometimes disappear from sight and then re-emerge. It makes me think they must have put some tracking device on my car."

"Can you see them?" Brad asked.

"All I can see is that it's a black sedan with tinted windows, probably a Mercedes. No chance to see a license plate. What should I do?"

"Head for the Nyack Boat Club where your father's yacht is moored. Drive slowly so I can get there first. Find the parking space closest to your father's slip. After you park, walk slowly toward the boat. I'll arrange a welcoming committee for these guys. Meanwhile, you could pray that this goes well," Brad suggested as he ended the call and headed for the front door.

Before Brad could reach the front door, Nigel called after him, "What's happening?"

"Allison's being followed. I'm on my way to meet her at the boat club."

"Take Antonio with you, Brad!" he called down from the top of the stairs. "He's experienced in such matters."

"Do you have a weapon?" Brad asked as he turned in the direction of Antonio.

"Heavy or light?" Antonio grunted tersely.

"Both."

From a drawer against the wall in the front lobby, Antonio withdrew an automatic assault rifle and several loaded clips, and the two of them headed out the front door in the direction of Brad's Yukon.

As they entered the car, Brad dialed up Foley. "Where are you, buddy?" Brad asked.

"I'm just a few blocks from Nigel's front gate. I'll be there in less than two minutes."

"There's been a change of plans." Brad said. "Meet me at the Boat Club ASAP. If you have your weapon, bring it. Allison's being followed."

Meanwhile, Sarah and Billy, coffee in hand, settled in place at the conference table and began leafing excitedly through the pages of the professor's e-mail messages and taking notes furiously as if they had suddenly unearthed a priceless treasure.

CHAPTER

19

OLEY WAS FIRST TO THE BOAT CLUB and carefully selected an obscure parking spot that would give him full view of any approaching vehicles. He checked his glove compartment for his revolver and made sure it was loaded. Then he glanced at his watch and waited in his car.

In less than two minutes, he spotted Brad's blue Yukon approaching. Brad parked in a space near Foley, with his car pointed in the opposite direction. Foley watched as Brad stepped out of his car and came toward him. Then he noticed that a giant of a man emerged from the other side of Brad's old SUV. What was even more threatening than the sight of such a huge man emerging from the SUV was seeing what appeared to be an automatic assault rifle in his hands wrapped in a black, plastic cover. Indeed, the man was a weapon himself, and that was all the intimidation anyone would normally ever need to encounter; he really didn't even require a weapon.

As Brad approached, Foley rolled down his car window.

"Meet Antonio," Brad said, gesturing toward the newcomer. "He's Nigel's new security guard."

"I can see he came prepared," Foley responded with admiration.

"Listen, Foley. I told Allison to park near her father's yacht. We need to walk over there and find a vantage point close to where she might park. I'll move my car closer there in case we get into a chase. We don't have much time to take our positions. Allison will be here any minute."

Foley emerged from his car with revolver in hand and began walking quickly in the rain along with Antonio in the direction of the marina where he knew the professor's yacht was moored. Brad moved his Yukon to an obscure parking place closer to the marina from which he knew he could exit quickly if a chase ensued. He climbed out of his car and took a position crouched behind an SUV, and there he waited. He could not see Foley or Antonio, but he knew they were close by. The only sounds he could hear were the sighing of the wind and the distant ringing of sailboat halyards striking their metal masts as they swayed with the waves. Yet louder still he could hear the pounding of his heart. Something inside of him warmed at the prospect that this time he would be the source of the surprise and not the people who ransacked his condo, put him in the hospital, killed the professor, and stole the professor's notebook.

Within a few minutes, Brad spotted the approaching headlights of Allison's car. As instructed, she wound her way slowly through the parking lot toward the marina and parked in the open place nearest her father's yacht. She seemed to pause a moment, looking in all directions to see the promised welcoming committee. Not far behind her came the black Mercedes. Seeing the approaching car, she emerged from her own vehicle, took out her umbrella, and began walking in the direction of her father's yacht. She passed within twenty yards of Brad, who was still crouched behind the SUV.

Brad watched as the Mercedes moved cautiously in the direction of the marina. The occupants turned off their headlights and parked near Allison's car with a good view of the marina. Brad wondered whether their purpose in tailing Allison was to gather information about her activities, intimidate her, or whether it was something even more malevolent. Allison had about reached her father's yacht and was preparing to climb aboard when Brad saw two men emerge from the Mercedes. They began walking quickly in the direction of the yacht. That was all the signal Brad needed. Still crouched in the shadows, he began moving noiselessly in the direction of the men, hoping to surprise them from behind. He had closed the distance between himself and the men to just ten feet when suddenly there came a flashing light and the sound of a car horn from behind him. Apparently there was a third occupant in the Mercedes, and he had spotted Brad and was alerting the others. The two men instantly spun in their tracks and reached for their weapons.

In a split second, Brad knew there was no time to reach into his coat and draw his one weapon against their two weapons. In an intuitive flash, he thought of the time and distance required for the arming of a torpedo fired from a submarine. He would become the torpedo. Brad lowered his head and rushed forward like a bull. He struck the closest man head-on in the solar plexus. He could hear the man groan with pain as he left his feet and sailed backward in the air. He landed with a painful thud on the wet pavement with Brad fully on top of him. The other assailant had now drawn his gun and was prepared to shoot. But rather than risk shooting his companion, he lifted his gun by the barrel high into the air to strike Brad with his full strength and finish the job that had been started on Brad only a few days earlier.

Just as he lifted his gun to the apex of the swing, a giant emerged from the shadows. Antonio grasped the man around the abdomen from behind. Brad thought he could hear ribs cracking as Antonio lifted the assailant off the ground and squeezed him in his vise-like grip. The man dropped his weapon and groaned with agony. Antonio lifted him higher and then carried him a few paces and threw him full force into the cold water of the marina.

Foley, not to be outdone, was running toward the Mercedes with his weapon in hand. The driver of the Mercedes, seeing Foley and realizing he could no longer help his companions, spun the wheel and stepped on the gas. With a squeal of tires, the Mercedes swung around and headed toward the exit. Foley ran after it until it became apparent that he could not intercept the vehicle. Firing his weapon at an unknown driver seemed too drastic a measure, but he did have the presence of mind to observe the license plate number. He recited it several times to remember it until he could write it down.

When Foley finally rejoined Brad and Antonio, still breathing heavily, he said, "The driver got away, but I got his tag number."

Antonio fished the one man out of the water of the marina. The other assailant was still lying on his back, unconscious, in the rain. Brad gathered up the weapons the two men had dropped.

"Well, would you look at that," Brad said excitedly. "This Glock seventeen is probably my missing weapon, but I see they have filed off the serial number."

Brad took out his iPhone and dialed 911. "This is Bradford Beck at the Nyack Boat Club. We have apprehended two armed assailants in an attempted murder or kidnapping. Notify Lieutenant Davis of homicide and send someone right away to take these men into custody."

Satisfied that the police were on their way, Brad quickly dialed Nigel's number and apprised him of the latest events. Nigel seemed especially pleased about Antonio's role in the episode and informed Brad that Billy and Sarah had also been finding a few surprises in the professor's e-mails.

Allison approached from her vantage point on her father's yacht where she had witnessed the entire ordeal. "That was quite a welcoming party," she said admiringly.

Brad smiled. "I don't think these two guys will be following you again anytime soon."

Within five minutes, two squad cars arrived with lights flashing. The police officers found six people gathered under the awning of the front entrance to the boat club. The two suspects, looking wet and subdued, were seated on the entryway steps, clutching their midsections. Hovering over them were Antonio, Brad, and Foley brandishing the assailants' confiscated weapons. Antonio had stowed his own weapon in the trunk of Brad's car.

Brad explained to the officers, "We apprehended these two men as they were attacking this young lady. These are their weapons; although I believe this Glock seventeen is one that was stolen from my condo a few days ago. Lieutenant Davis will want to interview them with regard to a murder that took place in Central Park last week. There was a third assailant, but he escaped in a black Mercedes with this license plate number." Brad handed the number that Foley had written on a piece of scratch paper to the lead officer.

Another policeman handcuffed the two suspects while a third officer read them their Miranda rights.

As two officers escorted the handcuffed suspects to the backseat of one of the squad cars, Brad could hear one of the assailants objecting, "We're innocent. We did nothing. These men attacked us. We want our lawyer."

"We will all testify that we saw these men pursuing this young lady in the dark with loaded weapons. At the very least, you'll get them on illegal possession of weapons; but if we're right, that's only the tip of the iceberg," Brad countered.

The lead officer motioned to Brad to accompany him to the other squad car while he ran a make on the Mercedes from the driver's seat. "That's interesting," the officer said to Brad. "That car is not registered to an individual but to a corporation. The corporation is called Navigational Technologies International. It's located right here in New York. I'm sure Lieutenant Davis will have someone follow up on that information."

After the officer had collected all of their names, addresses, and phone numbers for his report, the two squad cars disappeared into the night with the suspects in tow.

Brad turned to his comrades and said, "Let's go back to Nigel's place. He says Billy and Sarah have some surprises for us."

They then all got into their vehicles and headed in the direction of Nigel's trading center. This time, Antonio chose to ride with Foley, whose SUV offered him a bit more leg room.

CHAPTER

20

A LITTLE WORN AND WEARY, THE crew regrouped a short time later around Nigel's huge conference table, trying to make sense of how quickly they had found themselves so deep in such a dangerous mystery. It was well past the scheduled 8:00 p.m. meeting time when the group finally settled in, but their excitement had not waned. On one side of the dark mahogany table, Sarah and Billy sat with satisfied smiles behind a wide spread of paper strewn in a vaguely organized mass. The two grad students were clearly in their element as a myriad of archeological and historical details from the professor's e-mails filled their minds. Across the table from them, Foley, Allison, and Brad settled in with cold drinks and curious looks, anticipating some good news.

"Okay, guys. Let's see what you found," Brad started in after a big sip from his glass.

Spinning a paper toward Brad and Foley so they could read it, Sarah began earnestly, "Well you're not going to believe this, but it looks—"

"Whoa. Not so fast, Sarah," Nigel interrupted. "We need to cover a few things first."

He was slightly reclined in his oversized chair at the end of the table and spoke like he was commanding one of the many corporate board meetings he had presided over in his sixty-eight years of life. Leaning forward in his chair with palms pressing down on the mahogany, Nigel slowly and deliberately looked each participant in the eye as if to emphasize the incredibly high stakes of the investment each was about to make.

"As we know from the events these past few days and the death of our dear friend, Don, we have stumbled onto something very dangerous. Perhaps the greatest concern is that we don't fully know who we are up against and we don't have a good grasp of what is really at stake here. Those are not good conditions for us to be curiously wandering around, asking questions and making our interest known. After tonight, we will all need to take many more precautions and take this much more seriously than we have so far. While we don't have Don's entire journal, we may have reconstructed a good part of what he was trying to tell us. In fact, if what Billy and Sarah have uncovered is even remotely accurate, and I believe it is, we are all in much more danger than we ever imagined." Pausing for effect, Nigel nodded to Sarah to redeliver the punch line.

With all eyes turning now to Sarah, she began a bit slower this time. "Well, you're not going to believe this, but it looks like Professor Romiel discovered where the largest cache of ancient Egyptian gold has been hidden untouched for centuries or even millennia. It seems the ancient Egyptians buried an immense amount of gold and for some reason it has never been recovered."

"What?" Foley said. "How is that possible? How do you know he found it? Where is it?"

"That's incredible!" Allison exclaimed proudly as she suddenly imagined her father standing victoriously on a huge pile of gold in some enormous tomb in the Valley of the Kings.

"Until now?" Brad offered questioningly. "Never been recovered until now, you mean?"

"Well," Billy began, "it's hard to tell from the e-mails. You see, for example, in this message he mentions knowing where *IT* is. But that is as detailed as the professor gets. He doesn't actually mention the word *gold*."

"So what *do* we really know?" Foley continued. "So how did you come to this grandiose conclusion about the greatest hidden treasure in the entire universe?"

"Why are these people trying to kill us?" Allison suddenly wondered. "Do we have the treasure map or something? What does the e-mail say?"

"I don't know," Sarah replied. "We just have some curious entries."

"Curious entries!" a few voices exclaimed in unison, Foley again louder than the others. "What do you mean curious entries? Is that all we have?"

"All right. Settle down, everyone," Nigel stepped in. "Just settle down. There is a lot more to the story. You're not giving Sarah and Billy a chance to explain. Now listen. Sarah has a background in Egyptology, and this all makes a lot more sense to her. Billy also has a background in the history of that period. Allison probably also understands some of this. But, Foley, you and Brad need to hear this out from the top. And I hope it goes without saying that absolutely none of this information leaves this room. Don specifically wanted Brad's help to get out of this mess, and I think we need Brad to lead this investigation. So pay close attention and don't interrupt. Sarah, if you would please, from the beginning."

"Okay." Sarah nodded. "Let me see if Billy and I can explain this and make it simple." Sarah tossed her long, sandy-blonde hair back and took a deliberate sip from her black coffee mug. Gesturing to the pile of papers strewn in front of them, she said, "You see, the professor's e-mails are all centered around the Akhenaten period. Akhenaten was a very unusual pharaoh who reigned in Ancient Egypt for only about twenty years, and he is central to this mystery. Now, in all these e-mails, the professor is communicating general updates to his unknown sponsor, who we found out is some still-unknown corporate entity that provided a million-dollar grant to the professor through the Museum of Natural History. So, basically, each of these e-mails just gives a short accounting of the day's or week's activities and what the professor plans to do next in fulfilling the objectives of the research grant. There is no real correspondence, and by that I mean the professor used this e-mail account almost exclusively for sending these encrypted updates to his sponsor's e-mail account. There are only a few short e-mails where Professor Romiel actually received instructions from the sponsor, and they don't tell us much. But it is clear that the professor was focusing his research on the Opet and Sed festivals of the eighteenth dynasty pharaohs and particularly on the *heretic* Pharaoh Amenophis IV in the area of Thebes."

"Wait a second," Foley interjected again. "You said the professor was zeroed in on Pharaoh Akhenaten's time period. Who is this Amenophis IV?"

"He's the same guy," Billy replied. "A few years into power, he changed his name from Amenhophis IV to Akhenaten." Seeing the perplexed look on Foley and Brad's faces, Billy added, "I know it's a little confusing, but it will make a lot of sense in a minute. Let me try to explain it this way. Way back in fourteenth century BC, the richest guy in the world was Amenhophis III, the father of Amenhophis IV."

"So you mean Amenhophis III was the Bill Gates of ancient Egypt, and number four, a.k.a. Akhenaten, was his son?" Foley asked.

"Well, you could say that," Sarah agreed. "There is evidence that a single sculpture built in the Karnak temple was made out of more than five tons of pure gold, ten tons of copper, and over a thousand pounds of gemstones. He was loaded. And just think, he built a lot of solid gold and gold-plated monuments."

"Right," Billy continued. "Then number four, a.k.a. Akhenaten, came along and turned thousands of years of Ancient Egyptian

culture upside down. He forced everyone to suddenly stop worshipping a group of gods with their main god, Amun, and start
worshipping only one god."

"Let me guess, Aten or Aton, A-t-o-n," Allison chimed in.
"The sun god."

"Right," Billy continued. "Then Amenhophis IV changed his
name to remove *Amen* and became Akhenaten, meaning, 'He who
works on Aten's behalf.' Maybe it would help if you knew that recent DNA evidence has established that the mysterious boy king
Tutankhamen was actually the son of Akhenaten. You see how this
is starting to tie together?"

"So how could he change thousands of years of religion overnight? Didn't the people riot or something? I mean, wouldn't the
priests at least rebel and do something?" Allison continued with
her thoughts. "It seems to me that a persecuted religion generally
thrives because throughout history there are many examples where
people couldn't really change ideology with a sword, right?"

"Exactly, Allison! Hold that thought!" Sarah replied.

"Yeah, but hold on a second. What about Opet, Sed, and
Thebes; and what does all this have to do with the gold?" Brad
asked impatiently.

"Okay. Going back. What I said," Sarah replied, "was that the
professor's research was concentrated on the two huge temples of
Karnak and Luxor, which are located in an area called Thebes. It's
basically an enormous complex of temples dedicated to the many
Ancient Egyptian gods and the place where most of the important
festivals for the pharaohs took place. Here's the bottom line. It looks
like Allison's father figured out how and where a lot of really angry
priests took most of Akhenaten's gold and precious stones from the
treasury and hid them for a lot longer than anyone ever imagined."

"Wasn't all the loot protected?" Foley asked. "How could a
bunch of priests steal tons of gold with the army guarding it all?
How could it have stayed hidden all these years?"

"That's just it!" Billy exclaimed. "These priests were brilliant engineers, politicians, artisans, and planners. It's even recorded that many of the priests went on to become mayors and governors of surrounding regions. Many were prodigies who descended from an elite ancestry of mathematicians and engineers who constructed some the greatest wonders of the world, many things we are still trying to figure out even today. While the priests were no match for the most powerful pharaoh and his army in the world of fourteenth century BC, their cunning might have been light years ahead of the pharaoh and the military. The professor's e-mails suggest the clues are literally carved into the architecture, even 'standing in plain sight.' In one e-mail, he says the answer is in the keys of electrum. Professor Romiel's theory is that the priests somehow incorporated the unbelievable heist into one of their holy festivals when they could briefly gain full access to the treasury."

"Are you still with us?" Sarah briefly checked the faces across the table.

Brad responded, "I was with you until Billy mentioned the keys of electrum. What's that all about?"

Sarah replied, "All we know is that electrum was a kind of shiny, metal alloy that was used to coat the tips of the obelisks. It would reflect the sunlight for miles in every direction and served as a kind of beacon or position marker. We still don't know what the keys of electrum means except that we believe it holds the clue to the position of the treasure."

"I know about electrum," Nigel said. "It is a mixture of silver and gold that occurs naturally in deposits all over the world. In my business, you learn a lot about precious metals, even ancient ones."

Ignoring a few obvious expressions of disbelief, Sarah passionately continued with her presentation. "Okay. So then Billy and I went through this stack of paper and tried to narrow down even more precisely where the professor was looking. That's when we noticed that the professor kept reporting on detailed hieroglyphics about the Sed and Opet festivals."

"Okay," Foley interjected impatiently. "What's the deal with these festivals? Why do we care that they had a big party some four thousand years ago when all the loot went missing? If the key is in the electrum, then what does the Sed and Opet have to do with it."

"Good question!" Billy replied. "Here's why, Foley. Those parties were not your average backyard holiday barbeque. When the pharaoh threw a party, it went on for days, maybe weeks; and the whole region would show up and watch spectacular processions and parades that would stretch from one temple to another and another and sometimes even cross the Nile on boats and visit more temples and go on and on. I mean, check this out. I'm not kidding you." Billy flipped to one of printed e-mails and began to read the professor's notes. "'Recorded at Temple of Amun festival offerings: one million nine hundred and seventy-five thousand eight hundred bouquets, sixty thousand four hundred and fifty wreaths, fifteen thousand five hundred scented bouquets, a hundred and forty-four thousand seven hundred and twenty lotus bouquets...' Well you get the point. These festivals were enormous and so very well documented by the priests that even the quantity of flower offerings are carved on the temple walls."

"Yeah. It's kind of funny how they kept stats of everything." Sarah added, "They even measured the pharaoh's jubilee festival by the number of broken empty wine jars and left these ancient records for us to see how big a party they threw."

"It sounds like Billy at an NYU party!" Foley offered with a laugh. "Is there anything you don't keep stats on?"

Billy acknowledged his nerdy tendencies with a sarcastic smile at Foley and continued with his explanation of the ancient parties.

"The Egyptians had dozens of festivals, but the only ones the professor mentions anywhere are the Opet and Sed. The Opet festival took place every fall season and was a huge, two-week celebration that corresponded with an important point of the flooding of the Nile. After a huge procession from the Temple of Karnak down a route of about a mile straight to the Temple of Luxor, the priests floated barques of the gods across the Nile and back down the river to the Temple of Karnak. The Nile was the source of life for their advanced agricultural economy, and so they threw quite a party during the flood season.

"The other big festival was to honor the pharaoh in what is called the Sed festival, and it was probably the largest of all the celebrations the Egyptians ever held. For some reason, the pharaoh typically celebrated this festival only after thirty years of reigning, and he was celebrated as becoming a god at this jubilee. You might say it was a party thirty years in the making, and a lot of preparation and construction was involved. And here's where it gets interesting. Billy and I remembered from our studies that Akhenaten had one of the most controversial Sed festivals ever researched by archeologists. You see, his father, Amenhophis III, was one of the most successful pharaohs and ruled for more than thirty years. He celebrated his Sed festival and then his three-year kingly renewal festivals in years thirty-four and thirty-seven; and a fourth celebration was being planned when he died. But his son, Amenhophis IV, a.k.a. Akhenaten, recorded his first Sed festival in only his third year of rule. Many scholars believe this was evidence that Amenhophis III and the son Amenhophis IV had a co-regency and shared the throne for a few years, basically because it had to have been the father's Sed festival."

"Okay okay. That's all very fascinating. I get it. The Ancient Egyptians knew how to throw a party," Foley interjected again. "Look, guys. I've listened intently, but where is this huge treasure trove? What does all this have to do with it?"

Silence filled the room, the team glanced around, examining each other's expressions.

"We can say with confidence," Nigel began in a statesmanlike manner, "that the professor found the location of the treasure solely based on the knowledge of these two festivals and the keys of electrum, whatever that is. I'm sorry to say that what he discovered and revealed to his sponsor was probably what got him killed."

"Do you think the sponsor is the killer, Nigel?" Brad asked.

"I don't know, Brad. But I intend to put every available resource on finding out about this Navigational Technologies International group and everything else we can find on the source of the professor's secret funding. We've got a few mysteries to solve and not much time!"

CHAPTER

21

MEANWHILE, IN AN UPSCALE corporate office on the other side of the city...

"You fool! Why did you leave them at the scene?" the director asked angrily, his bloodshot eyes and wrinkled facial features telling a story of hatred, indulgence, and greed.

"I had no choice. They were waiting for us," the driver of the black Mercedes responded fearfully. "I was lucky to get out of there. They had guns and were coming after me too."

"I told you not to approach the daughter unless she was alone and defenseless. You disobeyed an explicit order!"

The driver, a swarthy Middle Easterner named Salah, resented being blamed for the mishap that evening. He believed he deserved respect for his many secret operations that demonstrated his loyalty to the corporation. Still, he knew better than to argue with the director. He knew he could disappear without a trace or suffer some nameless agony for less. Instead, he turned his shifty gaze away from the director's and responded with deference.

"What's going to happen to the others?" he asked, hoping to change the subject.

"I've already dispatched our lawyer to the precinct," the director responded. "We were monitoring police communications, and we know exactly where they were taken. He'll have them out of custody before anyone can question them. We're going to have to teach these people a lesson they will never forget. They have no idea who they are dealing with."

The director picked up a scrap memo from his desk and crushed it in his hand, his anger still seething. He was still upset that Professor Romiel's journal seemed to be missing the critical information they needed. And Romiel's cell phone offered them little useful information apart from the stored phone numbers of his daughter, Allison; Brad Beck; and his NYU departmental office.

At the precinct headquarters, two squad cars had arrived and parked in the rear parking facility, where the officers unloaded their two prisoners and jostled them roughly to separate interrogation rooms on the second floor. A police sergeant was preparing the interrogation procedure, while a routine check was being made of criminal records using fingerprints and identification documents in an adjoining room. The sergeant let each prisoner sit alone for a few moments as a kind of softening intimidation. Then he first entered the room with the prisoner, who complained of broken ribs.

"What were you doing at the boat club tonight?" he began.

The prisoner responded as he had been coached, "I'm not saying anything until my lawyer arrives."

"You had a stolen weapon in your possession," the sergeant continued. "Where did you get it?"

"I have nothing to say," the prisoner insisted.

"Do you know what the sentence is for criminal assault with a stolen weapon?" the sergeant demanded. "You and your partner could spend a lot of time in Rykers."

"Do you know what the penalty is for unlawful detainment and police harassment?" the prisoner responded sharply. "You could lose your job, and I'll be happy to testify to that effect. Now where's my lawyer?"

Just then, the door to the interrogation room opened and another policeman entered. He whispered in the sergeant's ear, "His lawyer's outside."

"Send him in," the sergeant responded reluctantly, all the while wondering how the lawyer could have arrived so quickly when no telephone call had been made. He noticed the smug sneer on the face of the prisoner as the lawyer entered.

Without even taking a seat, the lawyer demanded, "I insist that you tell me the charges against my client. And bring in his colleague right this minute. You have no right to interrogate these men without their lawyer being present."

"Fine. Now that you're present, I have a lot of questions," the sergeant replied. "First of all, why were they attempting an armed assault on a private citizen in the parking lot of the Nyack Boat Club tonight?"

"Armed assault? Did they actually accost the alleged victim? No! For all you know, they were trying to protect that person. These charges will never hold up in a court of law. Is that all you've got?" the lawyer demanded. "It appears that my client has also suffered injuries. If that was the result of police harassment, there'll be hell to pay!"

"That's not all," the sergeant continued. "They were in possession of a stolen weapon."

"A stolen weapon?" the lawyer repeated. "How do you know it was a stolen weapon? Did you match the serial number to a number on a list of stolen weapons?"

"Well, no, because the serial number had been filed off!" The sergeant retorted.

"Officer, I demand that you release both of these men into my custody. Clearly you have no charges that would hold up in a court of law. I doubt very much that your superiors would look favorably on another police harassment suit for unlawful detainment."

"Look here, what's your name?" the sergeant stepped up into the face of the lawyer, not waiting for answer. "We can hold these guys for twenty-four hours no matter what you say, and *if*—that is *if*—they make bail, *then* you can take your guys. You got it? Now get out of here. You can come visit your friends tomorrow."

Before the lawyer could even respond to the ferocity of the seasoned police officer, another officer entered the interrogation room with a cell phone raised in the air.

"Sarge, it's the chief! He says let them all go! Let them go now! No questions."

Dumbfounded, the sergeant snatched the cell phone from the officer and shouted, "What's going on here, Chief?" as he stormed out of the room.

Within minutes, the assailants were free and riding comfortably on black leather in the back of another sleek, black Mercedes. The smug attorney sat in the passenger seat, giving the driver directions to their next destination.

CHAPTER

22

BACK IN ANCIENT THEBES ON THE
eastern bank of the Nile…

The grand schemes of the great high priest,
Hemenhoreb, were fitting neatly into place like huge,
granite blocks carved with perfection by a master
stonemason. Only the arrogance of a heretical pharaoh could rival
the ingenuity of the schemes; and paradoxically, Akhenaten's ego
had become the cornerstone.

The elite *hemernetjy* priests of Amun had convened in secret for
several weeks now as the young pharaoh continued to issue decrees
claiming divine inspiration for every bold stroke undermining the
priesthood of his forefathers. The priest's planning and progress had
been difficult as new challenges faced them at every whimsical change
of the pharaoh. More wab priests and masons had been diverted to
assuage the ire and impatience of Akhenaten in the construction of a
small Aten temple to the east of the Great Amun temple. The pharaoh demanded the temple be placed in a prominent easterly location
even closer to the sun disk's morning arrival so as to catch the blessed
sun's rays before they reached Amun's worshippers. Under increasing
time pressure from the pharaoh, the masons used smaller stone bricks
called *talatat* instead of the more unwieldy large blocks used throughout the complex. Even with such ingenious methods to satisfy the impossible deadlines and expectations of the young pharaoh, his visions

kept exasperating. In short, Akhenaten's ambitions had exploded; and now, the Egyptian people were being told of a city paradise created entirely for the worship of Aten. The Aten temple was not enough; the pharaoh had to supplant the enormous spiritual center of Thebes with a new capital predictably named Akhetaten, "the horizon of the Aten," located some hundred miles to the north.

The Heretic, as they now called pharaoh under their breath, was moving very rapidly. With only a few short days left, Hemenhoreb summoned Bekenamun, his first priest, to accompany him aboard one of the vessels for a ceremonial practice voyage on the Nile portion of the upcoming procession. As the pharaoh would soon decree, this first ever combined Opet and Sed festival jubilee would become the last and greatest celebration of the Theban temples of Karnak and Luxor. The end of worship of Amun and the gods was at hand. The pharaoh, his viziers, and his army would see to that.

"Hemenhoreb, have you heard what the pharaoh is asking of the priests?" Bekenamun stated with exasperation as the two elder priests met outside the southern wall of Karnak under the late afternoon sun.

"What is it now?" Hemenhoreb replied with concern.

"We are to consider name changes to glorify only Aten. For now, it is only a request. You know already what comes after. Of course, I must not be slow to comply, as even the lowest priests have begun to make changes to please the pharaoh, even today."

"You will never become Beken*aten* to me, brother. The lines are being drawn, and our days are numbered. Come. We will discuss all that must be done." Hemenhoreb gestured down the avenue of monuments to the precinct of Mut. "We will walk the procession south to the Luxor Temple. You have much to tell me before we meet with Sekhmaret, who waits for us on the barque."

The two stately priests decorated in the ornate vestiges of their holy positions set out with a leisurely stride on the mile-long walk to the entrance pylons of the Luxor Temple. Three Hemnetjer priests accompanied them who were trusted with many critical details that would be carried out in just a few short days. The lush gardens that surrounded the temple complex and adorned the avenues were as verdant and full of blossoms as at any time Hemenhoreb could remember. Everything flourished in the fertile silt of the Nile—well, almost everything.

"Has he finished?" Bekenamun inquired, remembering that the role assigned to Sekhmaret, the high priest of Toth, was to acquire and prepare the largest barque possible. It was all part of the impending actions to dutifully honor the new god-pharaoh during the Opet festival procession with all the grandeur and glorification the young imbecile could absorb.

"I am told he has transformed the old obelisk barge of Amenhophis III and it will be a sight to behold," Hemenhoreb replied as an evil grin escaped his tightly controlled facial expressions.

His thoughts drifted briefly to the three-hundred-foot-long barge that had floated countless tons of granite and even a two-hundred-ton obelisk down from the southern quarries of the empire. This time, it would carry the finest musicians in the land to accompany the pharaoh's boats while serving a far more sinister purpose. There would be no barque for Khonsu, Mut, and Amun on this voyage. The time of the many gods was at an end. Yet this procession for Akhenaten would be an even grander and more significant form of worship for their gods. The priests had seen to it.

The leisurely stroll under the shade of trees, with colorful flowers and monuments perfectly spaced and aligned in a north-south axis adorning the walk, belied the deadly urgency of the matters at hand. Bekenamun quickly recapped for Hemenhoreb the events of the annual gathering of the Theban first priests. As was tradition, the high priests rarely met in full assembly with the pharaoh, as symbolically, their greatest obligations lay with their gods or at least the pretense of such full devotion. Akehnaten's viziers tried their best to prevent any redirection of funds from the pending projects at the new capital but, in the end, were no match for the political oratory of the priests and the prideful extravagance of a pharaoh desiring the most lavish of celebrations ever imagined. A fierce victory had been won with the power of words. The greatest army could not protect the pharaoh now.

"Oh great Akhenaten," Ptah's first priest, Asmetoreb, began with convincing humility, "only you have been called by the Aten to open the gate of heaven for the great multitude of the people of the two lands. By the gods, it is written you must be glorified in a Sed festival for your deification unto Aten at the earliest moment we can comply. Please consider our devotion and all the offerings of the gods for your supreme celebration. With your authority, we humbly pray that, in this season of Akhet, as the Nile flooding begins, your people will all celebrate your glorious deification together in concert with the greatest Opet festival ever conceived. So as your kingdom rejoices at the flooding life waters of the Nile, they will sing your praises from your Sed celebrations to the Opet festival; and all the blessings of your Lordship will be upon them. In this way, will you be glorified above any others who have come before you; and may you live forever."

In the end, Akhenaten was convinced that his full and proper glorification as the one lord of the two lands would require great contributions from all the Theban temples' treasuries and beyond. His decree was final and was at once self-serving and supportive of his glorious plans for monotheism and the sole worship of Aten, or so he thought.

"Now please tell me, Bekenamum, how are your people prepared with the treasury?" Hemenhoreb asked as the Luxor Temple came into view behind the beautiful date palms lining the avenue. The beautiful walk connecting the northern Karnak Temple with the southerly Luxor Temple stretched for just over one mile and had been a scene of parades and celebrations for many centuries.

He replied in a soft voice only slightly more audible than their sandals striking the path, "We have full access. The scribes have the accounts. We can begin even tomorrow at your word. As we speak, the treasuries are being consolidated. With eleven days of the Opet and twenty-four days of the Sed festivals, we have time for many trips, as much as the barge can carry."

"Very good, and here is Sekhmaret," Hemenhoreb observed as the tall, thin high priest approached them from the banks of the Nile with arms spread wide in greeting. A genius of navigation and naval architecture, it seemed there was no feat too great for his engineering calculations and vessel construction.

"Bekenamun, you will begin tonight. Let us work the numbers together now. The schedule will be for you and the treasury tonight. We might die for this, but those who believe and follow our markers will restore the faith. Amun be praised."

The five priests turned from the path and met Sekhmaret with warm greetings. All was going according to plan. The last preparations would be reanalyzed, recalculated, and ultimately finalized as the enormous barge floated majestically north down the Nile carrying the schemes of a bitter Theban priesthood and, soon, the greatest treasures the world had ever known.

CHAPTER

23

I T WAS LATE IN THE EVENING, YET THE
meeting continued at Nigel's trading center. Responding to
the big question still floating in the air, Billy began, "Foley, the
truth is we don't know exactly where the treasure is but only
that the professor was pretty sure about it, and he indicated as
much in these e-mails. However, for some reason he never pinpointed
the location for his sponsor. Perhaps he suspected that his sponsor had
devious intentions. I think he figured out that the treasure was hidden
under or very near the huge monolithic obelisks. Sarah thinks that's
completely implausible. She thinks the treasure was taken on a big
parade and hidden somewhere as part of the festivities."

"No! I think they hauled it off and buried it during the festivities when no one was watching," Sarah responded defensively.

"Okay. *Whatever*, Sarah. The idea of carrying all this extremely
heavy gold around and secretly dumping it in the middle of a party
seems even more implausible to me."

"Maybe these maps and measurements will help us locate the
treasure." Allison pulled out the pages Brad had rescued from her
father's journal.

"What maps are those?" several voices asked in unison.

"These are the pages Brad managed to hide before he was attacked. Remember, Brad and Foley showed them to us during our
first meeting. Maybe they'll give us some more answers."

With even more excitement, the group quickly examined the three pages of maps and data entries Brad and Foley had left at the center during their last meeting. Brad leaned in closer now, watching the young students expertly decipher the notes.

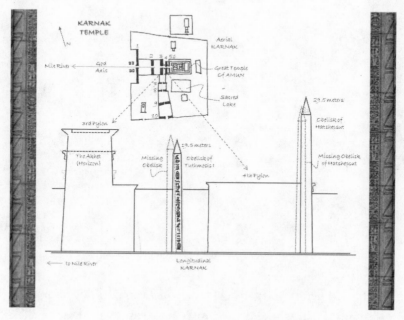

Annotated Map of Karnak Temple, Thebes

"I honestly don't even remember why I took those particular pages out of the journal," Brad explained with a wry smile. "So if they're not helpful, don't blame me. However, I'll certainly take any credit you give me for finding the treasure!"

Sarah and Billy were already muttering back and forth, exchanging pages and quickly coming to conclusions about the new information. Sarah was the first to speak.

"Looks good, people. Looks like Brad really snagged some key info. I bet this map of the Opet route probably passes right over the treasure."

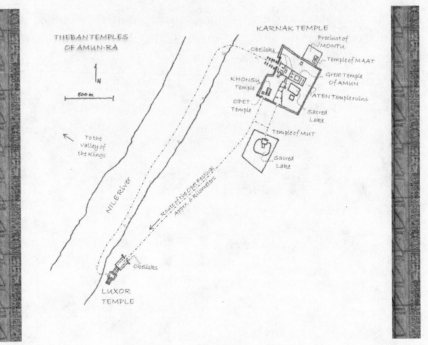

Annotated Map of Luxor Temple, Thebes

"Yeah! I thought you'd reach that conclusion!" Billy retorted in disbelief. "Then why did the professor measure all these obelisks he has listed here and was about to measure the obelisk in Central Park but has no data listed? Tell me that!"

Brad interrupted their dispute. "Foley, do you remember that article Allison read us the other day? It said the obelisks always appeared in pairs and that they…Allison, do you still have that article with you?"

"Uh no, Brad. It's back at the house."

"That's it, Brad!" Billy interrupted. "Many of the obelisks were in pairs. They were said to stand up over the horizontal lines of the temple. And the professor says here, 'The flat shape of the huge entrance pylon resembled the *akhet* or horizon.' So basically the temple symbolized the entrance point of the sun as it rose into the sky and the obelisks reflected the sun over all the earth. That obelisk in London was the sister obelisk to the one in New York, and

Professor Romiel needed to measure them. I think he was trying to figure out which obelisks cleared the *akhet*!"

"Then maybe Billy and Sarah are both right! Maybe the obelisks gave directions on the festival route about where to hide the treasure. Maybe they were markers of some sort," Brad suggested.

"What?" Foley exclaimed. "I'm so confused! Do we know anything useful at all? Opet, *akhet*, Aten, Sed, pylons, and parties; give me a break. You all are pulling this out of thin air. This so-called treasure could be anywhere."

"By the sound of it, Foley could be right," added Brad. "I mean, just look at this list of obelisks. How does this narrow anything down? Even if you found the right obelisk, what do we do next? I mean, what if the obelisk in Central Park is that obelisk? Then what?"

"What does 'clearing the *akhet*' mean, Billy?" Nigel asked.

"And," Foley continued, "the bad guys have all the e-mails and the whole journal—well, most of it anyway—and they probably already have the treasure well in hand. No offense, Billy and Sarah, but what's the point of chasing the professor's notes?"

"Okay. Okay. Here's the point," Billy exclaimed, holding up a page out of the professor's journal with a big smile. "Let me read something the professor wrote."

If I'm correct, then the priests of Amun emptied Akhenaten's treasury into the Nile with precise calculations so that it could be recovered after the restoration of polytheism. It had to be done quickly, and it threw Akhenaten into such a rage that he shut down Thebes and spent a good part of his reign defacing and destroying many of his ancestor's monuments to other gods. The treasure is still nearby, and these are the keys.

"What did my father mean, 'He shut down Thebes'? What are the 'keys'?" Allison asked.

Billy looked at the paper and flipped it over. "How should I know? I'm just trying to offer some possible solutions. There's nothing written after that. This is the back page, and on the front is the list of obelisks."

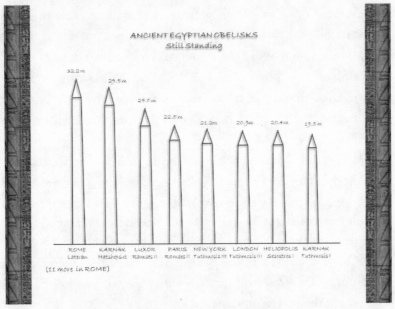

ANCIENT EGYPTIAN OBELISKS
Still Standing

Annotated Drawing of London Obelisk,
Thames Embankment, with measurements dated June 27.

"Hey," Foley said, "didn't you say one of the e-mails said the answer was in the *keys of electrum*? Maybe we should start with that."

CHAPTER

24

As the meeting at Nigel's trading center dragged on into the night, the sun's rays were slowly emerging on other side of the globe. It was now just past 5:00 a.m. Sunday on board the *Greifen 4* that lay at anchor in the waters of the Nile in the vicinity of Luxor throughout the night. The eighty-foot river tender held gently at anchor with the black-hulled bow pointing into the slow, northerly current. Despite a well-worn fifteen-ton deck crane that stretched above a buoy deck full of several huge cement block anchors, half a dozen red and green metal buoys, and hundreds of feet of solid steel anchor chain, the *Greifen* was far from an ordinary work boat. A series of advanced computers on the bridge had suddenly come to life and were rapidly collecting billions of data bits through an encrypted, long-range, wireless network while the ten-man crew slept soundly in their berths below.

Half a mile away, a large, burly figure emerged on foot from the darkness along the western bank of the Nile, giving quick orders in Arabic over a small, hand-held radio. Suddenly, three groups of men emerged in pairs at different intervals hundreds of yards apart along the Nile in the dim morning light. Each pair was carrying a portable control console and a man-sized mechanical device still dripping wet from the river.

"Shut off transmissions. Load the RemBots in the truck. We are done for the night," the lead figure ordered into the radio as the first call to prayer began to break the early dawn silence near Luxor. The men adjusted some electronics on the back of each of their remote bottom-scanning units and carefully lugged the motorized underwater vehicles to their pickup point along the dirt road.

"How many more days, Mahmud?" a voice crackled over the mike.

"Insha-Allah, until we find something, Ahmed. Now stay off the radio," the burly man ordered again in Arabic. "Report to the buoy yard again at sunset. The data will tell us if we need to relaunch tonight, so keep all units charged. Get some sleep. That is all."

Mahmud switched off the handset as a white box truck raced past him to collect the men and their equipment before the bright summer sun revealed any more of their covert activity. Mahmud pressed a speed dial number on his cell phone and waited for a voice on the other end.

"Yes?" the voice answered in a familiar English dialect.

"We're all clear. Please let me know if we have any good targets on this run. No troubles with the RemBots tonight and the search patterns should be complete. Look. I just don't know how many more days we can avoid suspicion..." Mahmud's voice trailed off.

"We'll let you know. It takes a few hours to examine the images. You know we have to find this, and everything from the old man points us right here. Come to the boat if you want to look yourself, but it should be obvious when we hit. Otherwise get some sleep and I'll call you after lunch."

The call ended, and Mahmud's eyes turned to the gentle waters of the Nile now reflecting a beautiful sunrise. How much longer could these waters hide the greatest treasures of ancient Egypt in its depths? Technology was on his side, but his luck had to improve. There was still too much area to cover and too little time. Tiredly, he brushed a fly from his face and decided to get a few hours of rest until the data results came in. Today would be the day. He could sense it. And he would need the rest.

CHAPTER

25

THE MEETING IN NIGEL'S CONFER-
ence room had now continued into the late evening
hours. Brad took the helm and concluded the meeting with a summary and a plan of action.

"Okay. It's getting late. We need to wrap this up,
summarize our findings, and plan our next step. Here's what we know
so far. First, there's a massive hidden treasure buried somewhere in
Egypt, possibly under the Nile River, and it's worth many millions of
dollars if not totally beyond measure. Second, Professor Romiel discovered the existence of the treasure and a means of locating it that he
called the keys of electrum. The location has something to do with the
obelisks he was measuring, and this information, or his unwillingness
to share it, is what got him killed. Third, we know that his sponsor was
willing to invest a lot of money to fund Don's work and get information on the location of the treasure. Also, we know that the sponsor
went to great lengths to remain anonymous even to Don himself. It
might be that Gunther at the American Museum of Antiquity is the
only person who could give us the identity of the sponsor, and he's
unwilling to do so. It's even possible that the sponsor, in collaboration
with a person or persons at the museum, was responsible for Don's
death. We have an e-mail address for the sponsor, but it doesn't reveal
who the sponsor is, and we must be especially careful about using it."

"We do have the name Navigational Technologies International, a corporation that might be affiliated with the sponsor in some way," Nigel interrupted.

"That was my next point," Brad continued. "We need your help, Nigel, as our first plan of action to get all the information you can about that corporation. What is the nature of their business? Who is the CEO? Are there other affiliated organizations? What projects do they have planned or ongoing in Egypt?"

Nigel nodded his agreement.

"My final point in summary is this," Brad continued. "We are in a race with time. The enemy has designs on getting to the treasure as quickly as possible. They have Professor Romiel's e-mails and most of his journal. They have already been working at accumulating information and chasing down leads for several months at least. They probably have some kind of search ongoing in Egypt as we talk. It is imperative that we begin our own search immediately. We have to send a team to Egypt as soon as possible and probably to those European obelisk sites the professor visited."

Turning his attention to Sarah, Brad continued. "Sarah, you indicated to Gunther at the museum that you want to pursue Don's archeological research in Egypt. As our next plan of action, I think you should give Gunther a follow-up call and see if he has heard anything from the sponsor. Be very careful. It's likely that the sponsor already knows who you are and what you're up to, and they might try to lead you into some kind of trap. Just try to get as much information as you can. We probably need you in Egypt with your archeological expertise and any contacts you have. If the sponsor will send you, so much the better because it can open a lot of official doors; but if not, we need to send you right away. We need contacts inside Egypt. I'd like you to make a list of all the contact professionals you know in Egypt so that we can consider them right away. Foley and I also have an old friend from Coast Guard Academy days who is now highly placed in the Egyptian navy, Moustafa El-Ezaby. You remember Moustafa, don't you, Foley?"

"Of course I remember Moose. He was a really big guy and a rugby fanatic while he was with us at the academy," Foley replied. "Last I heard, he was already an admiral in charge of their navy covert operations. Seems like it was just the other day he was a cadet trying to recite all of our Coast Guard sayings. Man, *Admiral* Moose! Wow! He's already making me feel old!"

"One final matter, and this might be the most important," Brad continued. "We need to decipher whatever Don meant by 'the keys of electrum.' We know it has something to do with obelisks and the measurements Don was taking. Billy, you seem to be thinking a lot about obelisks. Any ideas?"

"Well," Billy replied, "for starters, we know that they are huge, single-piece, multi-ton monuments the ancient Egyptians carved out of solid stone. The problem is that they are now scattered all over the world. You see, out of hundreds of obelisks erected by the Ancient Egyptians, there are only six still standing in Egypt. More than twenty other obelisks that still stand are now located outside of Egypt in places all over the world, including New York, London, Paris, Rome, and Istanbul. If I'm really going to investigate these keys of electrum, I need to start in Rome, where more than half of all the Egyptian obelisks are now standing."

"You're kidding." Brad replied. "Each of these obelisks weighs many tons and is one gigantic piece of stone? How were so many taken out of Egypt? If they are the keys to our dilemma, then it looks as if history has managed to lose them all around the world!"

"Exactly! Who would have ever believed so many these huge relics would be removed from their special places of honor. In fact, some actually weigh *hundreds* of tons, Brad," Billy corrected. "The tallest one in Rome is a single piece of stone over a hundred and five feet tall and weighs two hundred and thirty-five tons!"

"No kidding! Wow!" Brad exclaimed. "Well, I guess that explains some things. For one thing, it tells us that the ancient Egyptians had the engineering know-how to move hundreds or even thousands of tons of gold."

"Fascinating! Keep that thought, Brad," Nigel interrupted. "Did you know that the entire US gold reserve stockpile, the largest in the world, is considered to amount to only thirty thousand tons? Some experts believe that the Federal Reserve has been secretly loaning out gold to provide artificial support to gold futures trading and to keep the price of gold down, and they cannot buy back what they have loaned out without causing a huge spike in gold prices. So US reserves might actually now total only about fifteen thousand tons, half the stipulated amount. This means that a huge hidden cache of gold could become an incredible power source on the world commodities markets and could even determine the next world superpower. Even a few thousand tons could be seriously disruptive. Any attempts to corner the gold market could push price stabilization over the brink and precipitate a collapse in major world currencies."

"There might be a lot more to this mystery than even the professor realized. So I'm prepared to authorize use of my own jet waiting at the corporate hangar at La Guardia Airport to shuttle Billy to specified sites in Europe to follow up on the professor's notes and measurements. He should leave in the morning, or I should say later this morning," Nigel concluded.

"Awesome!" Billy exclaimed.

"I'm not sure that would be safe right now. At least we should all travel in pairs or have some kind of buddy system considering how much danger we are in," Brad cautioned.

"That's wise." Foley agreed. "What if Antonio goes with Billy? I'm sure he'd be safe with Antonio."

"Well, Antonio does know several languages," Nigel admitted, "but I was thinking after Allison's close call today she probably needs a personal bodyguard and driver until things settle down. He's the best I've got. And besides, with the trouble I'm going to stir up poking around, I might need his skills close by."

"Then what if I go with Billy?" Foley offered. "I mean, as long as we are passing around spending cards and vacation packages, you can sign me up for the European tour. I'll keep an eye on Billy for a few days."

"Great idea, Foley!" Brad added with a laugh. "Meanwhile, I need to take a commercial flight to Egypt, ASAP. As soon as Sarah hears from Gunther about sponsor support, I could accompany her on the next flight."

The receding adrenaline of the day's events was starting to sap the energy of the group as quickly as it had first arrived. The group was ready to adjourn. Allison was unconsciously spinning her long, brown hair with her fingers as a subtle streak of jealousy intruded into her thoughts. The idea of Brad running off on some adventure with the bright, attractive Sarah by his side definitely did not sit well at all. Sarah was only a few years younger than Allison, and her lifestyle as a full-time student projected an extra carefree and playful attraction she feared Brad would find hard to resist.

"I know some people at the Ma'adi Community Church near Cairo who would be glad to help us out," Allison blurted out. "I think if I went I could get some local help when we need it, and I know some resourceful ex-pats there too who know nothing of my father's work. Besides, I'm the only one here who speaks Arabic." As she spoke, Allison thought she caught a certain look from Sarah.

"Allison, I don't know about that," Brad responded gently. "Your father's friends might be compromised. He didn't know whom to trust down there, and meeting the wrong person could risk the whole element of surprise. We might need you to stay somewhere safe and give us support from the States. We might need you later if we come up with something."

"Look," Allison insisted more strongly, "I've been over there several times since I was a child, and I know my way around pretty well. If Sarah doesn't get sponsor support, I can set her up with me in the homes of some of my friends. I will be fine."

"Okay, Allison, but you might have to avoid places where people know you or your father, especially the archeology sites," Brad concluded.

"In that case," Nigel added, "We won't need Antonio to look after Allison and he could go with Billy. Foley, you could stay here and oversee some operations from this end."

"He's right, Foley," Brad agreed. "We need you here for several reasons, not the least of which is our project on the Hudson. And Susan would want to weigh in on your travel plans as well."

Nigel informed the group, "It's now past one a.m. Antonio will take Billy in my car to La Guardia at five a.m. That will give you both enough time to grab your passports and some clothes for the trip. And that will give us time to have a flight plan filed. Foley, would you please help Brad, Sarah, and Allison gather their things, make their calls, and be ready to board their departing flight to Cairo? I will have my secretary book for the first available flight from JFK tomorrow evening. We'll need the extra time to walk your passports through the embassy and get the necessary tourist visas. I'll alert my evening staff to begin a thorough search of Navigational Technologies International."

CHAPTER

26

IN ANCIENT THEBES, THE CONSPIRACY had reached its most critical point...

Hemenhoreb knew that everything was happening according to plan with the holy blessing of Amun. The pharaoh had fallen for their scheme. His pride had been his undoing! He had agreed to observe the Opet festival in concert with his Sed celebration of his ascendancy to godhood at the beginning of his reign. Even in this he had rejected the traditions of his fathers. The agreement of the pharaoh provided him with full access to the treasuries and use of the gigantic barque for transport. And now the treasures of Amun could be preserved until long after the pharaoh and his wicked heresy had disappeared from the blessed two lands. Hemenhoreb's own fate did not matter if only he could preserve the glory of Amun. Mother Nile will embrace the treasure under the watchful eye of Amun until there arises one with a mind of the gods who can unlock the treasure with the keys of electrum.

Bekenamun had begun the first of several voyages with the help of the priestly brotherhood to move the treasure in the darkness of night. Sekhmaret had guided them in the details of transport and placement of the massive treasure. Every detail would be followed perfectly so that nothing is lost. All had been calculated by Sekhmaret: the weight of each load and the length of the vessel.

The very size of each molten piece of gold would add to the safety of the treasure in its resting place. Each would rival the very obelisks for which the vessel had been constructed. That way no one person or group of persons could ever move the treasure without the engineering wisdom of the priests.

The secret final resting place was to be known only to the five high priests. Any workman who helped them in the project would do so with the sacrifice of his life, because only then could the secret be preserved. Otherwise, even if the workman was honest and devoted to the worship of Amun, Pharaoh Akhenaten could easily extract their secret by means of torture. The five had themselves sworn an oath and sealed it in their blood that if suspected of removing the treasure and apprehended, they would take their own lives for the glory and honor of Amun.

The most ingenious part of the plan concerned the placement of the treasure itself. The idea had come to Hemenhoreb as he stood in Karnak at the base of the mighty obelisk of Hatshepsut on the west side, the front side facing the Nile. The inscription and clue for generations to come, read as follows:

The Horus, Usritkau, Lord of the Vulture and Serpent Crowns [chosen by the goddesses Nekhebit and Uatchit], Flourishing in years, The Horus of gold, Divine one of crowns, King of the South and the North, Lord of the Two Lands, Maat-ka-Ra. She made [them] as her monument for her father Amen, Lord of Thebes, setting up for him two great obelisks before the august pylon [called] 'Amen, mighty one of terror.' It is covered over with a very great quantity of shining, refined electrum, which lights up Egypt like Athen [the solar Disk]. Never was the like made since the world began. May it make for him, the son of Ra, Hatshepsut, the counterpart of Amen, the giving of life, like Ra, forever.

As the inscription declared, Amun was symbolized by the august pylon, mighty one of terror, before which the obelisks were placed, with their pyramidians reflecting the glory of Aten, the solar disk. The placement point in the Nile would then be the point where the pyramidian of Hatshepsut's pyramid was obscured by the august pylon, the point where Amun could be seen to surpass Aten. The next key was to locate another point of reference to be taken in tandem with Hatshepsut's obelisk to provide a marker that was perpendicular to the flow of the mighty Nile, giver of life. Everyone knew that the obelisks were placed in pairs as a symbol of harmony, but the pairs were usually placed in parallel to the Nile and the rising sun, never perpendicular. The ideal marker was there before him: the remaining obelisk of Pharaoh Thutmose I, the father of Hatshepsut and the founder of the eighteenth dynasty. This obelisk, although smaller than the obelisk of Hatshepsut, also said on its inscription that it was dedicated by the pharaoh to his father, Amen-Ra. It was located west of Hatshepsut's obelisk; and together, the two obelisks provided a line of sight that was perpendicular to the Nile.

The irony flooded the consciousness of Hemenhoreb with immense satisfaction. The keys of electrum would be provided by the obelisks dedicated to the glory of Amun by the very ancestors of the heretic pharaoh. Their eternal devotion to Amun would prevail over the heresy of this transient fool. And the point of drop-off for the treasure would be the very point where Amun obscured the Aten to which this pharaoh claimed devotion. It was also satisfyingly ironic that this pharaoh would be sailing over the very point where the treasure was hidden while he was making his Opet Festival celebration. The irony was glorious! Although this Opet Festival was likely the last one that Hemenhoreb and his brothers would ever live to see, he could not wait for that day to come.

CHAPTER

27

THE MEETING HAD ADJOURNED AT
Nigel's trading center…

As Foley, Brad, Allison, and Sarah made their
way from the meeting to their cars waiting in Nigel's
parking lot, Billy gathered up the fragments of paper
dealing with obelisks, stuffed them carefully into his satchel, and
huddled briefly with Nigel.

"Look, Nigel," Billy said. "I think we should start where the
professor left off with his measurements and work backward. Since
we don't have any measurements from the Central Park obelisk, we
should start with the London obelisk; and perhaps that will help us
understand what he was looking for."

"I think you're right, Billy," Nigel responded. "So London will
be the first stop on your journey. You'll be in constant radio contact
with me through my pilot, so I can pass on any findings to Brad
immediately through a satellite telephone. I don't need to tell you
how important your research will be. It might be our only chance
to beat the killers to the location of the gold. And be careful. There
might be observers waiting at every obelisk location. That's why
Antonio is going with you. Here. I have also made some falsified
copies of the journal pages in case they fall into the wrong hands.
Keep the real pages completely secure, and let these be the ones
that someone might find."

Billy smiled at the satisfying thought that he was being entrusted with the task of decoding the keys of electrum and he would
soon be off to Europe on one of the most important adventures of
his young life with his own private jet and professional bodyguard,
all expenses paid. He shook hands warmly with Nigel in an enthu-
siastic farewell and started down the stairs in search of Antonio.
Somehow, he was not surprised to see Antonio standing near the
door, waiting with his bags already packed. Together, they went out
the door toward Nigel's waiting car on their way to Billy's apartment en route to the corporate hangar at La Guardia Airport.

As the two of them climbed into Nigel's chauffeured limousine,
Billy clutched his satchel with the obelisk papers tightly on his lap.
He felt amazed at the way events had come together to sweep him
into an adventure for which he had somehow been preparing all of
his life. He could not help but recall his childhood fascination with
obelisks and ancient history. This time, he would not only be calling
upon his knowledge of history but he would also be making history in a very personal and meaningful way. He turned and grinned
broadly at Antonio, who seemed far away in thought. Already, Billy
was measuring ancient obelisks in his mind as he fought back sleep
on the way to his apartment.

Meanwhile, Foley had motioned to Brad, Allison, and Sarah to
leave their cars and climb into his SUV and he would shuttle them
from place to place with JFK Airport as their final destination later
in the day. There would be no sleep as they made preparations for
the journey of a lifetime.

CHAPTER

28

L ATER THAT DAY, SLEEP WAS HIGH ON their list of priorities as the three of them boarded a commercial flight bound for Paris with a connecting flight to Cairo. Nigel's secretary had managed to reserve the last two business-class seats for Allison and Sarah, but Brad had not been so fortunate. He stowed his carry-on case overhead near the rear of the aircraft. Although part of him wished he could overhear the conversation between Allison and Sarah in the forward cabin, the other part was thankful for the quiet time to think, plan, and sleep.

It was satisfying for him to consider how the day's events had come together. Thanks to Nigel's diplomatic contacts, the tourist visas were issued amazingly in less than an hour on a Sunday morning. Sarah's phone call to Gunther at the museum had been somewhat unproductive, as she was told he was away on a business trip and might not return for a week or two. That was probably just as well, Brad thought, because he really did not want anyone at the museum to know of their plans. Brad's telephone call to Vice Admiral Moustafa El-Ezaby had gone through to Alexandria, and Brad had alerted his former classmate about the trip and had enlisted his help. He had scheduled the earliest possible meeting for the two of them at Brad's hotel in Zamalek, an island in the Nile

River that is the suburb of Cairo where most of the embassies are located. Allison, for her part, had contacted an American family in Ma'adi that she had known from her childhood in Egypt and her attendance at Ma'adi Community Church. The husband and father of the family would be working on assignment to an oil-drilling project near the Red Sea three weeks each month; but the wife and mother of three was overjoyed to learn of the visit, and she welcomed the company of Allison and Sarah in the family's rented villa for as long as they could stay.

Brad was thankful for Nigel's satellite phone in his carry-on bag that would allow him to be in encrypted contact with Nigel at least once daily. They agreed he would make contact in the early evenings Egyptian time that corresponded to late mornings New York time. By natural instinct, Brad began rehearsing his first moves for his arrival in Cairo. He would accompany the girls to the home in Ma'adi, where they would be staying. Then he would return and check into his hotel in Zamalek and wait for his meeting with Moustafa. He was already thinking that a Nile cruise would be an ideal way for the three of them to travel upriver to Luxor unobtrusively as tourists and learn what was happening in the area where Don Romiel had been conducting his research. His thoughts turned inevitably back to Central Park and the rude events surrounding the death of the professor. He remembered his cold, still body in the city morgue and the terse message in blood beside the obelisk in Central Park. He knew that Nigel would already be busy unraveling the corporate connections and that Billy would already be in London, avidly focusing on obelisk measurements. As he turned these thoughts over in his mind, the long-overdue call to sleep overtook him there in the back of the Boeing 747.

In the forward cabin, Allison and Sarah were also winding down a thorough conversation in which Allison had been sharing what to expect with her friends in Ma'adi, and Sarah was telling about her two earlier archeology internship trips to Luxor and

Aswan. Both women were obviously excited about the opportunity to revisit Egypt, but both were conscious of the importance of the trip and the danger they could be facing. Finally, they both drifted off into a deep sleep that was interrupted only by their change of planes in Paris.

CHAPTER

29

ON THE OUTSKIRTS OF LUXOR, in a small room darkened by thick shades to keep out the bright sunlight of the days, Mahmud lay sound asleep. A small, old window air conditioner unit struggled to keep the room's temperature comfortable while the noisy vibrations from the highest fan settings served to muffle some of the loud traffic noises outside. As the old mattress covered by only a few sheets attested, the barren apartment served only as brief rest stop between the nightly runs Mahmud had been spearheading for weeks along the Nile. Utter fatigue was setting in; and when the cell phone rang from somewhere on the floor near the mattress, Mahmud could hardly discern the ring above all the white noise.

"Huh?" Mahmud grunted as he answered the phone from his bed and pressed it awkwardly to his ear.

"Mahmud, we got something!" the voice on the other end exclaimed in accented English. "Are you awake? We got something!" he repeated.

Mahmud rolled off the thin mattress, dropping a few inches onto the hard-tiled floor still holding the phone, still trying to determine if he was awake or asleep.

"You got what?" he asked as he struggled to his feet. "What time is it?"

"Hurry to the ship! The RemBots found something on the run last night! You have got to see this! It's about two in the afternoon! Now hurry out and I'll show you!" The caller hung up abruptly.

Mahmud stared at the cell phone a moment, trying to confirm if the call had been real. In a flash, he grasped the reality: the treasure! In the time it took to put on his weapon, his clothes, and shoes, he was out the door.

CHAPTER 30

I
T WAS A HOT, DRY SUMMER AFTERNOON
with temperatures near 100 degrees Fahrenheit when Brad,
Allison, and Sarah rolled their carry-on luggage through
immigration and customs in the Cairo International Airport
and out into the brightness of the terminal parking lot. Brad
hastily donned his sunglasses and carefully surveyed the surroundings, wondering if anyone had anticipated their arrival. Soon, they
had given their destination to a transportation attendant, agreed on
a fare, and had boarded a white Toyota station wagon that served
as their taxi to Ma'adi. Allison and Sarah needed no reminder to
be cautious with their conversations in the presence of the driver.

Brad sat in the front seat beside the heavy-set, middle-aged
driver and took in the unfamiliar scenes around him. The traffic
was heavy and noisy with horns honking and cars and trucks and
an occasional camel busily weaving about every which way for
position, with no regard for lanes. Every stop brought Brad fresh
reminders of survival of the fittest as cars raced to be first through
each intersection. In the backseat, Allison and Sarah smiled with
recognition as they detected familiar scenes and smells. Soon, they
were speeding southward past Cairo down the Corniche along the
east bank of the Nile en route to Ma'adi.

Hoping to make conversation, the driver turned toward Brad and asked, "*Inta men eyn?* You from where?"

"America," Brad replied.

"Ah, Amrika," the driver responded with a pleasant sigh.

Brad suspiciously was not sure whether the driver's pleasure was due to genuine high regard for Americans or a secret longing for a substantial tip at the end of their journey.

Soon, the driver reached across to Brad with a pack of local cigarettes and offered in a friendly way, "Take cigar."

Brad, who didn't smoke, paused briefly, wondering if there was a polite way he could refuse.

Allison, in the rear seat, anticipated Brad's confusion and spoke to the driver in clear Cairene Arabic, "*Ma fish nafas.*" This, she explained to Brad, was a polite way of saying either that he was out of breath or that he had a breathing difficulty that made it hard for him to accept the offer of a cigarette. Brad's admiration for Allison rose.

The driver addressed his next question to Allison, realizing as he now did that she was fluent in Arabic. "*Fein fel Ma'adi?*" he asked, wanting to know exactly where in Ma'adi they were going.

Allison removed a card from her purse on which she had written the road number and the villa number where her friends were located. She was careful to give a nearby address to the driver that was not their exact destination.

When the three of them had finally climbed out of the taxi, Brad breathed a sigh of relief and helped remove the luggage. After he had paid the fare and tipped the driver handsomely, the driver smiled with a toothless smile and, with a loud "*Shokran,*" proceeded to drive off back in the direction of the airport. Brad thought best to be sure that the women were appropriately situated and then to find different transportation to his hotel in Zamalek. The three of them walked a short distance on the dusty road in the direction of their destination. The suburb seemed quiet and sleepy compared to downtown Cairo, and the sight of stately palm trees and gated villas dating from the British occupation era brought welcome tranquility. When they had arrived at their destination villa, they saw that the grated iron gate was shut; but asleep on a bench inside the gate they saw an elderly bearded man in a long, loose-fitting, beige-colored garment known as a *galabeya*. Allison woke him with a standard greeting in Arabic, and he immediately awoke and opened the gate to let them in. She explained that this was the *bo'ab*, or gateman, who was a kind of caretaker.

Mary Jo McCauley, the lady of the house, greeted them with a warm Louisiana accent and ushered them into a cool, comfortable living room with a high ceiling fan and offered them each a cold glass of *kerkaday*, a kind of hibiscus tea that was unbelievably welcome and satisfying. Brad explained that he needed to check into his hotel in Zamalek but that he would be back the next afternoon if he could arrange their booking on a cruise to Luxor. Mary Jo offered him use of their company car and driver parked just outside the gate, and Brad gratefully accepted.

CHAPTER

31

THAT SAME EVENING, AFTER BRAD had unpacked, showered, and settled into his hotel room in Zamalek, the telephone in his room rang loudly. It was Vice Admiral Moustafa El-Ezaby in the lobby right on time.

"C'mon up to room two thirty-two, Moustafa," Brad said. "I can't wait to see you again."

After a typical Egyptian hug, a warm *"Ahlan-wa-Sahlan"* expression of welcome from Moustafa, a brief exchange of pleasantries, and some reminiscing about their days together at the academy, Brad got down to business.

"Look, Moustafa," he said. "This is going to push the limits of your sensibilities, but I'm here to gather evidence about something terrible that is happening that is of grave concern to your government and to mine. I'm basing a lot on our friendship that you will believe what I am about to tell you. You see, I have reason to believe that there's an international smuggling operation that is even now staging one of the greatest heists of ancient Egyptian treasure ever. I only hope we're in time to stop them. You should also know that they have already murdered an American archeologist and they'll stop at nothing to get what they want."

"Yes, I do believe you. Please tell me everything you can, Brad," Moustafa responded quickly. "We have a lot of experience with people trying to plunder ancient Egyptian treasures. This sounds like a critical concern for us."

"Well"—Brad returned his friend's anxious gaze and, after pausing for a deep breath, continued with more details—"you understand that this is highly sensitive information, and someone has already been killed for bringing it to our attention. My friend, Dr. Don Romiel, an American Egyptologist, was murdered in Central Park more than a week ago. He had been working in Egypt on a project to gather information about the Akhenaten period of ancient Egypt. In the course of his research, he came across information about the placement of a massive gold treasure that we believe might be located somewhere under the Nile River in the region of Luxor. Professor Romiel might have uncovered a plot to remove the treasure, and he was on his way to enlist our help when he was murdered. We suspect his sponsor might be involved and are checking on that possibility. I'm here with two American colleagues, the professor's daughter and a former student of the professor, who is also an Egyptologist. I'm now thinking we need to go to Luxor surreptitiously, possibly on a Nile cruise boat tomorrow evening, and learn what we can learn."

"Brad, we will want to know whatever you uncover," Moustafa said. "You should know that we have a small naval terminal at Luxor, so that would be a good way for us to stay in regular communication. I can get you in touch with some friends there to make sure you have some support. Our government also has a couple of major exploratory projects ongoing in the Nile River that I know of. One is a two-year project administered under the Ministry of the Interior to map and install navigational aids along the entire route of the Nile River from Aswan to Cairo. You understand that my government has a number of concerns about navigation safety for tourism and commerce. The project is intended to improve commerce with buoy placement and other aids to navigation that we very much need. Maintaining those aids to navigation will become the responsibility of the Egyptian Navy and Coast Guard, and that's where I will eventually come in."

"The other project is a newly initiated river-bottom probing project designed to locate ancient artifacts buried in silt beneath the river bed between Luxor and Aswan. It is believed that a lot of important ancient artifacts were lost in the Nile as thousands of workmen transported items to Luxor from the quarries at Aswan. The secretary of antiquities, Dr. Housny, has raised a lot of foreign research funding for the underwater mapping project that is currently operating near the Aswan dam. I am much more familiar with the antiquities Nile project because they have need for some of our navy divers to help with that research effort. They are both very large maritime projects that are expected to last for years. I can definitely see how this could put any artifacts or treasures in the Nile at risk."

"Those projects could be critical pieces of the puzzle. So the river-bottom mapping is located in Aswan now? Where is the other project being based out of?" Brad asked.

"As I said, that's the responsibility of the ministry of the interior. All I know is that they have contracted with some international corporation to complete the project and they presumably have installed the buoys from Aswan approximately to Luxor. I guess they still have a few months remaining for the final navigational section to Cairo. I can get more details for you from the ministry if you like."

"By all means!" Brad responded. "I could use the name of the corporation, the terms of the project, and the names of any project personnel. Also, it might help to know who the responsible contact persons are at the ministry."

"Of course, Brad. I can probably get that information for you tomorrow. Is there anything else you need?"

"Now that you mention it, how can I get information about exactly where Professor Romiel was doing his research and who the people were whom he was working with?"

"That would be the province of a special department within the ministry of antiquities that oversees all archeological projects in Egypt. Your Professor Romiel would have had to get permission from that department. I can make some inquiries there as well if you like."

"Please do so," Brad responded. "We don't have enough information to work with at present. And time is critical. We might already be too late. But be very careful. We can't afford to alert certain people that we are here or that we have any idea about what they are up to."

After a few more minutes of conversation and planning, Brad accompanied Moustafa down to the hotel lobby, where he hoped to confirm a Nile cruise and provide details of the schedule to his friend. Brad was pleased that with Moustafa's help he was able to book passage for three on a cruise ship leaving Cairo at 6:00 p.m. the next evening and arriving in Luxor early the next morning. Although the cruise continued to Aswan, Moustafa arranged for them to leave the cruise and get reservations for a suitable hotel in Luxor. After agreeing to provide whatever information he could gather for Brad at a noon luncheon the next day, Moustafa said a warm farewell and took leave of his friend. Brad watched from the lobby window as his friend stepped into a government car driven by a uniformed military driver and sped away into the city lights and the warm Cairo evening.

CHAPTER

32

MEANWHILE, ON THE NILE RIVER near the city of Luxor…

Mahmud excitedly flung open the door to the mess deck. His eyes met a chaotic scene of papers, images, and printouts scattered across several small dining tables. Nearly out of breath and still tired, he had raced from his Luxor apartment to the buoy yard where he had taken a wooden skiff with a small outboard motor out into the Nile to rendezvous with the *Greifen 4*. Mahmud had scrambled up the worn rope ladder and, with bowline in hand, secured his small boat to a starboard stanchion and rushed inside the steel superstructure to finally hear the good news.

"Look at this, Mahmud!" one of the three ship's officers shouted, holding up some colored imagery on photographic paper. "You hit it! You did really well last night. We've got all kinds of TOI's just below the riverbed. Metallic! Very clear *metallic* ones and scattered like a treasure's debris field. It's perfect! Well done!" The second mate could not contain his exuberance and confidence that those targets of interest were much more than ordinary river garbage buried over centuries of silt shifts.

"Looks good all right," the gray-haired captain muttered with a slight German accent without looking up from the papers before him. "That notebook from the archeologist came in handy. All three RemBots produced a lot more hits the closer their sweep to Karnak. Seems we've been wasting quite a bit of our time to the south of the Luxor temple."

The captain and first mate continued to mark and measure some of the charts with a series of transparent overlays taped together and stretching the length of one dining table. Mahmud took the imagery sheet from the second mate and examined the reddish colorations that were splotched and scattered across a mostly gray background in a mesh of black gridlines.

"So these red dots could be the gold we've been looking for?" Mahmud asked, pointing to a corner of the grid sheet. "That's a big cluster up in that section, so what else can you tell me? How much gold do you think this is?"

Looking up, the captain motioned to an aluminum chair next to his table. "Have a seat, Mahmud. I'll walk you through it. Your department of the interior will be very proud of your work. You have done exceptionally well, and we will let Dr. Hezani know how much the recovery of the notebook has helped us also." Pushing aside a few images and pointing with a brass divider, the captain gestured to the chart and overlays stretched across the table.

"This is our Nile search map. Here, we have overlaid all the search patterns of the RemBots since this project started. Based upon what we were told initially, you can see we concentrated all of our efforts here to the west of the Luxor temple."

"Yes. We thought that since the ancients departed on vessels from here"—Mahmud pointed at the western edge of the Luxor temple that bounded the Nile on the east—"that it made the most sense for the gold to be dropped straight out into the Nile from the banks of these Opet shrines. Okay. Go on."

The captain ignored the interruption. "Well, you know how that worked out. See these drop sites? We craned up sediment and examined four target zones here and over here, and those were nothing."

"Then, based on what you said from the professor's records, we moved our search downstream to the north." Sliding the connected charts carefully over the table, the captain adjusted the view for Mahmud. "Your men ran the three RemBots in these patterns last night. You can see the lines are plotted there lightly in green. The section over here that looks like scribbling is where RemBot 1 got fouled for almost two hours. Propulsion got tangled up or something."

"Yes. I remember. Probably got wrapped in garbage or fishing gear. Thought it was going to be a mess last night," Mahmud acknowledged.

"Anyway, let me put this overlay down on the chart." Aligning a new transparency over the chart to several reference points, the captain delivered the best news last.

"Okay. You see this, Mahmud? These are last night's TOIs, and we have all three RemBots passing near this area for an excellent deep riverbed penetration scan from several angles. Each underwater platform's ground-penetrating radar gives us a very accurate depth reading and material composition estimate. Linked with GPS systems on board, we now have the precise location, size, and depth for crane extraction."

"Yes. Very nice. I see," Mahmud replied. "But please help me. How large an area is this treasure site? Do you have an idea about how much gold this could be?"

The captain leaned back from the table and smiled. "You know it is difficult and unwise to give you such numbers at this time, but I can tell you the main area we will target is approximately ten meters by four meters right here."

"Captain, do you notice something about the alignment of that spot to the temple?" Mahmud suddenly observed in surprise.

"What? The alignment of this treasure site to the Karnak temple? What? That it's due west?" the captain responded.

"Well, yes!" Mahmud exclaimed. "But notice that it lies exactly on what we call the god axis of the Karnak temple. If you go the other direction, south toward Luxor, that is called the pharaoh axis; and you see if you draw a straight line down the center of the temple on this east-west axis, it corresponds with the rising and setting sun as the ancients designed it. That same line of the sun passes directly over the temple out the entranceway and right out over the Nile on top of this treasure site! It has to be the treasure! It makes perfect sense now!"

"Captain," the first mate spoke up now, "what if we expand the search along that axis in the direction of the highest concentration of metal? It looks like we could find even more results in the tens of meters from this point to the shore!"

"Yes. I was thinking the same thing. Very good, very good." The older man rose slowly from his seat with a very uncharacteristic smile spread across his tough, weathered face. "It's time to get busy! We are going to need to get our hands on samples for Mahmud and his team back at the interior ministry. Let's plan on another Bot run tonight. I will have the system send out the next search patterns based on what we have learned today. Good work!"

With that, the captain left the mess deck, ducked the doorway, and made loud steps up toward the privacy of the bridge. It was time to give headquarters a call and prepare them for a new direction in gold futures.

CHAPTER

33

I N LONDON, IT WAS AN HOUR EARLIER than Cairo as Billy began his radio conversation with Nigel from the cockpit of Nigel's corporate jet parked outside a corporate hangar at Heathrow.

"Look, Nigel," Billy began. "We've been to Cleopatra's Needle at the Victoria Embankment. I've managed to confirm Professor Romiel's measurements. Apparently, it's an exact clone of the obelisk in Central Park. Both are about sixty-eight feet tall and weigh about a hundred and eighty tons. The hieroglyphs inscribed on the sides might differ somewhat, but it appears that the professor was most concerned with the measurement of the capstone or *pyramidian* at the top of the obelisk and not with the hieroglyphs. His measurements included the height of the obelisk to the base of the pyramidian, the height of the pyramidian itself, and the angle of the ascending sides of the pyramidian. Apparently, he was not concerned with the hieroglyphs inscribed on the sides of the obelisk because he knew that the inscriptions were added much later by Ramses II to commemorate his victories in battle."

"What do you think Don was looking for?" Nigel asked.

"I'm not sure yet," Billy responded. "My first thought was that he was trying to determine the direction of the reflection of the sun's rays off the electrum coating of the pyramidian. We know that on a clear day, the sun's reflections could be seen for at least fifty miles in all directions from the obelisk as the sun went through its daily cycles. In this way, I imagine that the electrum provided a kind of beacon that pointed to the location of the treasure."

"That sounds like a promising explanation," Nigel said.

"Yeah, only the reflections were too diffused and moved with the movement of the sun. And there is a more serious geographical problem with that theory."

"What problem?" Nigel asked.

"Well, it turns out that the London and New York obelisks were originally placed in the Temple of the Sun in Heliopolis by Thutmose III in about fourteen fifty B.C. The timeline works for us, because Pharaoh Akhenaten reigned from approximately thirteen fifty-three to thirteen thirty-six B.C., or a hundred years later than Thutmose III; but the geography is all wrong. Heliopolis is a suburb of modern-day Cairo that is located about three hundred and twenty miles north of Luxor. Professor Romiel was working in the Luxor area, where the Opet and Sed festivals occurred. This location problem shoots down my next theory also."

"Which is?" Nigel asked.

"Which is that the New York and London obelisks together formed a sighting line perpendicular to the Nile that served to pinpoint the location of the treasure. But since they were located so far north of the route of the Opet and Sed festivals that Professor Romiel was studying, that theory doesn't make sense either."

"So what do you propose as the next step?" Nigel asked.

"Well, I was going to suggest that we go next to Cleopatra's Needle number three. It's located in Paris at the Place de la Concorde. It's actually bigger than the New York and London obelisks, standing about seventy-five feet tall and weighing approximately two hundred and fifty tons. But there are two problems with that obelisk as well. First of all, the pyramidian is missing, and the French government reconstructed an artificial metallic pyramidian to replace the one that was lost. In the second place, that pyramid was also placed at the temple of the sun in Heliopolis. Its mate is still standing at the original site today, and we have the measurements of that one from Professor Romiel's notes. Because it is also from the Heliopolis site, it doesn't offer much information about the Luxor or Karnak Temple sites," Billy responded hesitantly

"So where does that leave us now?" Nigel queried impatiently.

Billy took another deep breath. "I now believe that our next stop should be Rome. It seems the ancient Roman emperors hauled off thirteen of the Egyptian obelisks to place them in Rome. Since there are only six obelisks left standing in Egypt and twenty-seven outside of Egypt, and thirteen of those are in Rome, I suspect the information we need could well be there in Rome. I see that Professor Romiel was especially interested in the Lateran obelisk, so named because Pope Sixtus V had it placed before the Church of Saint John the Lateran in AD fifteen eighty-eight. It's the granddaddy of all the obelisks, originally weighing about four hundred and fifty-five tons and rising forty-two meters or a hundred and thirty-six and a half feet in height. It's the only obelisk we know of that was set up without a mate. They think the mate was abandoned unfinished in the Aswan quarry when Thutmose III died, because it was found to have some cracks or fissures. The important thing is that this obelisk was originally set up at the Karnak Temple, which makes it a logical candidate to use as a marker for burying treasure during one of the festivals."

"Very well, Billy. Your next flight plan will be filed for Rome," Nigel agreed. "Did you encounter any suspicious activity near the London obelisk? I mean, were you being watched?"

"Nothing unusual," Billy reported. "Of course people were watching us, but that was probably just because we looked so strange, the two of us taking photos and measurements of an ancient piece of granite."

"Well, keep me posted on all developments and be very careful. The last person measuring these obelisks did not fare well, as you recall. I'll be in constant communication with your pilot."

"Okay, Nigel. That's it for now." Billy handed the radio headset back to the pilot with the words, "It seems we're now headed for Rome as soon as we can be airborne." He watched as the pilot confirmed the instructions with Nigel.

As Billy turned to rejoin Antonio in the aircraft cabin, the pilot, who had finished his radio conversation and had overheard Billy's earlier conversation with Nigel, spoke out of curiosity, "What's so important about obelisks, if I may ask? I mean, why would the governments of Britain, France, Rome, and the US even bother to take all the expense and effort to move those huge chunks of stone so far away from Egypt? They can't be worth that much trouble."

Billy welcomed the question on one of his favorite topics, and he was primed to rise heatedly to the defense of the ancient monuments. "Chunks of stone? Obelisks are symbols of enlightenment and civilization. They dispatch light and point upward. The fact that they were major markers of the most advanced civilization of the ancient world makes them tempting artifacts for later civilizations as a demonstration that they have finally arrived. Why do you suppose that the Washington Monument in Washington, DC, was constructed in the form of an obelisk? Obelisks have monumental cultural significance. They are a lot more than mere chunks of stone. According to archeometrology, the study of measuring systems used in ancient times, obelisks were designed to show harmonic relationships between mathematics, astronomy, geometry, biology, physics, and time. Their builders intended to use their dimensions and physical locations to encode messages about harmony and science."

"Wow. I didn't know they were that special," the pilot said.

Billy rejoined Antonio in the cabin lounge. He was comforted to see Antonio dutifully cleaning his weapon in the lounge, and Billy promptly apprised him of the next leg of their journey. Settling into a comfortable, leather-upholstered chair, Billy opened his laptop and began searching for information on the obelisks of Rome.

CHAPTER

34

O N THE BRIDGE OF THE VESSEL
Greifen 4, the skipper and first mate were checking the navigational instruments above the
drone of radio chatter and loud music blaring
from a CD player on the chart table. The morn-
ing sun was already delivering a searing heat that would only inten-
sify through the day. On the water two hundred meters from the
Nile's shore, the flies were still a major nuisance as they unmerci-
fully pelted the sweaty faces of the crew, with not even a hot breeze
to keep them away.

The first mate examined the ship's position on the digital navigation plot as he throttled the *Greifen* slowly forward with a few
intermittent thrusts of the engine.

"Okay now! I think we're directly over the target, Captain," he
exclaimed loudly above the blaring music.

Pressing a few buttons on the ship's GPS and a yellow, hand-
held unit, he set a digital marker to the current location. The captain made some additional notations; reset the settings on several
other electronic instruments; and took a seat in his red, cushioned,
aluminum chair.

"Ready?" the first mate asked as he turned to receive a nod from
the captain. "Okay. Throttling up. Will move a hundred meters into

the current and drop anchor. That should drift us back above the target when the anchor sets in the mud and just far enough to keep the anchor chain from damaging anything below."

The captain nodded his agreement and stood to his feet to fish out a vibrating cell phone in his front pants pocket. Waving flies from his face with his free hand, he flipped open the phone and answered gruffly, "Greifen here." He paused. Turn off the music," the captain ordered as he leaned into the call and covered his ear from all the noise. In a few moments of straining to hear, the captain ended the call with a simple, "Got it," snapping the phone closed and slipping it quickly back into his pocket.

"We've got trouble arriving from the US. That was headquarters," the old man explained to his first mate. "There's some kind of investigation going on. They want us to move faster. They will give us as much cover as possible; but we need to be even more alert, use deadly force as necessary. Pass it on to the crew and let's get the divers ready. I want to hoist something good before sunset. Got it?"

"Yes, sir," the mate responded; he knew when the old German was deadly serious.

CHAPTER

35

BACK IN ZAMALEK, JET LAG WAS BE-
ginning to take its toll as Brad entered the elevator to
return to his room on the second floor of the hotel. He
relished the small dinner he had ordered in the hotel
restaurant adjacent to the lobby. The coffee they served
came in a tiny *estekan*, and he was sure it would not serve his purpose
until he tasted it and found it was ultra-high octane. He was pleased
at all that had been accomplished on their first day in Egypt. The
meeting with Moustafa had been especially productive. He was glad
the girls were safe in the villa in Ma'adi, and now he had reservations
for their cruise up the Nile to Luxor the next evening.

There was no one in the corridor as he inserted his key in the
door to his room. His thoughts turned to Nigel and Foley and Billy
and Antonio as he entered his room in search of the satellite telephone stored in his luggage. He knew he should report in to Nigel,
and reception would be best on the small balcony overlooking the
street outside his room. Stepping outside onto the balcony, he could
hear automobile horns honking in the street below; and he felt the
warm evening breeze bringing the smells of the city as he oriented
the antenna and dialed up Nigel's encrypted phone number in the
light of a nearby street lamp.

Having dialed the number, he turned suddenly to take a seat in one of the two wicker chairs conveniently placed on the balcony. In that same instant, he heard the whine of a bullet as it ricocheted off the concrete wall beside his head. Instinctively, he fell flat to the deck on his stomach. He knew better than to stand and try to look in the direction from which the missile had come. He silently thanked God for his own sudden movement that had taken him out of the line of fire. There had been no sound of a shot, so the sniper's weapon no doubt was equipped with a silencer. He edged slowly toward the iron-grated railing surrounding the balcony, hoping the darkness hid him from view and wondering for a moment if he could find his assailant. Finally, he decided it was too dark and there were too many open windows in the buildings across the street. He crawled slowly back into his room and shut the door. He pulled the blinds tightly shut and moved away from the doors and windows. He considered alerting the hotel staff but then realized that this would only make matters worse and would make his mission a public event.

His next thought was that he had to find a way to contact Nigel. With the satellite telephone in hand, he proceeded cautiously out into the corridor outside his room and to a stairway leading up to the roof. After climbing several levels, he found at last that the stairway ended at a small door. He was pleased to discover that the door was unlocked and opened onto a deserted, flat roof. He quickly found a sheltered space not far from the door, where he sat, heart pounding, and once again dialed up Nigel's number.

"Hello."

"Nigel, is that you?" Brad asked anxiously.

"It sure is," Nigel replied warmly at the other end. "How goes the Egyptian expedition?"

"Well, I just dodged a bullet on the balcony of my hotel room here in Cairo. We can forget about the secrecy of our mission. Apparently they know we're here, and they're not happy about it."

"Good heavens, Brad! Have you reported it to the police?"

"No, not yet. We don't need an international incident to advertise our activities. The girls are safe with Allison's friends in Ma'adi, and I'm here tonight in a hotel in Zamalek. I plan to switch rooms and keep out of sight. Changing hotels will not help. Apart from that, things have gone well here. I met with Moustafa today and alerted him to the purpose of our visit. I meet with him again tomorrow for lunch to compare notes on a project the ministry of antiquities is conducting to map the Nile riverbed in the region from Aswan to Luxor. We have a reservation on a Nile cruise to Luxor tomorrow at six p.m. local time that should put us in Luxor the following morning where we are booked into a hotel. Do you have any more information about who we're up against?"

"Nothing definitive yet, my friend," Nigel replied. "The Navigational Technologies International Corporation that we have been looking into is part of an international conglomerate with tentacles in many sectors. Surprisingly, it's listed as a subsidiary of one of the largest commodities trading hedge funds based in New England, but tracing these connections is often a complicated process. In short, we don't know the names of any individuals yet. We do know that Navigational Technologies International has a project ongoing in Egypt that is financed by the Egyptian ministry of the interior. But I still do not know the nature of that project."

"I might be able to tell you more about that project soon," Brad responded. "What about the meaning of the keys of electrum that Billy is investigating?"

"I just finished talking with Billy," Nigel replied. "There is no clear answer to that question yet either. Billy has pursued several different theories, and he and Antonio finished their work in London and are on their way to Rome as we speak."

"Well, that's pretty much the situation, then," Brad concluded. "I'll try to call you tomorrow at about this same time."

Brad concluded the conversation with Nigel and tiredly made his way back down the stairway to his room. Once inside, he immediately phoned the hotel desk clerk.

"Do you have another room on the other side of the building? This room on the street side is too noisy for me to get to sleep," he said.

A moment later, a bellhop appeared at his door with a new key and escorted him to a vacant room across the hallway. He hung a "Do Not Disturb" sign outside his door; double-locked his room, propped a chair against the door, and settled in warily for a restless, fitful sleep punctuated by the cacophony of city horns and sirens outside.

CHAPTER 36

ORNING CAME LATE. IT WAS nearly 9:00 a.m. when Brad finally pried his eyes open and looked around his room. His sleep had been fitful with dreams of Coast Guard boarding missions gone awry and bullets flying too close for comfort. There were unforgettable scenes of bodies floating in water and the recurring sight of Professor Romiel stretched out in the city morgue. Brad was thankful for the light of day. As he slowly remembered the attack on his life the night before, he experienced spasms of despair. How could he carry out this mission against unseen assailants? Why had he ever agreed to bring Allison and Sarah along on this dangerous venture? What was he even hoping to find out here in Egypt? He reached for the drawer of his bedside table, hoping to find an English language telephone book that would have the phone number of Mary Jo McCauley so he could find out if the girls were okay and alert them to the most recent developments.

No such luck. There was no phonebook with local residence numbers. To his amazement, the only English language reading material was a beige-colored Gideon Bible. Brad was astounded that this vestige of his own Judeo-Christian culture would be found in such a remote corner of the earth. He had to admit that he was not a particularly religious person himself; but he had a lot of respect for those he knew who were, including Allison and her father. And he was curious enough to look more closely. Randomly opening to Exodus chapter 12, he began reading.

> Now the sojourn of the children of Israel who lived in Egypt was four hundred and thirty years. And it came to pass at the end of the four hundred and thirty years—on that very same day—it came to pass that all the armies of the LORD went out from the land of Egypt.

Of course Brad had heard about the slavery of the Israelites in Egypt and about the events surrounding their exodus from Egypt. He had even seen a movie about the exodus. But he had no idea that the length of their sojourn itself was greater than the entire history of the United States of America. Even more impressive was the fact that their sojourn in Egypt appeared to end at a predetermined day, as if some divine clock had been ticking to signify the end of that era. He thumbed backward in the book, trying to get some idea about how this period began. In chapters 46 and 47 of the preceding book, Brad read of how Joseph had been the first of his family to migrate to Egypt and how he had become prime minister in a time preceding a great famine. He had originally been sold as a slave to the Egyptians by his envious brothers; but years later, he had occasion to forgive them with the words, "You meant it for evil, but God meant it for good." Apparently, through careful planning and preparation, Joseph was enabled to save the known world of that day from death by famine. Here again, it seemed that the message was that God had orchestrated the events of history at both personal and international levels. Brad drew strange comfort at the thought that perhaps the events of his own life and now this weird adventure in Egypt were no accidents. Perhaps Allison had been right that there is a divine purpose behind our existence on this planet.

He learned additionally that, as a result of Joseph's administration during the famine, the wealth of the Egyptian nation—including its people, their gold, and their lands, and cattle—became the possession of the pharaohs. Only the priests and their lands were not subjugated by the pharaohs. And Joseph himself had married a priestess of On. This certainly explained to Brad how so much wealth could be concentrated in the hands of the Egyptian pharaohs and how the potential for animosity between the pharaohs and the priests could be ever present. He remembered the animosity and power struggles that grew between the clergy and the monarchies of Europe during the Middle Ages. He made a mental note to ask Billy or Sarah if there could have been any relationship between the details he had just now read and the reign of Akhenaten who was the focus of Professor Romiel's research.

By the time he had showered, dressed, and packed his things to check out of the hotel, it was approaching time for his luncheon meeting with Moustafa. In the lobby, he returned his room key and checked out of the hotel. He detected no awareness of last night's events on the part of the hotel clerk. He decided to sit in a large lounge chair against the back wall of the lobby to wait for Moustafa so he would have a good view of the entire lobby and not be too close to the window nearest the street. Sitting there, he pondered how the enemy had known of his presence in Egypt so quickly. Then it dawned on him that, when he had checked into the hotel, he was required to let the desk clerk make a copy of his passport. Whatever government department had access to that information would know immediately of his presence in the country and the location of any hotel where he might be staying. He was thankful the girls' location was not disclosed in the same way.

Within a few moments, Moustafa arrived and walked straight up to the place where Brad was seated.

"Hi, Brad! Did you sleep well your first night here in Egypt?"

"Not so well, Moustafa," Brad replied. "Apparently, our adversaries arranged a welcoming committee for me. I dodged a bullet on the balcony outside my window last night."

"I had no idea you were in so much danger or I would never have let you stay in a public hotel. My sincerest apologies," Moustafa said with deep concern written on his face.

"Let's go eat, and we can discuss the details," Brad said, changing the topic.

Irrespective of the events of the previous night, Brad was feeling especially hungry for what had now become a combination of breakfast and lunch. The two of them made their way to the hotel restaurant.

"Moustafa, before you share what you learned from the ministry of the interior and the ministry of antiquities, I have a question," Brad began. "Who would have access to my passport information when I leave it with the hotel? I'm wondering how my assailant last night learned of my arrival and of the room number where I was staying."

"Well," Moustafa replied, "that information is routinely passed on to the immigration control bureau within the ministry of the interior. They maintain a databank of all foreigners in the country. Are you suggesting that someone there is responsible for the attack last night?"

"I don't know," Brad answered. "But it seems unlikely that the hotel staff would try to assassinate tourists in their own hotel. They would have too much to lose in negative publicity. And I'm not aware of anyone else who knew where I am staying."

"I can investigate that possibility. At least I can determine the chain of information flow and find out who had rapid access to your location. We are actually a very technologically sophisticated country, you know," Moustafa added jokingly to lighten the mood. "Ours is an IBM culture. *I* stands for *Insha'allah*, 'if God wills.'

B stands for *Bokerah*, 'tomorrow.' And *M* stands for *Ma'alesh*, 'it doesn't matter anyway.'"

Brad laughed as the waiter brought their order, but he also remembered that his friend had been one of the brightest students at the academy and he had completed a degree in electrical engineering during his time there. He knew that Moustafa himself was certainly technologically sophisticated. Brad was also aware of something else that most people did not know. That was the fact that the Coast Guard Academy was the most selective of all of the US military academies, including West Point and Annapolis. The US Coast Guard Academy in New London, Connecticut admitted only eight percent of their applicants, which was even more selective than Harvard or Princeton. More impressive still was the acceptance of a handful of foreign military candidates like Moustafa. These young men and women had cleared keen selection processes both at home and in the US and were destined for distinguished leadership roles in their own country. Admiral El-Azabi was a fine example of such.

"Tell me," Brad asked, "were you able to find out anything at the two ministries?"

"Actually, I received some useful information this morning. Here in Egypt, we have a ports and lighthouse administration that falls under the ministry of maritime transport. Unlike many of our bureaucracies, this one is particularly efficient, economically oriented, and is headed by a rear admiral named Hosni Khattab. He was able to give me some details of the Nile navigational mapping project. I'm sure he assumed my interest had to do with our navy's expanding roles in maintaining aids to navigation on the Nile."

"I'm all ears," Brad said.

"Well, first of all," Moustafa began, "the Nile navigational project was contracted out to an international corporation by the name of Navigational Technologies International. They were given a seventy-five-million-dollar contract for the project with a two-year directive to deliver an IALA region A system of fixed markers and buoyage all along the Nile to enhance maritime commerce from Aswan to Cairo. They're using their own black-hulled boats with specialized equipment for mapping and buoy placement. They have an international crew of ten persons, including divers and technicians; and they have an Egyptian liaison officer who reports to the ministry of the interior for contract compliance."

"IALA A? Oh, what is up with that? You Egyptians drive on the right side of the road and the wrong side of the river!" Brad said with a laugh, recognizing the International Association of Lighthouse Authorities (IALA) region A that is used mainly in Europe and Africa where the red and green buoy system is reversed from IALA region B. Brad interrupted Moustafa again with this tangential thought.

"You know what I never understood, Moustafa, was why do the Japanese also drive cars on the wrong side of the road but use the same IALA B system for navigating waterways as the United States? Could we possibly make international travel any more confusing? Anyway, sorry. What about the other project, the bottom-scanning for ancient underwater artifacts at Aswan?" Brad asked.

"Well, as I explained yesterday, that project is being funded by the ministry of antiquities. But the project has only just begun. It is currently a nineteen-million-dollar project. I know more about that project because the divers are some of my own men. Using sophisticated electronic sensors, they will probe deep beneath the river bottom in search of artifacts that we believe were lost through maritime mishaps in ancient times. We expect this will be a very rewarding venture, as the Ancient Egyptians were one of the most active maritime cultures in world history. You can only imagine what thousands of years of ancient waterway traffic has generated for us to recover. The teams of scientists and archeologists are using a specialized research vessel on loan from the French government. We have quite a lot of security and constant presence of Egyptian experts and authorities. I really don't see how this project would be a significant risk to our antiquities.

"I also asked about your friend, Professor Romiel. I was told that he had an apartment in the Luxor area close to his research work. But he left suddenly a couple of weeks ago with no explanation to his colleagues. They seemed to be concerned about his whereabouts and his well-being. They said that his apartment had been trashed and there were threatening messages left there. No one seemed to know what that was all about. I didn't tell them about his murder in New York City."

"That information is all very useful, Moustafa," Brad responded. "It sounds to me like we should pick up the trail at Professor Romiel's apartment in Luxor. We no longer have to worry about keeping our presence a secret, because they already know we're here. I also want to gather more information about the riverbed mapping project. That corporation you named, Navigational Technologies International, turns out to be a corporation we already have under surveillance in conjunction with Professor Romiel's murder."

"Listen, Brad," Moustafa said after some reflection, "in view of what happened to you last night, I need to provide you with some protection. The last thing we need is a dead American tourist on our hands. I'm dispatching a military car and driver for your transportation needs around Cairo, and one of my own special forces men will accompany you from now on. I know you can handle yourself; but he has the local knowledge, is fully armed, and will give your adversaries reason to pause."

"Thanks, Moustafa. I can use the help, especially since my two young lady companions are not very good in a street fight."

Moustafa excused himself and went out the front door to his waiting car to tell his driver to radio for another car and driver with military escort. After several minutes, he returned and went to the desk clerk to enquire about the management of passport information. He returned to Brad momentarily.

"Brad, something's not right here," he said. "There's a car parked across the street with two occupants who are obviously watching this hotel. The odd thing is that it's a government car and the license indicates that it belongs to the ministry of the interior. Also, when I asked the hotel clerk about your passport information, he said that the information was passed on to the ministry of the interior, and they had sent an agent yesterday to enquire about your room number. Something's very strange here."

CHAPTER 37

BILLY AND ANTONIO ARRIVED IN
Rome within a few hours of Billy's conversation with
Nigel. The hour was late, so they spent the night on
board Nigel's corporate jet parked beside the corporate hangar at the Rome International Airport. Late
into the night, Billy continued his online research into the thirteen ancient obelisks of Rome and compared the information with
the pages he had from Professor Romiel's journal. One by one, he
found what he could find about each of the obelisks listed in the
journal and compiled a companion notebook in an effort to determine what the professor was looking for.

By far, the most fascinating information he had amassed concerned the obelisk known popularly as the Lateran obelisk because
of its placement before the Church of St. John Lateran at the Piazza
de San Giovanni in Laterano in 1588 by order of Pope Sixtus V. It
was the largest obelisk ever made, weighing an estimated 455 tons
and reaching 42 meters or 137.8 feet into the sky when its base was
included. Billy found this information especially relevant because
that particular obelisk had originally been placed in the solar courtyard at Karnak Temple in Luxor. Pharaoh Tuthmosis III had ordered its construction during his reign from approximately 1504 BC
to 1450 BC, but he died before its completion. It lay on its side on

the south side of Karnak Temple for approximately thirty-five years until his grandson, Pharaoh Tuthmosis IV, had it erected during his reign from approximately 1426 BC to 1415 BC. So, in this case, Billy realized, finally both the geographical and chronological information were appropriate. Because Pharaoh Akhenaten was believed to have reigned for about seventeen years—from 1353 BC to 1336 BC—this giant obelisk had to have been a prominent feature rising into the sky above the Karnak Temple throughout his lifetime.

As he fought off the urge to sleep, Billy pondered what significance the dimensions of this great obelisk might have. He remembered reading about the tendency of ancient Egyptian architects to achieve a kind of mathematical harmony and to encode spiritual messages in their structures. What did the professor see in these measurements? Why had he taken measurements of so many of the obelisks? What were the keys of electrum?

Antonio and their pilot were already asleep on the special beds provided in the main cabin, and Billy could hear their rhythmic breathing and low-volume snoring as he himself finally turned off his laptop, closed his eyes to the world, and drifted off into a deep sleep.

CHAPTER 38

BRAD TOOK LEAVE OF MOUSTAFA in the lobby of the Zamalek hotel after Moustafa had introduced his new military escort to him. Kosar Yousef was a special forces officer in his thirties with a determined look, a muscular build, a holstered pistol, and an AK-47. Brad quickly discovered that Kosar spoke English fluently and that he was Coptic, meaning that he was descended from an ancient sect of Egyptian Christians who comprised nearly twenty percent of the total Egyptian population. They had their own orthodox Catholic tradition, with their own priesthood, pope, and monastic orders. Brad was grateful for Kosar's presence not only for the protection he provided but also for his unique perspective on the culture in which he found himself.

Together, Brad and Kosar exited the hotel from a side entrance and got into the waiting military car with uniformed driver that Moustafa had arranged for them. The car that had been parked in front of the hotel had disappeared, and the tempo of the city had slowed markedly in the heat of the afternoon sun. No one appeared to follow as their car crossed the small bridge to the eastern bank of the Nile River and turned right into the Corniche en route to Ma'adi and the villa of Mary Jo McCauley.

On the way, Brad thought best to learn what he could about his new bodyguard.

"Well, Kosar," he began, "with a family name like Yousef, does that mean that you descended from the Joseph of the Bible who used to be prime minister in Egypt?"

"That is a distinct possibility," Kosar replied tersely.

"I don't know if Vice Admiral El-Ezaby informed you, but we used to be classmates at the US Coast Guard Academy. I'm here to look into the affairs of an American professor who was doing archeological research in Luxor. I'm here with his daughter and another Egyptologist whom you will meet in a few minutes. There are people here in Egypt who, for some reason, are violently opposed to our presence. That's why I'm especially grateful for your presence."

"Who are those people, and what kind of threat do they pose?" Kosar asked.

"I wish I knew," Brad replied. "I do know that one of them took a shot at me outside the hotel last night. By accompanying us, you'll be facing some danger as well."

"I know a few things about danger," Kosar volunteered. "Hopefully I can even the odds in your favor."

Soon, they arrived in front of Mary Jo's villa and found the same wizened *boab* inside the gate sleeping on the same bench in the shade of the same giant palm tree. After a few traditional greetings, Brad and Kosar left the car and driver parked outside, and they were ushered in through the front gate to the front door of the villa. Inside, Mary Jo was engaged in cheerful conversation with Allison and Sarah in the large living room as they entered. They had been reminiscing about Allison's childhood friends from the Ma'adi Community Church and about blessings they had experienced over the years. They were all visibly shocked at the sight of Kosar with his AK-47.

Brad quickly explained, "Vice Admiral El-Ezaby has assigned Kosar here as military escort for our protection. Someone took at

shot at me at the hotel last night. I booked our Nile cruise departing to Luxor tonight at six p.m.; but in view of the fact that our
adversaries now know I'm here, I'm having second thoughts about
taking you ladies with me after all. I think you'll be a lot safer here
with Mary Jo."

"Wait a minute!" Allison objected. "We signed on for this trip
regardless of the danger. Besides, it was my father who was killed!
We didn't come this far to sit and drink tea."

"That's right!" Sarah agreed. "We need to follow through on
this, and we're just as safe with you and Kosar as we ever would
be here in Ma'adi. Besides, we probably know a lot more about
Professor Romiel's work than anybody else you could find."

Brad could see that his arguments were futile. And he had to
admit that he was glad they were along, especially Allison.

"Well then," he said. "You'd better pack and get ready. Our
cruise boat leaves in two hours. Meanwhile, I need to fill you in on
what has been happening."

"Now hold on just a minute, all of you!" Mary Jo interjected.
"Two hours is plenty of time to sit down and enjoy a decent home-
cooked meal. My children have a swim meet at the Cairo American
College international school nearby right after their classes, so they
won't be home before you leave. Just sit down right now and take a
deep breath. It'll be ready in two shakes."

"Yes, Brad," Allison agreed. "We're all packed and ready, and
Mary Jo has key lime pie cooling. You and Kosar look as if you
could use some food before we begin the cruise."

And so it happened that the five of them sat down to a full-
course Southern meal, the first one Kosar had ever tasted. It was
apparent that this assignment was not going to be so bad for him
after all. Brad quickly shared the events of the past day and what he
had learned from Moustafa and from Nigel.

An hour and a half later, they bid thankful farewell to Mary Jo
and boarded their military car en route to the Cairo boarding point

for their cruise up river. Thankfully, the cruise boat crew did not think it unusual that a soldier with a machine gun would appear to accompany them. They seemed glad for the protection and readily made a place for Kosar, as if they had been told to expect him. Kosar, for his part, cautiously made his way around the foredeck and examined the cabins that had been assigned to them—one for Allison and Sarah and an adjacent cabin for Brad and Kosar.

With a sudden vibration and churning of the weathered boat's engines, they were quickly underway. The late-afternoon view of the banks of the Nile was spectacular as the sun declined toward the west. They could even see the silhouette of the Great Pyramid on the Giza Plateau to their right. Sarah explained that all of the pyramids and pharaohs' tombs were located on the western side of the Nile, in keeping with the direction of the setting sun. Pharaoh Akhenaten, however, commensurate with his radical views about monotheistic sun worship, during his reign had attempted to change tradition and move burials to the side of the Nile toward the rising sun, even as he had moved his capital eastward away from Thebes and Memphis to his newly constructed city of Akhetaten, dedicated to the worship of Aten. Of course, his seventeen-year reign was just the blink of an eyelid in the grand scheme of thousands of years of Egyptian dynastic rule, and his plans were ultimately doomed to failure. Even his own tomb was eventually raided and his mummy never found. Interestingly, Akhenaten's temple, dedicated to mono-theistic worship of Aten, was much later transformed into a church by ancient Coptic Christians. Paintings of saints and angels are still visible on the walls. Perhaps the Christians felt a kindred spirit with Akhenaten's bold monotheistic faith and his minority status.

CHAPTER

39

O N THE NORTHERN SIDE OF THE
Mediterranean Sea earlier that same day, Billy
had managed to dress hurriedly and eat a hastily prepared breakfast before joining Antonio
in their rented car at the Rome International
Airport. Antonio's fluent Italian was a huge asset as he instructed
the driver to take them to their first destination: the Piazza de San
Giovanni in Laterano. Billy was awestruck as the giant obelisk came
into view above the horizon. It seemed incredible that this—the
largest of all Egyptian obelisks—had actually been transported here
by ship nearly 1,700 years ago. By now, it had been in Rome almost
as long as it was in Egypt.

They asked the driver to stop the car, and he and Antonio got
out and began walking across the crowded piazza in the direction
of the obelisk. Billy began recalling how the obelisk had come to its
present location. Originally, its construction had been ordered by
Pharaoh Thutmose III, who reigned in Egypt from about 1500-1447
BC. The pharaoh died before the obelisk could be erected or its
intended mate could be cut from the quarry at Aswan. It lay on its
side at Karnak for about thirty-five years until it was finally erected
by his grandson, Thutmose IV. The Roman Emperor Constantine I
(AD 306/323-337) had ordered the obelisk removed from Egypt and

taken to his new capital at Constantinople. Eventually, however, the obelisk was instead brought to Rome after Constantine's death by his son, Constantius II, where it was erected in AD 357. But oddly, it disappeared entirely from view sometime thereafter.

Billy would never question the wisdom of Pope Sixtus V in ordering a search for the lost obelisk in 1587. Eventually, it was found beneath twenty-three feet of rubble in the ruins of the Circus Maximus Coliseum. It had been lying there on its side, buried, for centuries, broken into three separate sections that were later rejoined. Fortuitously, the burial had only served to preserve more clearly the hieroglyphs that had been carved on its sides. The pope had also ordered a giant cross constructed atop the pyramidian along with his own papal heraldry symbols. Thus, the obelisk came at that time to symbolize the geographical heart of Christendom.

Although the tip of the pyramidian was no longer visible, Billy had no difficulty in confirming the measurements recorded by Professor Romiel. Clearly, Professor Romiel's focus had been on the height of the obelisks and the dimensions of their pyramidians. But what did all this have to do with the keys of electrum and the location of the treasure? A few conclusions seemed obvious to Billy. First of all, because electrum was the metallic coating placed over the pyramidian, the secret had to do somehow with the pyramidian atop the obelisks. In the second place, the professor had referred to the keys plural, so it was likely that the secret had to do with more than one obelisk. This would also explain why the professor had taken measurements of so many of the obelisks. Use of two obelisks placed perpendicular to the Nile River would also potentially provide a line-of-sight locator for placement and eventual retrieval of the treasure. And finally, as Billy had concluded earlier, it made sense to limit inquiry to those obelisks originally located near the Karnak Temple, because that is where the professor had focused most of his research.

Billy jotted down a few of these random thoughts on his notepad and began walking slowly across the piazza in the direction
of their rented car. For a few seconds, he was deep in thought and
thoroughly oblivious of his surroundings. He failed to notice the
silver Fiat sedan with tinted windows that had entered the piazza
at high speed on a collision course with him as he sauntered across
the street. From a high vantage point on the other side of the street,
Antonio had taken in the entire scene immediately. He drew his
semi-automatic pistol and quickly fired two warning shots into the
air to alert Billy to the danger. Billy heard the gunshots and froze
in his tracks. He turned his head to see what had drawn Antonio's
attention and saw the Fiat barreling down upon him. He jumped
back one step just as the car's side view mirror caught his shoulder, spun him around, and knocked him headlong into the gutter.
Antonio squeezed off several rounds at the car, and there was a
sound of shattering glass as the car sped off into the distance and
disappeared from sight.

CHAPTER 40

NIGEL AROSE BEFORE SUNRISE, dressed quickly, and went to his New York trading center in another part of the same building. The older he got the less he felt the need for sleep. Besides, he had a lot on his mind; and sleep did not come easily. He was gratified to see that two of his traders were still busy at their monitors. They worked in shifts throughout the night to take advantage of developments in the worldwide currency and commodity markets. He marveled at how it was possible for most of the people in the world to be oblivious to fluctuations in world markets. People seemed more conscious of changes in the weather than of changes in the economy that could affect their lives much more seriously. He poured himself a cup of hot coffee as he quickly looked over their balance sheets to check any new activity, positions entered or exited overnight.

He noticed immediately that the US dollar had fallen precipitously against other major currencies and the price of gold had skyrocketed another 10 percent over yesterday's New York close. He wondered if there had been some major calamity or whether the driving force was merely speculation. He remembered once hearing Paul Volcker say when he was chairman of the Federal Reserve Bank that his greatest fear was not rising unemployment or falling stock prices but the rising price of gold. Gold price appreciation seemed to Volcker to suggest that investors were losing all confidence in the economy and in government monetary policy, and this was his worst nightmare.

This thought turned his mind back to his most serious problem of the day: the safety of his friends in their quest for information about the death of Professor Romiel and about buried Egyptian gold. Above all else, Nigel prided himself as a problem solver; and here was a problem more challenging than any he had faced in his many years of anticipating market developments. Who had murdered Don Romiel and why? What had his friend discovered in Egypt, and where exactly was it located? Was there some sort of overarching conspiracy here; and if so, what did someone hope to gain? What did Don mean by his cryptic messages, "A-T-O-N," and the keys of electrum?

In a very real sense, Nigel felt responsible for the fate of his young friends. He had sponsored their travel to Europe and Egypt; and without his encouragement, they would not be in the danger they were facing. Already there had been another attempt on Brad's life. Where would all this lead? He knew he had to find some answers and find them quickly. He wanted to have some definitive information for Brad when he called later that morning. He turned his disciplined thoughts back on the trail of Navigational Technologies International, the corporation involved in the incident with Allison.

Because Navigational Technologies International was a publicly traded corporation registered with the Securities Exchange Commission, Nigel had already been able to amass a wealth of information about it. He learned the address and phone number of the corporate headquarters in nearby New York City. He learned the names and ages of the CEO and the CFO, but their salaries were listed as "not available." He learned that they had thirty-nine full-time employees and that their shares traded on the Nasdaq

Stock Exchange under the symbol NVTI. He learned that their market capitalization was only about 40 million dollars, making it what is known as a small cap stock.

What got Nigel's attention instantly was the reported finding that the corporation had negative book value, negative cash flow, negative operating margins, and negative future earnings estimates. Someone was fronting a lot of money just to keep this corporation in business. Next, Nigel decided to investigate the actual shareholders in the corporation. He learned that there were no insider direct shareholders but that 90 percent of the corporation was owned by institutional investors. When he tried to determine just which institutions were involved, he found to his amazement that nearly all of the shares were controlled by a single hedge fund by the name of Equity Asset Fund Advisors (EAFA). It was highly unusual that a single hedge fund would take on so much risk in a single corporation.

Because hedge funds are largely unregulated entities, the trail seemed to end abruptly at that point. Nigel knew that hedge funds were typically investment funds that invested in a broad range of assets privately on behalf of a small number of wealthy or large investors. Usually, each investor was required to put up a minimum investment of around one million dollars; but some hedge funds required a lot more than that. Nigel did have a close friend who was a behavioral economist at Pennsylvania State University's Smeal School of Management who happened also to be an expert on hedge funds. He decided he would ask his friend for information about that particular hedge fund. With any luck, he would have some definitive information in hand before Brad called later that morning. He left a message on his friend's voice mail to call back as soon as possible.

Nigel also still had the e-mail address of Professor Romiel's sponsor, which they could use as a final trace on the sponsor's location. He needed to develop a plan to use that e-mail address to best advantage. For that, he needed to call a brainstorming session

with Foley and get Brad's final agreement as well. He called Foley's
cell phone and found him still eating breakfast at home. Being extremely cautious about what they said on the phone, they arranged
a meeting together at the Nyack Boat Club that same morning.
Nigel said they needed to make plans for their next sailing venture,
but Foley easily read between the lines.

CHAPTER

41

SUNSET ALONG THE NILE RIVER PRE-
sented a panorama of unparalleled beauty. The heat of
the Egyptian summer day had subsided dramatically; and
the only sounds to be heard were the low murmur of the
boat's engines, the wind whistling in one's ears, and the
occasional cry of a white egret searching for a final meal before
nightfall. The stars slowly began to appear with casual ownership in
the night sky, and Brad began to understand that it was no accident
that astronomy had played such an important role in ancient Egypt.
It was almost possible for him to forget the crisis that had brought
them to this place.

Following dinner as they were returning to their cabins, Brad
noticed Allison leaning against the railing and staring off toward
the lights along the shore.

"What are you thinking, Allison?" he asked.

"I'm beginning to understand why my father loved this place so
much. Look at those bright stars. Those are the same stars that the
pharaohs looked up at millennia ago. It's hard to imagine how many
generations have played out their existence along these shores. They
all had individual aspirations."

"What are your aspirations?" Brad asked intently.

"Well, for one thing, I want to find out what happened to my father. You might say I'm on a quest for meaning. I seem to be obsessed with a need to understand why all this has happened. Does that seem odd to you?"

"Not at all," Brad responded seriously. "It might seem a strange coincidence, but when I was in my hotel in Zamalek this morning, I had very similar feelings. I mean, I had just been shot at; and I was wondering what we were supposed to be doing here anyway. I was even wondering why your father had singled me out to help him through this difficulty. You might even be interested to know that I found a dusty Bible in the desk drawer and I read about some of those people who used to live along these shores thousands of years ago. In particular, I read about one man named Joseph who came here as a slave and wound up as prime minister. He seemed to find special meaning in his sojourn in this land. He went through a lot of troubles, years of imprisonment and separation from family and friends; but in the end, he was convinced there was some divine purpose in it all."

"Yes," Allison said. "I know that piece of history well. Coincidentally, that was one of my father's favorite accounts. He used to say that it was ironic that the pharaohs went to such great lengths to remove Joseph and his people from the historical record, even though Joseph had done so much to preserve their civilization. I suppose they didn't want to record their own shortcomings for posterity. I mean, they didn't want to record that their long experiment with slave labor ended in the humiliation of the Exodus. Dad spent much of his life looking for archeological records of the Jewish sojourn in Egypt. I remember how excited he became the day he learned that archeologists had recovered chariot wheels at the bottom of the Red Sea. That proved the Red Sea crossing was not a myth, and even the fact that the chariot wheels had eight spokes enabled Egyptian historians to establish that they belonged to the time of the eighteenth dynasty of the pharaohs and the reign of Thutmose IV. The biblical connection was really why Dad was so interested in Akhenaten. Dad believed that Akhenaten's foray into monotheism was the result of the influence of Judaism. One Egyptian historian even believes that Akhenaten was related maternally to Joseph through Joseph's wife, Asenath, who was the daughter of Potipherah, priest of On.

"But you were right when you said that Joseph, or Zaphnath-Paaneah, as pharaoh renamed him in Egyptian language, found meaning and purpose in his life, despite all his troubles. And that's exactly what I meant when I said I was on a quest for meaning. In the end, Joseph was able to see the hand of God in his suffering; and he was even able to forgive his brothers who had sold him into slavery. But I'm afraid I'm not there yet. I mean, I still can't forgive the people who killed my father. I suspect Joseph couldn't forgive either until he understood the purpose behind it all."

"Well, that revelation was a long time coming to him," Brad responded. "I mean, Joseph had many years to see those purposes unfolding. By contrast, we're in a race with time. We have to get some answers today and some tomorrow or it might be too late. I think the three of us need to meet together now in my cabin to plan for tomorrow. And I should be calling Nigel to report in before long."

With those words, the two of them found Sarah and assembled together in Brad's cabin while Kosar, weapon in hand, leaning against the bulwark in the shadows outside the cabin door, kept a watchful eye up and down the deck.

"You know," Brad began in his usual methodical way, "tomorrow morning, early, we will be in Luxor. We still have no word from Billy or Nigel about the meaning of the keys of electrum. We will need to connect with some of Allison's father's colleagues and locate his flat. I also no doubt need to see if there is any underwater research activity happening in the river. Any ideas about how we can do all that without raising too much suspicion?"

Sarah responded first. "First of all, I want to say that I have great confidence Billy will find some answers for us soon. He lives to solve problems like this one. As for tomorrow, I still know several of the archeologists who are currently involved in various kinds of research in the Luxor area. Perhaps we should go first to the temple at Karnak and see what's happening there and see if I can recognize anyone. I know from previous visits where the archeologists usually have lunch and where they live and work. They often used to get together to discuss their work in the evenings. I have a good excuse for coming here because Egyptian archeology is my area of study and Professor Romiel was my professor. For all anyone knows, I am here to gather data for my graduate research."

"I suppose I have an excuse for visiting as well," Allison said. "By now, many of them will know of my father's passing. They will understand if I have come to see where his final work was being done. If I say that I'm collating his research, that will give me an excuse to ask a lot of questions about what he was doing. I have, in fact, given some consideration to writing his biography."

"That all sounds plausible," Brad said. "For my part, I'm a friend of the family along to provide assistance. I believe we should stick together. Kosar will have to follow at a distance and not raise too much suspicion. We'll find out what we can and keep a close eye out for trouble. Kosar tells me that Moustafa has arranged for government accommodation where we can stay and store our things. Any other thoughts or ideas?" Brad paused. "Good. Now that we have the semblance of a plan," Brad continued after seeing that there was no further comment, "it's time for you both to return to your cabin. I can see that we all need a good night's sleep before our busy day tomorrow. Kosar will escort you back and check out your cabin. Meanwhile, I need to phone Nigel and see if we have any news from Billy. I'll see you both in the morning, early."

CHAPTER

42

MEANWHILE, BACK IN ROME...
Antonio raced across the street toward the piazza in the direction of Billy. Cars screeched to a halt, and onlookers stared at the sight of the big man running with a weapon in hand. A small crowd had gathered around Billy as he sat up in the gutter, looking around absently for his glasses. He clutched his left shoulder that had absorbed most of the force of impact. Antonio instinctively helped Billy to his feet, picked up his notepad and glasses, and disbanded the crowd of onlookers by saying, "*Totto e sotto controllo.*" ("Everything's under control.") However, as he led Billy quickly in the direction of their car, he was not entirely certain that was the case. "Are you all right, Billy?" he asked nervously. It would not do for anything to happen to this young man on whom so much depended. Antonio's whole purpose on this trip was to protect Billy.

"Sure. I think so," Billy replied. "What was that all about?"

"Clearly that was a deliberate attempt on your life," Antonio replied. "We need to be much more cautious in the future. I believe I gave them something to think about though," he added with a smug note of satisfaction. "Let's get back to the airport and rethink our plan of operations."

Antonio helped Billy into the car and instructed the driver to return to the airport quickly by a route different from the one by which they had come. All the while, Antonio was watching behind to see if anyone was following; but no one seemed to be in pursuit, and the silver Fiat sedan did not reappear.

As they wound their way through the noisy, crowded back-streets of Rome, Billy stared blankly at his notepad. A new question swept over his consciousness with disturbing force.

"How could they possibly have known we were here? It wasn't as if we had traveled by commercial carrier or had announced our arrival by using credit cards or public telephones."

It seemed very unlikely to Billy that their opponents would have been waiting at the piazza against the possibility that someone might someday arrive with questions about the obelisk. The fact that the attack took place at the piazza implied that he was getting close to the answer, or perhaps their assailants only wanted him to think that he was getting close. How could they have known? He knew he had to ask Nigel about this. For the first time, an element of cold fear began to rise like an ugly specter within him.

Meanwhile, he turned his thoughts back to the problem at hand—the meaning of Professor Romiel's reference to the keys of electrum. He now firmly believed it referred to the placement of the treasure in relation to the location of the obelisks. The ultimate question for him, and the question that Professor Romiel must have been occupied with was, "Which obelisks?"

Billy reasoned that the obelisks had to be ones that were located at the Karnak Temple complex at the time of Akhenaten's reign. And very likely, there were two obelisks that were positioned in such a way that they would enable a line-of-sight placement of the treasure in the Nile River. He knew that he had to get back to their plane and the Karnak Temple drawing that had been taken from Professor Romiel's journal. Likely, that would give him the clues he was missing.

Then another thought rudely entered Billy's mind. If they know where we are, the plane is not safe. It could be a target. He looked at Antonio seated nervously beside him.

"Antonio, I'm thinking that our plane could be a target if they know where we are. Perhaps we should find lodging somewhere else."

"You read my mind, Billy. We need to secure that plane and go somewhere more defensible. Let's hope they haven't already discovered the plane's location."

As their car reached the airport and approached the spot where their plane was parked, they noticed immediately that something was not right. The entry door to the plane was open, and the boarding ramp was down. They had left instructions with the pilot to keep the door closed. Antonio was first up the ramp with his weapon drawn. They entered the plane with a shock. The inside of the plane was in total disarray; and there on the floor, unconscious, was their pilot, blood running from a long gash in his forehead. Billy rushed in to look for his briefcase with the critical maps and documents.

CHAPTER

43

N IGEL WAS PREPARING TO LEAVE for his morning rendezvous with Foley when his phone rang. Wilson, the Penn State University expert on hedge funds, was returning his call. He was glad Wilson was calling back on the same secure line on which he had originally placed his call.

"Hi, Nigel. I got your message. You sounded as if it was urgent. What can I do for you?"

"Wilson, you're just the man I need. You remember our last conversation about hedge fund data? It seems I now have a critical need to find out all I can about one particular hedge fund. The name of the fund is Equity Asset Fund Advisers (EAFA), and I need to know everything you can unearth—details like assets under management, positions held, fund managers, addresses, and the names of any investors you can find."

"You might be in luck, Nigel. I happen to know a little about that fund but only because it is so large. Usually, that kind of in-formation is impossible to find. The fund is based in Waterbury, Connecticut; and the manager's name is Dmitri Karlov. He's a quant, one of those Wall Street geniuses who has won international acclaim for his mathematical derivatives-pricing models. There's no way I can tell you what the fund is invested in; but, given his background, it's a sure bet that it involves highly leveraged positions in commodities and currencies."

"What about gold?" Nigel asked.

"No doubt, given the size of the fund, they have positions in all the precious metals," Wilson replied. "It's rumored the fund has over a hundred billion in assets under management. But they never disclose who their investors are or what their holdings are, for obvious reasons. With that kind of money, they must have international reach. Probably they manage money for some oil sheikhdoms and some large international corporations."

"So you don't have any idea who their investors are?" Nigel continued.

"Look, that's information nobody has except the IRS and the SEC; and then only if the hedge fund has chosen to reveal it. I'll go to my files and gather any further information I can find, and I'll call you back this afternoon."

Nigel thanked Wilson and concluded the conversation. He then proceeded directly to one of his most trusted traders on duty.

"Today, the first order of business is for you to gather everything you can on Dmitri Karlov and his hedge fund, Equity Asset Fund Advisers," Nigel said. "Check with our friends at the SEC if necessary. I need to know everything you can find on who his investors are and what his positions are in gold and other commodities and currencies. Especially, I need to know about large money transfers into and out of his hedge fund. If you need to tell the SEC we're on the trail of some insider trading schemes to get their cooperation, so be it."

With those words, Nigel turned and went down the stairway and out the front door to keep his scheduled meeting with Foley. His adrenalin was rising, and his heart was beating faster—sure signs he was finally getting close to some answers. He got into his car and signaled to his driver that he needed to go to the boat club. His driver could tell that he was in a hurry, so he wasted no time with small talk as he sped through the side streets by the most direct route.

Nigel could see Foley's car parked near the boat club entrance. As they stopped near the entrance, Nigel gave a few quick instructions to his driver.

"Wait for me here. Keep your eyes open. If you see anything suspicious, any cars coming or people waiting, call me on my cell phone immediately. I should be back in about thirty minutes." With that, Nigel entered the boat club in search of Foley.

It was another cloudy, rainy day—not one in which you would expect much activity at the boat club, especially in the early morning hours. Nigel was disappointed to see that his friend, Hoshi, was not there; but somehow, Foley had still managed to find a hot cup of coffee and a seat at a good table.

"Hello, Nigel!" came his greeting. "What do you hear from our friends abroad?"

"Not all the news is good, I'm afraid. Brad has had another attempt on his life, and Billy has still not unraveled the mystery of the keys of electrum. I'll need to get back to the office soon to be sure to intercept any messages from them today. We are making some progress on another front, however; and that's why I called for this meeting. Do you remember the e-mail address Professor Romiel was using to correspond with his sponsor?"

"Sure," Foley replied. "You mentioned sending a tracer message to that address to locate the sponsor, and Brad suggested you wait until we have more information and a plan."

"Well, I think I have narrowed our search to three entities of interest. One, of course, is the museum you visited, where the curator knows the sponsor but will not reveal his identity. Another is the corporation, Navigational Technologies International, which was involved in the attack on Allison and probably in the burglary and attack at Brad's condominium. It seems they also have a government contract ongoing in Egypt called Nile Shipping Lanes

Management. Now, I have learned that this corporation is a wholly owned subsidiary of a hedge fund based in Connecticut. That is the third entity of interest. The hedge fund presumably has leveraged positions in gold and currencies. Do you see where this is headed?"

"You're saying that the hedge fund might have a burning desire to get its hands on a large cache of Egyptian gold," Foley surmised.

"Exactly," Nigel responded with excitement. "But to be sure who is behind the professor's death, we need to pinpoint the precise location of the sponsor. I believe we are ready now to send a tracer message. What do you think?"

"I agree," responded Foley. "But what would you say in the message?"

"My thought is that we should send the message from Professor Romiel as if he were still alive and arrange a meeting somewhere neutral. That should really shock them and throw them off balance. And I think it's time to bring the police into this. But first let's get some input from Brad about the exact message and the timing of the message. By the way, what are the chances you could conduct your work project from my trading center? I mean, I could really use your help, what with Antonio gone and things heating up."

"Well, why not? I'll just tell my coworkers that I'm briefing Brad on their progress today, and I'll follow you back."

With that, Foley placed a cell phone call to a foreman on the Hudson River turbine project and explained his plans. Then Nigel and Foley left the boat club by the same door they had entered.

Stepping outside into the parking lot, Nigel could see the dark clouds and feel the brisk wind in his face. He held his hat on his head with one hand as he approached his vehicle.

"Now where's my driver?" Nigel asked aloud with consternation while Foley was still within hearing range.

They both stopped in their tracks and peered at the vehicle and around the parking lot. The car was still parked where Nigel had left it, but the driver was nowhere to be seen.

Nigel reached for the rear passenger door handle with his free hand. The blast was deafening. With a blinding flash, the car door itself came off its hinges and lifted Nigel off his feet and propelled him twenty feet back from the car. Flames and heavy, black smoke engulfed the vehicle. Foley was stunned and knocked to the ground; but being several yards behind Nigel, he sustained no injury save a terrible ringing sensation in his ears. He could see that Nigel was lying on the pavement beside him, unconscious, his hat gone and his clothing in smoldering tatters.

Instinctively Foley reached for his cell phone and dialed 911. "Send an ambulance to the Nyack Boat Club," he said, still dazed. "There's been an explosion. And alert Lieutenant Davis of police homicide division that there's been another attempted murder here. Tell him to come at once."

Foley then attempted unsuccessfully to revive Nigel. He spread his own overcoat on the nearby sidewalk and lifted Nigel and placed him on top of his coat, wrapping him as best he could to prevent the onset of shock. There, he waited for the ambulance and police as a crowd of bystanders began to appear and stare at the flaming vehicle.

CHAPTER

44

AT THE ROME INTERNATIONAL Airport, Antonio was doing his best to revive their pilot while Billy went back and forth between the cockpit and the main cabin, trying to find documents and assess damage.

"Thank God he's still alive," Antonio said after feeling his pulse and lifting him easily from the floor and setting him on the lounge sofa.

"Yes, and thank God they took the wrong ones; I mean the right ones," Billy responded with excitement. "Nigel gave me a set of false documents with altered maps and measurements. That's the set they took. The real set is still here in the restroom where I hid it beneath the plastic lining of the trash receptacle."

Antonio motioned to Billy to say no more. He thought it very likely that the assailants would have left some electronic bugging equipment, and he didn't want to take any chances that their conversation was being overheard.

Their pilot was beginning to regain consciousness, and he became the total focus of their attention.

"What happened?" the pilot murmured as he reached toward the wicked gash on his head.

"We thought *you* might be the one to tell *us*." Billy responded. "We found you unconscious here on the cabin floor."

"I remember now. There were two of them," the pilot said. "They showed me badges and said they were from airport security and they needed to check our papers. I let them in, and they hit me."

Billy sat down and took a deep breath. "Look," he said to the pilot. "We must now make some serious decisions. Do you think you feel well enough to summon Nigel on the radio? I need to speak with him right away."

"Well, sure. I'm still a bit wobbly, but I can call Mr. Pearson right now. Let me just check the cockpit to see whether the instruments are all okay."

The pilot rose to his feet and moved slowly and uncertainly in the direction of the cockpit. Billy was right behind him, mentally composing his message to Nigel. Meanwhile, Antonio began packing his personal belongings in preparation for their next move. Then Antonio began looking around with his trained eye for any bugging devices the assailants might have left behind.

A few moments later, the pilot had established radio contact with Nigel's office; and he passed the headset and microphone to Billy.

"Hello, Nigel?"

"No. This is Brian, Nigel's trading partner. Nigel went out to a meeting this morning. He wasn't expecting your call so early in the morning. He's past due to return and should be back at any minute. Can I take a message?"

"Just tell him to call Billy Heckman as soon as he returns. It's urgent."

Billy terminated the call and returned to the main cabin. There, he could see Antonio applying a bandage from the first aid kit to the pilot's head wound. Antonio silently motioned to the other two to step outside the plane. Once outside, the three of them walked to a corner of a nearby hangar to a spot where they were obscured from sight behind a dumpster.

"Were you able to get through to Nigel?" Antonio asked Billy.

"No. He was away from the office. But I left a message to have him call as soon as he returns."

"Okay," Antonio continued. "Here's the deal. I found an eavesdropping device hidden in the cabin. And there's more. There's also a GPS signaling device in the cabin under the sofa that is broadcasting the plane's location. I'm pretty sure that those devices were not there when we left Heathrow. The good news, therefore, is that their intention is probably not to blow up the plane but to gather information about our plans and movements. What do you think we should do?"

"I think we should set them up," Billy replied. "Let's let them overhear us saying we have found the exact location of the treasure and we have to fly to another location to verify our findings before we tell anyone. We can let them know that the documents they got are counterfeit. We can lead them into a trap and find out who is behind this once and for all."

"Great idea!" Antonio responded. "Only we don't even have to fly to another location to set a trap for them. There's something I haven't told you. I have family nearby, right here in Rome, family with underworld connections." At the sight of his companions' shocked faces, he shrugged and said, "How do you suppose I learned what I know about weapons and security? All we have to do is lure these thugs to the right location and my family will do the rest."

"Excellent!" Billy replied. "You go ahead and set it up with your family right now." Turning to the pilot, he said, "You need to stay with the plane and take Nigel's call when it comes in, but don't give away the details of our plan; and this time, keep the plane door locked."

Antonio hastily made the arrangements in his native Italian via cell phone, and the three of them reboarded the plane.

CHAPTER

45

BACK ON THE NILE RIVER EN ROUTE to Luxor...

After the women had left with Kosar to return to their cabin, Brad reached for the satellite phone and prepared to call Nigel. That very instant, the satellite phone began to buzz.

Good! Brad thought. *Nigel is calling me this time, right on schedule. He probably has some news from Billy.* "Hello, Nigel?"

"No, Brad. It's Foley."

Foley rehearsed the events of the morning for Brad. Nigel was in intensive care, unconscious. Shrapnel from the bomb would have killed him, but he was partially shielded by the limo door. Nigel's driver had still not been found. Lieutenant Davis was back on the case with renewed vigor. He had finally bought into their story of a premeditated murder of Professor Romiel. In view of the most recent events, Foley had told him everything he knew, including details about Professor Romiel's journal, their visit to the museum, their travels to Europe and Egypt, and their suspicions about an international conspiracy to steal Egyptian gold. Lieutenant Davis said that, in view of the international implications, it was now necessary to bring the whole matter to the attention of the FBI. So it was now a federal matter. Interpol had probably also been alerted.

"What about Billy?" Brad asked. "Have you heard anything from him?"

"He called here while Nigel and I were at the Boat Club and said it was urgent that we return his call. I called back as soon as I could, but the pilot said there had been some serious developments and Billy could not speak with us right now. He said he would call back later with details."

"That's not good," Brad said. "We'll be in Luxor tomorrow morning, and I was hoping for some word from him about the location of the treasure by now. Did Nigel have any information before his injury?"

"Nigel said he had learned that the corporation involved in the attack on Allison was wholly owned by a hedge fund in Connecticut. They were also part of a project to improve Nile shipping lanes. He was preparing to send a tracer e-mail to Professor Romiel's sponsor, but he wanted to talk with you first."

"I think it's time to go forward with that tracer message to the sponsor. Here's what I believe we should do. You remember when I was stationed with Coast Guard intelligence at the office of naval intelligence in Washington, DC? Well, we had a lot of interaction with the FBI on drug interdiction cases. I got to know one of their cyber crimes agents, Darrell Tilson. If he's still with the Bureau, I know that he is easily capable of running the trace, and that would maintain FBI's involvement. Meanwhile, please keep me posted on Nigel's condition and call me when you hear *anything* from Billy."

"Sure thing, Brad. I was also planning to move my base of operations here to Nigel's office so I could monitor communications."

"That's perfect, Foley. While you're at it, could you also ask Lieutenant Davis to post a guard at Nigel's hospital room? I don't want anyone trying to finish the job."

"He's already done that, Brad. And there's one more thing. When I got here to Nigel's trading center, I learned from one of his traders that Nigel had asked him to check with personal contacts at the SEC for unofficial information about that hedge fund in Connecticut. You would not believe who their principle investors are. Take a deep breath and listen to this! The two largest investors are Mark Wyatt, the billionaire CEO of the Chicago-based computer search engine corporation, and Connecticut Senator Charles Lodge, the Chairman of the Senate Banking Committee."

There was a brief pause as Brad let the ramifications fully sink in. "Wow! If they're involved, it would explain a lot of things. For one thing, it would explain their need for secrecy. For another, it would explain where they got the technological sophistication to gather information on us and our movements. Do pass that information on to Tilson at the FBI."

"Will do, Brad! And you take care. I'll call you as soon as I hear anything from Billy."

With that, they ended their conversation, and Brad set about recharging the batteries of the satellite phone as he awaited Kosar's return to his cabin. After a few minutes, Brad welcomed Kosar back to his cabin. Kosar assured him that he had left his handgun with the women and had shown them how to bar their cabin door from the inside after his departure.

CHAPTER

46

BACK INSIDE THEIR PLANE AT THE
Rome International Airport, Billy and Antonio executed their plan with precision. Billy announced, for
the benefit of the listening device, that he had finally
discovered the exact location of the treasure. He said
it was right there on the Karnak map all along, the real map that
he had hidden and kept from the thieves. Now they needed to telephone Brad Beck directly in Egypt as soon as possible. To do so,
they would need to call from a safe phone, not the plane's radio that
they now believed to be compromised. Antonio related accurately
the fact that his family owned a small motorcycle assembly business
on the outskirts of Rome. He gave the address of their warehouse
and said that would be an ideal place from which to call. Together,
they agreed aloud on a time of about one hour that it would take
for them to arrive at the warehouse. Billy said he would take the
Karnak map with him so he could give precise directions to Brad.

As they stepped out of the plane, Antonio had yet another surprise for Billy. Gone was the car with the driver Antonio had hired.
In its place was a small commercial truck. The driver of the truck
smiled broadly at Antonio and pumped his hand in an affectionate
greeting. Then he opened the rear gate of the truck. Inside were two
shiny new Moto Guzzi Norge 1200 Italian motorcycles.

"You want the silver one or the red one?" Antonio asked Billy with a grin. As the driver helped him unload the two motorcycles, Antonio added, "Hang on tight. This twelve hundred cc model has ninety-five bhp at seventy-five hundred rpm with a six-speed transmission."

Billy chose red and eagerly loaded his briefcase with a few personal effects and donned the red helmet that was provided. Antonio stored some weapons and ammo in a compartment under his motorcycle seat, waved farewell to the driver, and started his machine with a roar.

In a moment, the two of them were flying through the side streets of Rome with the wind in their faces. Pedestrians heard them coming at a distance and offered a wide berth. Billy was thinking how different this was from his life as a student, how much he would love to have one of these of his own, and how he wished Sarah could see him now. It was as if he had somehow made a magic transformation from the study of history to the crafting of history on his own. He could see that Antonio had chosen their mode of transportation in order to negotiate the narrow streets and arrive at the warehouse before any of their guests. After a few more bumps and harrowing curves, they rounded a corner in a vacant quarter of the port district and saw a large warehouse with the words "Moto Guzzi" painted high above the entranceway. The sliding front door was open in anticipation of their arrival, so Antonio drove in through the entrance with Billy not far behind him.

The floor was brightly painted concrete, and it looked clean enough to eat from. Motorcycles were stacked on rows of metal racks, and some were in position to be crated for shipment. At one end was a shop where final testing and adjustments were conducted. There was a distinct smell of engine oil. Four men approached them from the back of the warehouse with smiles and warm handshakes. Two of the men were as big as Antonio. Billy surmised they must be Antonio's brothers or uncles. The most unusual thing about them was that they all carried automatic weapons. They looked as excited and eager, as if they had just been given front-row seats at a prize fight.

Antonio introduced Billy to his family and gave a few explanations and instructions in Italian, and then everyone took positions. It was decided that Billy and Antonio would be seated on chairs at the shop in the rear of the warehouse in plain view from the front door. The others would hide behind crates and racks on both sides.

They didn't have to wait long. Two cars appeared and parked in a side street across the street from the front entrance. Billy recognized one as the silver Fiat that had almost run him down earlier. A sheet of colored cardboard had been taped over the left rear window where Antonio had shattered the glass that same morning. Five ominous-looking characters emerged from the cars and ambled across the street toward the front entrance. It was a safe bet that they held weapons beneath their loose outer clothing. The driver of one of the cars stayed behind, possibly as a lookout to watch for oncoming traffic.

Three of the men walked hastily in through the entryway and directly toward Billy and Antonio, while two of the men stood at the entryway watching in all directions. Clearly, they were in a hurry, seeking to prevent Billy from divulging the location of the treasure. The closest of the three—a tall, swarthy man—removed a handgun from his coat pocket and spoke in English with a Middle-Eastern accent.

"You're coming with us. We want the map and whatever else you've got in that briefcase."

It all happened quickly. There was a sudden clicking sound somewhere to the right of the speaker. The forwardmost thug made the mistake of turning quickly to fire a round in the direction of the sound. There was a hail of automatic fire from several directions, and the man fell writhing to the floor. The two men nearest the spokesperson could see they were outgunned, so they did not reach for their weapons; and they offered no resistance. One of the men standing in the doorway took partial cover behind the front door and fired his weapon blindly at the motorcycle racks. There was another burst of automatic fire, and that man too fell to the ground with his weapon dislodged on the floor beside him. The remaining three men raised their hands in a show of surrender.

Outside, they could hear the squeal of tires as one of their two vehicles sped off away from the warehouse in the side street where it was parked. Family members pushed the surrendering thugs to their knees and disarmed them as Antonio and one of his brothers quickly hopped on the red and silver motorcycles and roared out through the doorway in pursuit of the escaping vehicle. They knew something that the driver of the escape vehicle did not know. The side street the driver had chosen was a dead end and offered no route of escape. A short distance into the side street, Antonio and his brother stopped their motorcycles and parked them end-to-end, blockading the exit. Then they took positions behind the motor-cycles with their automatic weapons raised in plain sight.

The driver of the escape vehicle managed to turn his car around at the end of the street, but he was now left with only two alterna-tives. He could surrender or he could attempt to run their blockade. Fortunately for him and for the pristine condition of the two mo-torcycles, he chose the former of the two alternatives. A few min-utes later, Antonio and his brother marched the disarmed driver through the doorway into the warehouse. Three of his companions were seated on the floor in the middle of the warehouse. The bodies of two of their associates were stretched out beside them. All of their weapons and identification cards had already been gathered.

"We need to find out who's behind these guys," Billy said to Antonio.

"Yes," Antonio agreed. "And we need to get our information before we bring the police into this."

The driver who had tried to escape was known to Antonio's family. He was a local thug for hire. They began to ply him with questions. Billy wasn't sure what was being said in Italian, but it appeared that it was having an effect as the driver stared down at his dead companions on the floor and began talking. After a few minutes, Antonio said to Billy, "We need to get back to the plane. I'll tell you what we learned when we get back. My people are going to call the police now, and it's better that we're not around when they come."

This said, Billy and Antonio got back on the motorcycles and retraced their route back to the airport.

Billy's mind was racing as they sped through the side streets. He was curious to hear more from Antonio about their assailants. But he sensed that they might now have stirred a hornets' nest, and he was eager also to leave Rome. Doubtless there were more thugs where these had come from, and he saw no need to give them a slow-moving target. At heart, Billy abhorred violence, especially when it was directed at him. It was also becoming apparent that all of their visits to obelisk sites were only confirming the professor's measurements and were not providing any new clues to the meaning of the keys of electrum. What he now needed most was time to think without interruption.

CHAPTER

47

MORNING WAS BEAUTIFUL AS the warm sun made its stage entry over the horizon and the cruise boat finally docked in Luxor. The Nile seemed narrower and cleaner here than downriver in Cairo. Also, the fertile valley did not seem to extend as far on either side of the river. Life was quieter and its pace slower here. The pace of life seemed inversely proportional to the distance upriver. It was hard to imagine that this place had been the center of civilization millennia ago. Brad and his companions shared a satisfying early breakfast on board the boat and contemplated the next phase of their adventure.

Kosar was eager to make contact with military representatives on shore; and that was not long coming, because several officers were there waiting for him on the dock. He exchanged a few words with them and quickly returned to advise Brad that a car was waiting to take them to their lodgings. Before finally disembarking, Brad cautiously surveyed the surroundings with his keen eyes. He was still pondering the significance of the large, black-hulled ship anchored in the middle of the Nile that they had passed about a mile downriver. He could just make out the words *Greifen 4* painted on its bow that was pointed upriver. Brad wondered if this could be one of those vessels engaged in the Nile navigation project. He made a mental note to gather more information from the authorities on shore.

The other tourists on board the cruise boat must have thought that Brad, Allison, and Sarah were important celebrities, what with their armed escort and the VIP greeting party that met them as they walked down the gangplank. Several uniformed personnel also carried their luggage to a waiting government vehicle. Sarah and Allison seemed delighted with this familiar ancient setting, and even the dust and the dry heat seemed like old friends to them. They could hardly wait to find transportation to the Karnak temple complex that was located approximately a mile downriver to the North. Brad was more reserved and vigilant, like a wild animal trying to decide whether he was the hunter or the hunted.

A few minutes later, their car passed through a guarded gate and stopped before a military housing complex that appeared to be a cross between army barracks and VIP officers' quarters. Armed guards were small consolation to Brad, who knew that their adversaries had sufficient resources at their disposal to buy sympathy anywhere they wished.

Brad's first big surprise came as they entered the lobby of the central VIP accommodation. There, standing in the lobby, waiting for them in full dress uniform, was Vice Admiral El-Ezaby.

"Moustafa!" Brad volunteered with shock as he went forward to shake his friend's hand. "I didn't expect to see you here."

"I flew in last night, Brad. It seems my government is placing a very high priority on this business, and they have put me in charge. And there have been some important new developments. Are these your companions?"

"Yes. Vice Admiral El-Ezaby, allow me to introduce Allison Romiel and Sarah Johnson. Allison's father, Dr. Donald Romiel, the Egyptologist who made the original discovery of the treasure, is the one I told you about who was murdered in New York. Sarah here was his student at NYU. They both are fully aware of the situation as we understand it."

"Please accept my sincere condolences, Miss Romiel. You can be assured that we will do everything in our power to apprehend those responsible," Moustafa said.

"Thank you, sir," Allison responded.

"Pardon me for rushing things," Vice Admiral El-Ezaby continued. "You must all be tired from your journey. Please take a few minutes to take your belongings to your rooms. Shall we meet back here in about fifteen minutes? We can share more details then over a cup of hot tea in the officers' lounge."

CHAPTER 48

BACK IN NEW YORK, FOLEY WAS feeling a curious admixture of anxiety and boredom as he gazed blankly at the oak-paneled walls of Nigel's office. His anxiety stemmed from the fact that Billy was long overdue in calling. What could be holding up his report? He supposed that Billy and Antonio were probably enjoying the scenery as they toured the ancient cathedrals of Rome or strolled through the city and dined at a street-side bistro. He imagined that both Billy and Brad were having more eventful and enjoyable times than he was, confined as he was here within the four walls of Nigel's office. His boredom grew out of the fact that he was never an eight-to-fiver and never wanted to be restricted to an office and a desk. He preferred the unpredictability of the open seas.

He had already phoned the nursing station on the floor of the hospital where Nigel was confined. There was no change in his status. He was still unconscious and in critical condition from the bomb blast. A police guard was still seated outside Nigel's room. Foley wished he could again confer with Nigel or Brad about his next step, but he knew it was important for him to continue monitoring communications from Nigel's office. Foley had serious doubts that they would be able to get to the bottom of this puzzle without Nigel. Foley also found himself wishing that Lieutenant Davis was more forthcoming about the lines of his investigation, but he suspected that he probably knew more already than Lieutenant Davis had been able to discover.

Following Brad's instructions, Foley had managed to contact FBI Agent Darrell Tilson in their cyber crimes division. The conversation had been brief but productive.

"Agent Tilson? My name is Foley Arnold. I'm a former Coast Guard officer who served together with Brad Beck. I'm calling you now on a secure line. I believe you collaborated with Brad when he was assigned to Coast Guard intelligence in Washington. Well, Brad has asked me to contact you about a matter of grave mutual concern. We're investigating the murder of an American professor and a conspiracy to destabilize international commodity markets. We believe the conspiracy might have tentacles reaching to the halls of Congress. I can't say more now, but we need to talk in person. And we need your advice and assistance to identify the source of some electronic communications related to the case. Unfortunately, I'm stuck here in an office in Nyack, New York, because I need to monitor communications with Brad. What are the chances you could join me here ASAP? This is really a life-and-death matter."

Agent Tilson remembered Brad with considerable respect and admiration. Unfortunately, because his own office was located in Washington, DC, and because he was busy on several other cases, he could not join Foley in New York at this time. However, he had a close colleague by the name of Mark Lindgram who was also in the cyber crimes division, and he was based in their New York City field office. He was confident that Mark would be able to provide the support Foley needed. Tilson would call Lindgram immediately and ask him to contact Foley at once. So now Foley was not only waiting for a call from Billy, but he was also awaiting Agent Lindgram's call from the nearest FBI office.

Fortunately for Foley's depleted store of patience, his phone rang in Nigel's office about five minutes later.

"Hello! May I speak with Mr. Foley Arnold, please?"

"This is Foley Arnold. Is this Agent Lindgram?"

"Yes. I was just notified that you might have need of my assistance. What can I do for you?"

Foley gave Agent Lindgram a brief description of the problem as well as the address of Nigel's office. He was pleased to learn that Lindgram had already been informed about the case and the recent murder of Professor Romiel, and he estimated he would be able to join Foley at Nigel's office in about forty-five minutes.

Foley lost count of the number of cups of coffee he had downed before radio communication finally came through from Billy.

"Billy! What's been going on? Why haven't you called in earlier?" Foley asked.

"Foley! Is that you? Where's Nigel?" Billy responded with questions of his own.

"Look, Billy. Nigel's in critical condition in the hospital following a car bomb attack this morning. That's why I'm here in his office maintaining communications. We're hopeful he'll recover; but at his age, everything is uncertain. What about you? What's been going on over there?"

"Well, some goons tried to run me down this morning as I was checking Professor Romiel's measurements on the Lateran obelisk. Then, when we got back to the plane, we found they had beaten up our pilot and ransacked the plane. Fortunately, they didn't get their hands on the real journal pages. But we found they had put a listening device and a tracking device on the plane. We used the listening device to set a trap for them, and Nigel's family took them out. I mean, two of those thugs are now dead; and four others are in the hands of the police."

"Wow! I misjudged you, Billy. When you didn't call in, I was sure that you and Antonio were out dining on linguini and Italian wine. I see that you've had your share of excitement at that end," Foley responded.

"That's not all. Before we called in the police, one of the thugs confessed that they had been hired by some international naviga- tion and shipping company with offices in Rome. I'm betting it's the same company Nigel was checking on. The good news is that I finally think I have an idea about the meaning of the keys of elec- trum and the location of the treasure. In order to be sure, we must fly to Luxor and check out the maps and measurements. Please tell Brad we're coming as soon as we can file the flight plan and get the necessary permissions. Oh! I almost forgot. We trashed the listening device and managed to stow the tracking device on a flight bound for Buenos Aires."

"Roger that!" Foley replied. "I'm sure Brad will be glad to see you. He's been holding his breath for more information about the keys of electrum and the location of the treasure. Also, you should know that the FBI is now involved at this end, and we think the in- stigators of this plot might be highly placed political and corporate powermongers."

After a few more hurried exchanges, they terminated their con- versation. Billy set about preparing for the next leg of their journey, and Foley made ready for his forthcoming meeting with Agent Lindgram.

CHAPTER 49

I T WAS A COLD, DARK EVENING IN central Connecticut. Not a single star was visible in the misty night sky. The darkness suited Senator Lodge well as he drove his late model Mercedes quickly along the narrow country roads. Normally, he would have a driver and a body-guard along; but the clandestine nature of this meeting dictated that he travel alone. He had also made sure that no one knew his destination—no one, that is, except Dmitri, whom he was going to meet. Dmitri Karlov had, in fact, called this urgent meeting using telephone code signals the two of them had developed over the years. Senator Lodge was always hesitant to meet face-to-face with Dmitri, but he knew better than to question Dmitri's judgment. After all, Dmitri's cunning and financing had gotten him elected to three terms in the Senate and now had maneuvered him into his powerful position as chair of the Senate Finance Committee. Besides, Lodge was curious about recent developments concerning their scheme. He knew, for example, that Professor Romiel was not being as cooperative as they had originally expected.

As Lodge finally reached the front gate of Dmitri's country estate, he was given visible reminder of how far the two of them had come since they had shared a dorm room at Harvard. The enormous gate was opened electronically by a guard from an internal security post. The drive to the manor wound ostentatiously through rows of trees and gardens with colorfully lit fountains. The main building of the estate rivaled his senate office building in size and easily surpassed it in architectural beauty. He knew it also had its own subterranean network of offices and secret passageways. Outside the main entrance, he stopped his car, stepped out, and handed the keys to a deferential valet.

Lodge was pleased to see his old friend waiting for him at the top of the front steps. His own arrival had obviously been announced. They exchanged smiles and a warm handshake. Dmitri was short and stout with a receding hairline that made him look Napoleonic, in keeping with his ambitious aspirations. He walked with an air of confidence that would befit someone who owned the world. Lodge, by way of contrast, shuffled along with a slower gait that supported his bulging midriff, with his solid white head of hair betraying decades of worry. Dmitri led him through the massive front door into a reception area that might as well have belonged to Buckingham Palace.

As they ascended a circular marble stairway, Dmitri remarked, "I've included Mark Wyatt in our meeting this time. He has a lot invested in our project as well, and you know that he has supplied us with much of the enabling communications technology. He's waiting in our conference room."

"Are you sure it's all right to include him? I mean, I haven't actually discussed our operations with anyone else until now," Senator Lodge shared with hesitation.

"Don't worry, Charles. Wyatt has as much to lose as any of us. He's fully committed, and he has already been very helpful," Dmitri insisted.

When they had reached the top of the stairway, Dmitri led him down a hallway and into a posh conference room with a high-vaulted ceiling and expensive paintings on the walls. A tall, thin Wyatt stood immediately and greeted Senator Lodge with a polite handshake. From the empty glasses on the table, Lodge concluded that Dmitri and Wyatt had already been talking for a while before his arrival. He was genuinely curious to know just why Dmitri thought it important to bring them together at this time. Dmitri poured a drink for Senator Lodge and offered a refill to Wyatt.

"Gentlemen," Dmitri began, "you are no doubt wondering why I thought it necessary to meet in this way. You were both aware of our decision to commission Professor Donald Romiel to assist us in locating the treasure. To say the least, that has been a delicate part of our project. We funded his research but provided him with no information about us or our intentions. Fortunately, we had help from our colleagues at the American Museum of Natural History, so our own involvement is untraceable."

"Yes. I was wondering about that. Has he located the treasure yet?" Senator Lodge blurted out impatiently.

"Charles, I'm afraid Romiel deduced the nature of our operation, at least our designs for the treasure, and he decided to become a free agent. It's a pity too. He was beginning to provide very helpful information. Of course, we had to put a stop to our arrangement with him."

"I hope he will not be a threat to our plans," Lodge interrupted ominously.

"Professor Romiel is no longer with us," Karlov responded soberly. "He met with an accident in Central Park two weeks ago. It's too bad really. We had offered him more money and even a powerful position in the New Order, but he refused. His foolish religious convictions blinded him to the opportunities. He had the nerve to cite the Ten Commandments and say, 'Thou shalt not steal.' He was definitely going to become an embarrassment to us. These people who believe they are ultimately accountable to some unseen and all-seeing deity sicken me. In their preoccupation with a world to come, they are not capable of understanding the progressive cause of making this present world better. Unfortunately, before his departure, he was able to share some of his research findings with friends and family in the New York area. Thanks to Mark here and his eavesdropping technology, we've been able to retrieve Romiel's journal and to follow the activities of his associates and their attempts to beat us to the treasure. They have not been able to make a move without our knowledge. Care to comment on that, Mark?"

"Well, yes." Wyatt proceeded methodically, like a physician describing his diagnosis and treatment. "You must understand that our search engine technology allows us to snoop on any people searching the web and record their locations and communications. We have ancillary satellite communications technology that has enabled us to keep a close eye on people of interest to us. In this way, we have learned that the opposition has divided itself into three groups. We have followed one group to Europe to observe their efforts to understand Professor Romiel's research. We have also kept a close eye on a second group that tried to elude us in Egypt itself. The third group is based in New York, and we have successfully halted their work through a program of intimidation."

Dmitri interrupted. "Both of you should know that it has been in our power through our associates in Europe and Egypt to eliminate this opposition at any time, but I have decided to follow their efforts to learn what we can from them. You see, the professor left us with an incomplete record of his findings. We know the approximate site of the treasure but not the exact location."

"I expect to have in hand the final piece of the puzzle at any moment. And then we can eliminate these people and carry out the final stage of our plan. I have already positioned us with leverage in the worldwide currency and gold markets in such a way that the entire world banking system will be under our control within a few days of my command. Charles, have you taken the steps we discussed?"

"Yes. Of course," Lodge responded. I mentioned to the president confidentially that we could soon be on the verge of a worldwide banking crisis. He is prepared to declare a state of emergency whenever the time is right. He might be young and inexperienced, but he knows on which side of his bread the butter is, so to speak. Our colleagues at FEMA and Homeland Security know what to do at that time. The Federal Reserve is already overextended beyond repair. Thankfully, we will be able to bring order out of chaos. The people will regard us as national heroes."

The three of them seem pleased—almost self-righteously so—at the success of their efforts so far. They were convinced that their cause was noble and that it would justify any steps necessary. They were encouraged also by their belief that wealth was power and that whoever controlled the wealth controlled the power also.

CHAPTER 50

BACK IN LUXOR, BRAD, ALLISON, and Sarah assembled in the lobby and followed Vice Admiral El-Ezaby to the officers' lounge, where they were each presented with a tiny *estekhan* of hot tea. They soon discovered that the most powerful brews came in small containers.

Moustafa began the conversation by sharing that he believed they had uncovered a conspiracy within the ministry of the interior. "When I saw that car parked outside your hotel in Zamalek, Brad, my suspicions were aroused. You should know that some highly positioned persons within the two ministries, interior and antiquities, have had their mutual jealousies. The secretary of antiquities enjoys considerable prestige and international celebrity status. This has not gone unnoticed by some of his rivals in the other ministry. Whether their motives are to embarrass the secretary of antiquities or to get their hands on illicit gold or both, they appear to have hatched a plot to collaborate with foreigners to locate massive treasures hidden during the eighteenth dynasty. Before we can arrest the people involved, we need to gather evidence and establish exactly who the conspirators are. Above all, we must prevent them from removing gold and ancient artifacts from the country."

Brad's thoughts turned to the black-hulled ship anchored just down river. "Moustafa, we passed a research vessel of some sort about a mile downriver from here. It reminded me of one of our own Coast Guard buoy tenders, but there were some subtle modifications. Could that be one of the vessels chartered by the ministry of interior to map the Nile River bottom?"

"That's the one I was telling you about, Brad. The *Greifen 4*. They have an international crew of ten people and an Egyptian liaison officer who reports to the ministry of the interior. In addition to providing a complete map of the river bottom, they have been contracted to place initial aids to navigation in the river to assist tourism and commerce."

Brad turned to Allison and Sarah and continued with excitement. "That's it! Allison, your father wrote in his journal about a suspicious vessel in the river near Karnak. And listen to this! It just occurred to me that the abbreviated form of *aids to navigation* commonly used is *A-T-O-N*! That could explain the cryptic message your father left in the park. He must have realized that the underwater mapping operation is somehow related to the gold theft, and that's what got him killed. I need to get back in touch with Foley about this as soon as possible."

"You're right, Brad! That must be it," Allison responded excitedly. "They must be part of this whole evil plot. But how can we catch them? I mean, you can't just confront them about it. They would deny any involvement."

"Moustafa," Brad continued, turning back to his friend, "we need to put that vessel under twenty-four-hour surveillance, and I might need to get aboard to inspect their operation more closely."

"Wait a minute!" Sarah interrupted. "Aren't we forgetting something? There has to be some archeological connection. If they could locate the treasure just by scanning the river bottom, why would they need Professor Romiel's research? And why did they go to so much trouble to steal the journal? I think Professor Romiel knew exactly where the treasure is located, and they have not yet been able to find it. We still need to decipher the location. We can't just abandon Professor Romiel's research. We still need to find out what he meant by the keys of electrum."

"We haven't forgotten the importance of Professor Romiel's research, Sarah," Brad replied. "Even now, we're waiting for word from Billy about the meaning of the keys of electrum and the exact location of the treasure, but we have to proceed with what we know. We know that that ship, the *Greifen 4*, is involved in this crime; and we have to prevent any further theft of the treasure. We will follow through on our original plan. We still must check out the professor's flat here in Luxor tomorrow, and we need to make contact with some of the archeologists who worked with him. But first, I need to phone Foley and find out if Billy has contacted him and if he has had any further word on Nigel's condition. Tonight, I want to get on board the *Greifen 4* and find out what's going on there."

"There's one other matter, Brad," Moustafa said. "The secretary of antiquities himself is coming here tomorrow. He will want to be fully briefed on everything we know. I've been working closely with him because he's using several of my divers on the Aswan project. He knew Professor Romiel personally, and he is perhaps the foremost expert in the world on ancient Egyptian history. He will be a great asset in this business. One of my jobs is to keep you all alive until he comes."

CHAPTER 51

I T WAS APPROACHING NOON LUXOR time when Brad made his way back to his room and the satellite phone. He knew it would still be early morning in New York, but it was urgent that he contact Foley. A few moments later, a sleepy-sounding Foley responded at the other end.

"Foley, it's me, Brad. I'm sorry for dragging you out of the rack so early, but I needed to touch base with you right away. First of all, is there any news about Nigel's condition?"

"He recovered consciousness last night. He's still very weak and suffering from some serious burns, but the physicians say he's on the mend."

"And what about Billy? Has he been in contact with you?"

"Yes. Billy called in late last night. He's survived several skirmishes in Rome, but he wanted me to tell you that he thinks he has some insights about the exact location of the treasure and they are flying in to Luxor today to join you. I don't have the exact time of his arrival, but he said it would be around noon your time."

"That's perfect timing! Now what about the FBI cyber crimes investigation tracing the sponsor's e-mail address? Did you contact Agent Tilson in Washington?"

"I have big news on that front! Agent Tilson put me in touch with Agent Lindgram in their New York field office. We've had several sessions together. These technophiles are wonderful! He's already traced the sponsor's e-mail address, and you won't believe who the sponsor is. The e-mail led us straight to the personal computer of Dmitri Karlov, the hedge fund manager in Connecticut. And that's not all. It seems the SEC has had their eye on his hedge fund, Equity Asset Fund Advisers, and a federal judge has now authorized a wiretap on all of their phones. Several big fish have been caught in the net already. The biggest is Connecticut Senator Charles Lodge, the chairman of the Senate banking committee. Lodge and Karlov have been in contact almost daily for months now. It seems that the two of them were roommates in college. There've been no arrests yet. They're still gathering evidence, but it appears that this conspiracy has some very tall branches."

"Wow! A lot of things are starting to come together," Brad responded. "You'll be interested to know that we think we have deciphered Professor Romiel's message in blood, *A-T-O-N*. Remember that he wrote in his journal about a suspicious vessel in the Nile River near Karnak? Well, that vessel is still here; and it belongs to the corporation Navigational Technologies International that we've already had our own dealings with. The point is that it's a research vessel involved in mapping the Nile bottom and placing aids to navigation in the river."

"Of course," Foley said. "Aids to navigation is A-T-O-N. After my tours aboard buoy tenders, I can't imagine why I didn't think of it sooner. The professor was sending a message to you, Brad. That research vessel is somehow involved in this whole plot!"

"Yes, and Moustafa has been very helpful at this end to provide support. We now have most of the Egyptian government behind us. The only problem is that another part of the Egyptian government is involved in the conspiracy, so we need to proceed with caution. In any case, you've really made my day, Foley. I'd better sign off now and go meet Billy. Please give our fond regards to Nigel and tell him that everything is proceeding as planned. Once Billy joins us, we should have more news about the location of the treasure.

Brad could hardly contain his satisfaction as he finished his conversation with Foley. A broad grin spread across his face. He now felt better than he had felt at any time since the news of Professor Romiel's untimely death.

CHAPTER 52

THE GULFSTREAM PILOT TURNED to Billy and reported matter-of-factly, "We are on approach to the Luxor airport. We should be on the ground in fifteen minutes. You and Antonio should fasten your seatbelts."

Billy returned to the main cabin of the plane, took his seat, and stowed his laptop. It was about 11:30 a.m. local time, and he could see that Antonio was taking a well-deserved nap with his seatbelt fastened. Billy saw no need to wake him. Billy could hardly wait to see Brad and Allison and especially Sarah. He imagined with a smile that their adversaries were right now looking for him somewhere over the Atlantic as the plane with the tracking device approached Buenos Aires. And now, at last, he could visit Egypt and see the historical landscape that he had only read about. Unlike Sarah, he had never personally visited Egypt. From the window at his side, Billy could see far below the long dark ribbon that was the Nile River with a green belt of arable land on both of its sides. Beyond that, there was nothing but dry, sandy desert as far as the eye could see.

Billy took another hard look at Professor Romiel's map of Karnak in his hand. *The clue had been right there all along,* he thought to himself. He noted the thin line the professor had traced connecting the remaining obelisk of Hatchepsut to the presumed location of the obelisk of her nephew or stepson Thutmose III. Originally, Billy had thought this was some sort of temple wall; but no. That could not be. The line ran east and west, perpendicular to the Nile. And, when extended, it overlapped perfectly with the route of the Opet Festival. The irony was not lost on Billy. If he was right, the priests had chosen the monuments of Pharaoh Akhenaten's own ancestors offered in dedication to Amun as the means of hiding the ancient treasury from the heretic pharaoh who had strayed from the worship of Amun. What Billy still did not have was a vertical point of triangulation, a good navigational fix for determining how far out into the Nile the treasure had been dropped. For that, he would need to examine the temple structure more closely.

These thoughts were racing through his mind as he heard the squealing sound of the plane tires touching down. Antonio jerked into semiconsciousness as he gazed around. His eyes met Billy's, and he quickly realized that they had arrived at their destination. After the plane had taxied to a full stop, Billy stowed the map in his briefcase and they began gathering their luggage and equipment for the next phase of their journey. Billy hoped that Brad and the others had received the message of their flight and would be there to meet them.

As the plane door opened and Billy began his descent down the stairway, he could see three black limousines approaching. *They must have gotten my message, and this must be the official welcoming party,* Billy thought to himself with satisfaction. He and Antonio waited at the bottom of the stairway as the three vehicles parked and several dignitaries in dark suits and ties disembarked and approached them smilingly.

"Welcome to Egypt, Mr. Heckman," the leader of the welcoming party exclaimed with a warm handshake. "I am Hamid Marzouk, Deputy Minister of the Interior. We have been sent to welcome you and escort you to the hotel where the other members of your group are awaiting you. I'm sure that Mr. Bradford Beck, Miss Allison Romiel, and Miss Sarah Johnson will be delighted to see you again. Please step into our vehicles. It will take us only about fifteen minutes to join the others."

This time, Billy thought it best to take the pilot along with them; so as soon as their luggage was safely stowed in the back of two of the vehicles, they all took seats. Billy and Antonio sat together in the middle row of seats in the lead vehicle, and the pilot took a seat in the vehicle directly behind them. They were thankful for the heavily tinted windows and the refuge they provided from the intense sunlight.

"I trust you had a good flight and are not too tired from your journey," Mr. Marzouk began affably as the limousines started into motion. "I understand you have made some progress in your search for the buried treasure," Marzouk continued.

Billy was surprised and shocked that Marzouk knew so much about his business. No doubt Brad had shared some details about the information Billy had communicated with Foley earlier. As he pondered a discreet reply, he felt a sudden stinging sensation in his neck. Within seconds, the smiling face of Marzouk slowly faded from his consciousness.

In an instant, his eyes had closed and his body had gone limp in the same way Antonio had slumped in the seat beside him. Suddenly, the conversation reverted to Arabic language; and Mr. Marzouk began a series of terse commands to the driver and the other occupants of the vehicle.

"Take me to my ministry office. Then take these visitors and their luggage to our dock warehouse. Tie them up and lock them away in a quiet place. They should be unconscious for another six hours. They will be safe there. Mahmoud will know what to do with them."

CHAPTER 53

BRAD RUSHED BACK TO THE OFFICERS' lounge, where he could see Moustafa, Allison, and Sarah were engaged in casual conversation about Moustafa's experiences at the Coast Guard Academy and beyond. Allison painfully related some of the details of her father's murder to explain to Moustafa how they had become involved. In actual fact, however, they were merely waiting for Brad so they could order lunch together and hear the latest news from stateside.

"Lunch will have to wait," Brad volunteered hastily on entering the lounge. "Billy believes he has finally deciphered the meaning of the keys of electrum, and he is joining us today. He will be arriving at the airport at any moment, and we need to go meet him. And there's other good news. Nigel is conscious and his condition is improving. Also, the FBI has identified Professor Romiel's sponsor as a hedge fund manager in Connecticut; and they are closing in on the conspiracy."

The mood brightened considerably as Moustafa immediately ordered several vehicles to shuttle them to the airport to welcome Billy and Antonio. Sarah's eyes brightened visibly while she entertained the possibility of seeing Billy again and hearing him explain how he had unraveled the mystery of the keys of electrum.

Sarah was more pensive as she sat in the limo beside Brad and asked for more details about Nigel and the conspiracy. Moustafa radioed ahead to the airport to learn if any private flights had arrived or were about to arrive at the Luxor airport coming from Rome. They were all delighted to learn that a small corporate jet had landed not quite fifteen minutes earlier.

Speeding over the hot, bumpy roads, they soon made a sharp turn and the tiny airport came into full view. They saw the high, wire fence that surrounded the entire landing field; and they could see several planes parked on the ground. They approached the landing area through a heavily guarded side gate. Seeing Moustafa in an official vehicle, the guards saluted and allowed the two-vehicle caravan to pass. They were able to drive right out onto the runway and approach the area where they could see that a small, corporate jet was parked. Approaching the plane, they could see it was already vacated and closed up.

"They must be inside the building by now. Let's go into the waiting area through the passenger entrance," Moustafa suggested.

Once inside the building, they could see that it was nearly deserted at this time of day. A few officials were visible behind a ticketing counter, and two janitors were busily mopping the tile floor.

Moustafa approached the desk with his entourage and enquired concerning the corporate jet parked outside the building. The attendant explained that an official welcoming party had already received the passengers and it had not been necessary for them to pass through the terminal building. Moustafa asked curtly who the welcoming party was and when they had arrived. The attendant explained that they were high officials from one of the ministries and they had left the airport about ten minutes ago. He had not actually seen the officials, and he could not tell which ministry they represented.

Moustafa was irate. No one seemed to have any information about the welcoming party or where they were headed. Turning to

Brad, he explained in English, "Someone has already received Billy and Antonio. Supposedly it was some sort of official welcoming party, but no one here knows anything about it. Let's ask the guards at the gate on our way back to headquarters and see if they know anything more about this."

The guards nervously explained to an impatient Moustafa that three official black limousines from the ministry of the interior had passed through just a few minutes earlier. They did not recognize any of the passengers, but they had to let them pass because it was official business. They had no idea where the limousines were headed.

Moustafa explained that he needed to return the three of them immediately to the visiting officers' quarters while he himself inquired at the offices of the ministry of the interior to learn what was happening. Something was very wrong, and he intended to get to the bottom of the matter at once. Brad prevailed upon Moustafa to take him along after they had deposited the girls in safekeeping. It was about 12:45 p.m. when Brad, Moustafa, and two armed guards left the visiting officers' quarters in one of the same limousines they had taken to the airport.

B ack at the visiting officer's quarters, Sarah stormed into the lobby. She was hurt and angry—not just because Billy was not there at the airport as expected, but also because she and Allison had been so unceremoniously dumped at the visiting officers' quarters while Brad and Moustafa set about responding meaningfully to the new situation.

"Do you think Billy is all right?" Sarah asked nervously as her anger gave way to fear.

"I'm praying he's all right. Probably just a bureaucratic mix-up with the limousines. Besides, Antonio is with him, and they will get it all straightened out. Things take a while in Egypt," Allison replied.

Turning to Allison, Sarah said, "Well, I can't sit here and do nothing. I think it's time you and I did some investigating of our own. Let's round up Kosar and go over to Karnak Temple. I'll bet we can find some archeologist I know who also might have information about your father's work."

Allison hesitated momentarily but finally agreed. She was still very eager to know more about her father's work and what had happened to him. Also, she considered that they would be safe with Kosar. And besides, she was at least as adventuresome as Sarah, and her knowledge of Arabic language was far superior.

Kosar was hesitant, knowing he was responsible for their safety; but in the end, his reluctance was no match for the persistence of the two women. The driver and the remaining limo they had taken to the airport were still parked in front of the building. Kosar took his loaded automatic weapon and boarded the limo with the two American women and ordered the driver to take them to Karnak.

CHAPTER

54

I T WAS NO SECRET THAT BOTH ALLISON
and Sarah were eager to get back to the colossal ruins of
Karnak Temple. Allison had fond childhood memories of
walking with her father and mother among the gigantic
colonnades. Those were among the happiest days of her
life. For Sarah, this Karnak-Thebes-Luxor historical region and
the tombs across the river had been the central focus of her short
academic and professional career.

It was a hot, dry summer afternoon at the Karnak Temple complex as their military driver searched in vain for a shady parking
place. The two women donned their sunglasses and broad-brimmed
hats as they stepped out of the car into the centuries-old dust and
eagerly preceded Kosar on foot toward the complex, Kosar, with
his loaded weapon, only a few steps behind them. They passed by
a long row of lion sphinxes that had long since been effaced by
political and religious opposition. They entered the temple complex at the western gate from the Nile side and were once again
awestruck as they passed the first pylon and entered the forecourt.
Several tour groups were milling about with their Egyptian tour
guides, speaking variously in English, Italian, German, French, or
Japanese, according to the needs of each group to understand the
historical significance of the ancient monuments.

Allison overheard one English-speaking guide saying, "This temple was the national shrine of Egypt for over two thousand years."

Moving at a deliberate pace, the three of them proceeded past the second pylon and entered the Great Hypostyle Hall. The cool shade among the one hundred and thirty-four giant columns provided welcome relief. Allison reminisced over scenes of her childhood and gazed about in search of obelisks that might have been her father's most recent focus. Sarah, for her part, was scanning the crowd in search of familiar faces from among the archeological community. Kosar grasped his automatic weapon firmly and furtively glanced in all directions in anticipation of any potential threat.

Passing beyond the third pylon, they saw them. First, on their right was the ancient obelisk of Thutmose I, the great-great-grandfather of Akhenaten and the father of Queen Hatchepsut. And beyond, in the distance, they could see the one taller remaining obelisk of Queen Hatchepsut. Allison's heart skipped a beat as she reached out and touched the rose-beige granite of the ancient obelisk of Thutmose I.

Sarah volunteered the information that Thutmose I was a warrior king who reigned about thirty years from 1546 to 1516 BC. He did much to consolidate the upper and lower regions of Egypt from time of the defeat of the Hyksos kings to the north and the conquest of Nubia to the south. During his reign and that of his daughter, Hatchepsut, and grandson, Thutmose III, Egypt was at the zenith of its power and its dominion extended across the Euphrates into Syria. He erected two great obelisks here, both about 19.5 meters high and weighing about 143 tons. At the time of construction, they were the largest obelisks at Karnak, befitting his kingly stature. The matching obelisk was reported by European visitors to have stood nearby as recently as the AD eighteenth century; but now, only a few remaining pieces could be seen strewn about and other pieces could be found in foreign museums.

Sarah squinted in the sunlight as she pointed up the western face of the obelisk. "On each face of the obelisk," she said, "the column of hieroglyphs gives the names of Pharaoh Thutmose I. At the top on each side is the dedication to Horus, Mighty Bull, beloved of Maat. Here on the western face, it says Thutmose made the obelisk as a monument for his father, Amun-Re, lord of the thrones of the two lands, erecting for him two large obelisks at the double gate of the temple, the pyramidians being of electrum. Obviously, the precious electrum has long since been looted and removed in just the same way that these crooks we're dealing with are trying to remove gold treasure from Egypt today."

"Interestingly, he calls his god, Amun-Re, his father," Allison volunteered. "I wonder if he had the same concept of God as a powerful creator and father that I hold as the object of my faith. For example, Jesus taught His disciples to pray, 'Our Father which art in heaven…,' and spoke of God as a loving, all-knowing Provider who wants to commune with His follower children."

"I doubt Thutmose had the same views about God that you and I have," Sarah responded. "For one thing, he believed in a whole pantheon of gods and considered that he himself was a god. Part of his worship and commemoration of Amun-Re as his father-god was likely to certify and establish his own claims of godhood to his subjects. When the Egyptians saw these obelisks with their pyramidians brightly reflecting the sunlight, they were reminded of their god, Amun-Re, and his descendant-god, Thutmose I. It was believed that the pharaoh reaffirmed godhood status at the time of the Opet Festival, which we have discussed. There is a strange resemblance here to the politics of our day, as some followers of political rulers seem comforted to ascribe godlike status to their own rulers. I suppose certain people find safety in the belief that their leaders are not subject to human error."

"My father used to marvel," Allison mused, "that the Egyptians had thousands, perhaps hundreds of thousands, of monotheistic

Jews living among them for four centuries, and yet they persisted in polytheism. That's why he spent a lot of time in search of artifacts that would establish the time of the Jewish sojourn and the Exodus and anything else he might learn about the Jews of that time. He was delighted, for example, when he learned of the discovery at the bottom of the Red Sea of chariot wheels dating to the eighteenth dynasty, consistent with the account of the Exodus. Because the Jews were viewed as the blue-collar workers at the time, perhaps the discrediting of Jewish views about monotheism in that day was not unlike the discrediting of biblical Christianity on the part of the social elite in our own country today. It is said, for example, by our own social elite that the middle class ignorantly clings to guns and religion. In any case, anti-Semitism is still alive and well today as it was at that time."

"I wouldn't say the Jews had no influence on religion in Egypt at that time," Sarah responded. "I'm sure you know that some Egyptologists believe that Pharaoh Akhenaten's conversion to monotheism and his name change from Amenhotep IV to Akhenaten was the result of Jewish influence through some of his own Egyptian relatives who were distantly related to the patriarch Joseph by marriage. Your father held that view; and probably because he was my professor and mentor, I tend to agree with him. I never told you, Allison, but your father had a profound influence on me and on many of my classmates. Before I met him, I didn't take many of the historical claims of the Bible seriously, but now I take the Bible as the point of reference for all of history. And I share his view that God is in control of all of history. I also agree with his view that the unfolding events involving the nation of Israel serve as a kind of timetable or clock for all of human history."

"Thank you for sharing that, Sarah. Those words mean a lot to me. You know, Sarah, when I see all these vast temples a thousand years in the making only gathering dust today, it reminds me of something my father told me: 'True religion is not about monuments and ceremonies, it is about having a relationship with God, about caring for the widows and the orphans, and sharing God's love. That is what really matters.'"

Allison turned away silently and struggled to hold back the hot tears of fresh memories of her father by walking briskly forward beyond the fourth pylon in the direction of the obelisk of Queen Hatchepsut. As the two of them rounded the 29.5-meter, 323-ton obelisk, the tallest of all the Karnak obelisks, they were suddenly shocked out of their reveries. There standing at the base of the obelisk along with several other scholarly-looking foreigners was someone Sarah recognized immediately.

"Dr. Gunther, what are you doing here?" Sarah asked with amazement and an inexplicable tinge of fear.

"I might ask you the same question, young lady. Sarah Johnson, isn't it?" Gunther, the deputy curator of the American Museum of Natural History, responded.

CHAPTER

55

BRAD AND MOUSTAFA CONSIDERED their next move as the military car and driver took them and one armed guard at breakneck speed toward the government office complex inside the city of Luxor. Brad was reminded of scenes of the Indianapolis 500 as the driver leaned heavily against each turn. They soon came to a full stop alongside a tall building topped with an Egyptian flag and displaying an inscription in Arabic and English declaring that this was the "Luxor Central Office of the Ministry of the Interior of the Arab Republic of Egypt." As Brad, Moustafa, and the armed guard stepped out of their vehicle, they were unaware that their approach had been carefully observed from inside the building. Ascending the marble staircase in front of the building, Moustafa received a crisp salute from an armed guard standing beside the front door. Another guard opened the door so the three of them could enter hastily. Once inside, they noticed the polished, black marble floor and a metallic front desk with a uniformed receptionist.

"Who's in charge here?" Moustafa demanded in standard Cairene Arabic.

"Director Mohsen Al-Kateeb," came the polite but nervous response of the receptionist.

"Please tell him that Vice Admiral Moustafa El-Ezaby must see him immediately on an urgent matter of national security."

Following a brief telephone call to the office of the director, the receptionist motioned to another uniformed attendant and instructed him to escort the party to the director's office on the top floor. They entered a large elevator, and the doors soon opened to a red-carpeted hallway before a suite of offices. Their military escort introduced them to the middle-aged, heavyset administrative assistant stationed at a desk outside the door to the director's office. She announced their arrival by telecom and quickly stood and opened the door to the office for them with the expression, "*Et Fuddle!*"

Brad could see that the director was a gaunt-appearing man in his fifties with a full moustache and a balding head. Somehow, his features reminded Brad of the pictures of Anwar Al-Sadat that he had seen many times before. The director appeared suspicious and coolly reserved as he motioned for them to take seats on any of the black leather chairs arranged in a semicircle in front of his large walnut desk.

"Admiral El-Ezaby," he said expressionlessly in perfect Egyptian English, a dialect that had evolved from the time of the British occupation, "you said that you have come on a matter of national security. Please tell me how I might be of help."

Moustafa began politely by thanking the director for seeing them on short notice and by introducing his companion, Brad Beck. Then he wasted no time in stating his business.

"We have learned that three government cars from this office have just intercepted and detained a party of international specialists who are here in Egypt to protect our national interests. His Excellency, the secretary general of antiquities, has arranged a meeting with these specialists to take place here in Luxor tomorrow. If you do not insist that these experts are released immediately, there will be hell to pay. Of course, you might have no personal knowledge of these developments. In any case, there will be a formal inquiry; and you understand that your office at minimum could see position replacements and even prison sentences."

"Admiral El-Ezaby"—the director was visibly shaken and replied angrily with a tremor in his voice—"this is the first I have heard about any of these charges. I can assure you that no vehicles from this office were dispatched for any such purpose. Furthermore, I very much resent your tone. You dare not make such vicious accusations without proof. You can be sure that your demeanor in this matter will be reported at the highest levels."

"I have spoken in the interest of national security, which is my job," Moustafa replied without blinking. "You can be sure that the disappearance of these specialists has already been reported at the highest levels, and you can expect formal inquiries to proceed within twenty-four hours. Director Al-Kateeb, since you obviously have chosen not to be cooperative, we are leaving now. You can expect to hear from your superiors in Cairo very shortly."

With that, Moustafa turned in his tracks and stormed angrily out of the office with Brad and their armed guard keeping pace close behind. No word was spoken until after they had left the building and entered their waiting vehicle.

"You certainly were direct, Moustafa," Brad said admiringly.

"I have found the only way to deal with these bureaucrats is to be forceful and direct. Now we shall see the effects of our confrontation." With that, Moustafa picked up his cell phone to respond to an urgent call.

T he door of the director's office had barely closed behind them when the door to an adjoining office opened and the deputy minister of the interior rejoined the director. He had overheard the entire conversation.

"Hamid, they already know that you kidnapped the Americans," the director intoned impassively. "You must release them immediately. Find some way to release them without implicating this office. There is going to be an inquiry. You must let them go unharmed."

Hamid Marzouk responded, half in anger and half in fear, "I can't do that. They know who I am. It will be too dangerous for me and for you if we let them go."

Director Al-Kateeb walked to the window of his office and watched the military vehicle in the street below drive off hurriedly, carrying the American and Vice Admiral El-Ezaby.

"You're right, Hamid," the director finally said. "This situation is much too dangerous."

Slowly and deliberately, he walked back to his desk and removed his handgun and silencer from the top drawer. Turning suddenly, he fired two shots at point-blank range. Marzouk fell lifeless to the floor. In the next instant, the director was on the telephone to Mahmoud at the dock warehouse.

"Mahmoud, there's been a change in plans. We need to release the captives immediately. Have they recovered from the sedative yet?"

"Not yet, sir." Mahmoud replied. "They're sleeping like babies in the next room. And we have retrieved some very interesting information in their luggage. It seems they managed to pin point the burial site of the treasure, and the line of placement is marked on one of their maps."

"Excellent!" the director responded. "Here's what I want you to do. Keep the map with the treasure location. Then, have the hostages and their luggage taken quickly by private car to a remote site on the other side of the city. There can be no witnesses. Place them where they will awaken undisturbed and wander back into the city. But I need you to come here right away with a tarp to clean up an accident we have had here in my office. I need you to do all this immediately. Meanwhile, I want you to tell the captain of the *Greifen 4* to move to the treasure location on their map and begin extraction tonight under cover of darkness. We must load up everything we can get and start downriver before dawn. This is the final deadline. You can dispose of the body at the bottom of the river on your way to Cairo tonight. Do you understand?"

"Perfectly."

The director put down the telephone and stared with disgust at the pool of blood widening on his office floor. He knew he had some explaining to do in his meeting with the American archeologist tonight. This mess would need to be cleaned up before then. If all went well, the situation could yet be saved. Otherwise... But there could be no otherwise.

CHAPTER

56

TIME STOOD STILL, AND SARAH felt speechless for an eternity as she stared into the steel, gray eyes of Dr. Daniel Gunther. As circumstances would have it, they suddenly found themselves standing together unexpectedly at the base of the great obelisk of Queen Hatchepsut. Sarah swallowed hard, but her mouth went dry as she searched for words to explain her sudden appearance there at Karnak Temple.

"Well, Dr. Gunther," she began slowly, "I finally did find a sponsor to help me with my research into the Akhenaten period. That's how I was able to return here to collect data for my graduate research. By the way, did you ever hear back from Professor Romiel's sponsor? I tried to contact your office, but they said you were out of town."

Gunther glanced furtively at Sarah, at Allison, and then at Kosar a short distance away. He took a deep breath, smiled, and responded calmly, "How pleasant to see you here! Unfortunately, Professor Romiel's sponsor has not yet responded to my inquiry. I'm here on other museum business this week. I can continue to pursue the matter on my return if you like; but if you already have a sponsor, perhaps it is no longer a consideration. Have I met your companions here?"

"I'm sorry! This is Allison Romiel, the late professor's daughter. She spent her childhood here in Egypt; and because of the sad circumstances of her father's death, she felt this is where she needed to come to get away. Kosar there is along for protection. He is also here because of the unfortunate circumstances of Professor Romiel's passing. With regard to Professor Romiel's sponsor, by all means, please keep asking," Sarah responded. "I have learned that you can never have too many sponsors," she added with a smile.

"Well, had I known you would be here, I might have arranged for us to meet formally and discuss our common concerns. Unfortunately, my schedule now is very tight and is dictated by the interests of the Egyptian government. I expect to be in meetings throughout my visit. Perhaps we can get together when we are back in New York City." With that, Gunther returned to his party and they continued walking back toward the temple entrance.

After Gunther and his party had passed beyond earshot, Allison commented, "That was a shock! Brad and Foley expressed some suspicion about Gunther regarding my father's murder. I wonder what he is really doing here now. We have to tell Brad about this."

"Yes. It wouldn't surprise me at all if Gunther himself isn't trying to tie up loose ends regarding your father's research. He would be the first person the sponsor would contact. If that's the case, he is lying about trying to connect me with the sponsor. He definitely knows a lot more than he is saying," Sarah concluded.

For an instant, the two of them exchanged a knowing look; then they both turned to gaze up at the magnificent, ninety-seven-foot obelisk of Queen Hatchepsut. They felt a certain inexplicable pride as they thought of the woman who skillfully ruled the most powerful civilization of her day.

"Before we go back and share about Gunther," Sarah said, "I just want to point out that over there to the east beyond the wall is a smaller temple called the Temple of the Hearing Ear. It was there that the common people were allowed to approach and offer prayers to Amun. There is a foundation there that is believed to have been the location of the largest obelisk of all, the Lateran Obelisk that was removed to Rome. That obelisk was erected by Hatchepsut's coregent nephew, Thutmose III. He seemed to be in competition with her because he walled off her obelisks from public view and defaced many of her inscriptions. Three generations later, Akhenaten appeared on the scene, who was the focus of your father's research."

"It's interesting how each generation sought to outdo the previous generation," Allison said. "I mean, Hatchepsut's obelisks had to be higher than those of her father, Thutmose I; and then Thutmose III had to outdo Hatchepsut.

"Now that I think about it," Allison continued, "it's interesting that the tallest obelisk was taken away to Rome and some of the other smaller ones survived here in place. It's a little like the biblical proverb 'Pride goes before destruction, and a haughty spirit before a fall.' And again, 'The meek shall inherit the earth.' The pharaoh with the biggest ego over time is the one who suffered the greatest destruction of his works. I hope the same principle will find application with our adversaries, who must similarly have a huge lust for power in order to do what they have done."

As Allison craned her neck to gaze back up at Queen Hatchepsut's obelisk, she suddenly pictured herself as a young girl sitting on her father's knee. Percy Shelley's famous poem, "Ozymandias," was one of her father's favorites, and he had quoted it often to Allison. She now whispered the words out loud as though reciting it with her father.

> I met a traveler from an antique land
> Who said: Two vast and trunkless legs of stone
> Stand in the desert. Near them, on the sand,
> Half sunk, a shattered visage lies, whose frown
> And wrinkled lip, and sneer of cold command
> Tell that its sculptor well those passions read
> Which yet survive, stamped on these lifeless things,
> The hand that mocked them and the heart that fed.

And on the pedestal these words appear:
'My name is Ozymandias, king of kings:
Look on my works, ye Mighty, and despair!'
Nothing beside remains. Round the decay
Of that colossal wreck, boundless and bare
The lone and level sands stretch far away.

57

MAHMOUD ORDERED TWO OF his coworkers to back the white Toyota van into the warehouse. They were then instructed to load the three unconscious hostages, bound and blindfolded, into the back of the van along with their luggage.

"Take these visitors and their luggage to the *wadi* on the eastern side of the city and release them there. Don't let anyone see you and don't let them identify you. When they wake up, they can find their way back into the city and no one will be the wiser. Then come back here immediately. I have another job for you after that."

Next, Mahmoud called the captain of the *Greifen 4* by cell phone and instructed him to move the ship directly above the presumed location of the treasure and make ready for extraction.

"Tell your men to prepare for a long night," he added soberly.

A day later in the desert east of Luxor...
      It was late afternoon, and the sun was low on the horizon when the dry breeze whistling across the hot Egyptian landscape nudged Billy to consciousness. He had no idea where he was as he removed his blindfold and looked around him. There on the sand beside him were his two companions and their belongings. He first

removed the blindfold from Antonio and shook him to consciousness. The drug's effects wore off slowly, and Antonio began to sit up and move his arms.

"How did we get here?" he asked Billy.

"I don't know," Billy replied as he turned his attention to their pilot. "The last thing I remember was the limo ride with that Marzouk character. They must have drugged us."

Billy checked his belongings carefully. "It looks like they took the map of Karnak that marked the location of the treasure."

Instinctively, Antonio struggled up the side of the ravine in which they found themselves so he could get a better sense of their location. In the west, he could make out a row of mountains along the horizon; and in the distant foreground were some buildings and vegetation he could barely make out. He assumed that that must be the direction of Luxor.

Turning to Billy and the pilot, he called down, "Let's gather up our luggage! We have a bit of a walk ahead of us."

About forty-five minutes later, the three of them arrived, thirsty and dusty, at one of the roads on the outskirts of the city. Pausing every few minutes to set down their luggage and catch their breath, they finally came to a small shop with groceries and cold drinks. Explaining their predicament to the shopkeeper as best they could, they finally convinced him to call the authorities and send a car for them, but not before he graciously presented each of them with a tall, cool glass of Kerkaday.

The most welcome sight of all came about twenty minutes later when two military vehicles arrived at the shop and there, getting out of the forward vehicle, was Brad and his officer friend, whom Brad soon introduced to them as Vice Admiral Moustafa El-Ezaby. Their relief and jubilation was beyond measure; and Brad was quick to point out that they probably had his friend, Moustafa, to thank for their release.

"Tell us exactly what happened," Brad said to Billy as the military vehicles sped them back to their VIP officers' quarters.

"All I remember is that we were met at the airport by some official from the ministry of the interior who said his name was Hamid Marzouk. He said you had sent him. They must have drugged us, because we blacked out soon after we got into their limousines. That's all we can remember," Billy said.

"Hamid Marzouk! I know him," Moustafa declared suddenly. "He's the deputy minister of the interior. I knew there was some connection with that ministry in all of this. I didn't know that he was here in Luxor."

"That's not all," Billy interrupted. "They searched our belongings, and they took the map of Karnak Temple showing the presumed location of the treasure that was marked by Professor Romiel."

"Okay. That settles it," Brad responded angrily. "Moustafa, we need to take a boarding party to get on that vessel tonight. Any further delay could be disastrous."

"I agree." Moustafa nodded. "Let's go back to quarters and draw up a plan of engagement."

A little while later, as the sun began to settle upon the mountainous horizon, they arrived back at the military compound. As they entered, they were pleasantly surprised to see the women, Allison and Sarah, waiting for them in the lounge. The relief and joy was visible all around in the bright eyes and smiling faces.

Brad recounted briefly the events at the offices of the ministry of the interior and the trip out into the outskirts of the city to retrieve Billy and his colleagues.

Allison then interrupted impatiently, "We're delighted that we are all here together safe and sound at last, but I have another bit of shocking news to share. You'll never guess who was at Karnak Temple this afternoon. Dr. Daniel Gunther. He said he was here on museum business, but I didn't believe a word of it."

Brad explained to Moustafa that Gunther was the deputy curator of the American Museum of Natural History in New York City. Their paths had crossed before when they were trying to get information about Professor Romiel's death.

"The pieces of this puzzle are starting to come together at last," Brad said to the group. "I only wish Foley could be here to join us in our boarding attempt tonight."

"No matter, Brad," Moustafa said. "I have several trained men right here who are up to the task. I think Billy and the others should retire to their rooms and rest up for our meeting with the secretary of antiquities tomorrow. Meanwhile, you and I can discuss the events of tonight together."

CHAPTER

58

I N ANOTHER PART OF THE CITY, AT THE office of the Luxor director of the ministry of the interior, the American archeologist had arrived for a scheduled meeting.

"Good evening, Dr. Gunther," Director Al-Kateeb said warmly. "You will be pleased to know that things are going according to plan."

"That's not exactly the way I have interpreted the events of the past several weeks, Mohsen; but I will be happy if you can convince me otherwise. By the way, where's Hamid Marzouk? He was supposed to join us in this meeting as well." Gunther's manner was imperious, not at all the phlegmatic demeanor usually expected of a museum curator who was a guest in a foreign country.

"Look. We've had a few complications here," Al-Kateeb explained nervously. "Hamid is no longer part of this operation. He was, shall we say, careless. But I have some very good news. We have been able to retrieve Professor Romiel's map of Karnak with precise indication of the location of the treasure. We are on track to retrieve the treasure this very night."

"That's welcome news! Let's hope you're right this time, Mohsen. As you know very well, our friends in America have a lot invested in this project; and they do not like disappointments. The failure of your attempt on Brad Beck's life was one of those disappointments. Their patience is wearing thin. What's more, I know about the arrival of the flight from Rome today. Where are you keeping the passengers?"

Al-Kateeb was visibly taken aback by Gunther's awareness of recent developments. "We met them at the airport according to plan, and we took them to a place for safekeeping," Al-Kateeb answered. "But then we had an unexpected visit from Beck and a companion of his who is a vice admiral in the Egyptian navy. Somehow, they knew we had abducted the passengers on their arrival here in Luxor. Of course, we denied all involvement, and they can prove nothing. But we decided to release the prisoners in the desert because we knew there would be an inquiry and we didn't want to be linked to their disappearance. Hamid was seen escorting the visitors from the airport. That's why Hamid is no longer with us. We were, however, able to retrieve Professor Romiel's map from them before we released them. Our vessel is positioning to extract the gold even now as we speak."

"You fool!" Gunther ranted at Al-Kateeb. "Now they too will know the exact location of the treasure. Our chances of getting to the treasure before they know about it have now been greatly diminished by your bungling. And Hamid was our key contact within the ministry. He is the one man who could guarantee that we could get the gold out of the country."

"Dr. Gunther, I think you are far too anxious. I told you that we are even now about to extract the gold. And you have overestimated Hamid's role in all of this. He was just a figurehead. Who do you suppose he relied on actually to get gold and artifacts out of the country? And if you must know who bungled the attempt on Brad Beck's life, that was Hamid's work. No. Things are still very much under our control. We are closer than ever to reaching our goals."

For an instant, Al-Kateeb thought to himself that perhaps he should eliminate this pompous American as well. He could manage to dispose of the gold very well by himself without foreign interference. But no. He realized there were too many foreign participants already for him to change the plan. And he had seen enough to know that the international consortium of which Gunther was a part had power and reach and ruthlessness he could only imagine. Nevertheless, he would watch this American infidel closely from this point forward. One false step, and this foreign fool would become the scapegoat for all their failed plans.

"Look here, Gunther," Al-Kateeb continued, "I happen to know that the secretary of antiquities has called a meeting with Beck and his companions here in Luxor tomorrow. They will be tied up in meetings the whole time that we are moving the gold downriver. We will move the treasure right out from under their noses."

"What time is that meeting?" Gunther asked. "I am well acquainted with the secretary of antiquities, and I might be able to insert myself into that meeting to find out what they are doing."

"That doesn't sound like a very good idea to me," Al-Kateeb responded. "The meeting will likely be held soon after the secretary general arrives on the first flight from Cairo, but we have not been given an invitation. You do not fully realize the complexity of our relationship with that ministry. You could alert them to our involvement in this matter."

"Yes, and I could also divert their suspicions," Gunther responded. "I want you to get me an invitation to that meeting. Pull whatever strings you have to. I must learn what they know. If we have already removed the gold by then, I can distract them. If not, I can gain critical information."

CHAPTER

59

THE SUN WAS SETTING IN THE west at the end of yet another cloudless day. The red beams of the sun bled down from the mountaintops into the dusty valley below as they had done for millennia before. Mahmoud and two helpers loaded the motorized skiff they used to transport men and equipment from shore to the *Greifen 4*. This time, their cargo included the body of Hamid Marzouk that they had stowed in a large wooden crate to avoid detection by any onlookers from shore.

Their orders were clear. They were to assist in the extraction of the gold and travel downriver with the boat once the gold was loaded into the buoy-shaped containers. Then they were to dispose of the body in the river with heavy weights. Mahmoud was pleased that this stage of the operation had finally arrived. The situation was getting far too tense for his liking, and the delays in finding the treasure had taken a murderous toll on his patience.

As they boarded the vessel and delivered their cargo, Mahmoud could see thankfully that the *Greifen 4* was already positioned at the critical point opposite Karnak Temple. He could hardly wait to get to the operation center to learn of their success in detecting the treasure. Although they had passed over this region before with their scanning equipment, obviously they had missed the target. As the sky darkened and the stars began to appear slowly overhead, there were other preparations taking place on shore of the Nile that Mahmoud knew nothing about.

Brad and Moustafa and five Egyptian navy seals had assembled under cover of darkness on the shore between Karnak and the *Greifen 4* but slightly to the south, farther upriver, to allow for the current. The seven-man boarding party was watching quietly from the shore as the motorized skiff approached and offloaded its crew and cargo onto the buoy tender. The original plan called for a black rubber inflatable raft to carry them to the boat, but Brad suggested instead that they swim to the boat. It was not far to go, swimmers would be less visible, and he knew that Moustafa and his navy seals were much better swimmers than even he. Another couple hours passed well into the night until a few deck lights were extinguished and activity on the buoy tender stilled altogether. Dressed in military black wetsuits and each armed with a knife and a handgun, they waded quickly and silently out into the deeper water and began their silent approach to the *Greifen 4*. The confidence and pride of the Egyptian navy seals could be seen on every face as they noted the willingness and skill of their own vice admiral to take part in the operation.

Within fifteen minutes, they had arrived undetected at a dangling rope ladder on the starboard side of the boat. The main deck was only about ten feet above water line, so it was an easy climb to slip over the rail and onto the deck. Brad was first over the rail and onto the work deck, and he took refuge behind a large buoy crane. As the second man slipped over the rail, he was suddenly spotted by a member of the crew who was patrolling that side of the deck. Weapon in hand, the muscular crew member rushed toward what he thought was a single intruder. For an instant, the deck guard was distracted as he caught sight over the rail of the oncoming boarders. In that same instant, Brad was upon him with all the advantage of surprise. Brad struck the crew member with a solid right elbow directly to the soft left temple of his head. The crew member crumpled unconscious to the deck with his automatic weapon lying beside him. Brad picked up the weapon and motioned to the rest of the team to slip over the rail onto the deck. Instinctively, Brad tied the unconscious man's hands together with a short piece of nylon rope he found lying on the deck.

Once the boarding team was aboard, they proceeded swiftly according to plan. Brad, Moustafa, and one other team member headed for the operation center on the bridge, where they suspected the only crewmembers still on watch would be located. Two others proceeded in a clockwise direction around the deck, and the final two went counterclockwise to clear any resistance. When the deck was confirmed clear, the team moved silently down to the berthing areas, catching a majority of the crew defenseless in their bunks. Once the entire crew had been subdued, the plan was to inspect the cargo, searching for any gold or artifacts they might find. Brad and Moustafa entered the operation center and took the captain and a crewmember by surprise.

Brad, still holding the automatic rifle, shouted to the captain, "Get down on the deck! Face down now!"

Moustafa, for his part, recited the Egyptian maritime arresting laws and proceeded to restrain the captain with plastic wire cuffs. "Now on your feet!" Moustafa ordered as he pulled the graying sea captain up from his kneeling position.

The captain complied immediately, ordering his crew to offer no resistance. Then he objected vehemently to the boarding, calling the boarding party pirates. He insisted that he and his crew were operating under contract with the Egyptian government and any opposition would be in violation of international law. Brad secretly hoped they could quickly find evidence of criminal activity to justify the authority they had been given for this boarding. The last thing he needed was to spark an international incident that could also prove embarrassing to Moustafa and his men.

The boarding team moved deftly in the darkness and began a total space accountability search of the vessel. The crew members were searched for weapons and then ordered to sit in a central area on deck while the cargo search was carried out above and below deck. This turned out to be a lengthy and tedious operation because the vessel had so many compartments that had to be unlocked and inspected. After at least an hour of diligent searching, the boarding party still had found no evidence of treasure or artifacts. Mahmoud, seated on the deck with the other crewmembers, was breathing a sigh of relief that his men had actually been unsuccessful so far in locating the treasure at the designated coordinates.

Brad was asking the technicians on board about the nature and function of the underwater scanning equipment, and Moustafa was just about to call off the entire boarding operation when one of his men entered the operation center with shocking news. The boarding party members had pried open a wooden crate in the hold; and inside was a human body, fully clothed, with two bullet holes in the head. The body, they said, could not have been dead for more than a day.

That definitely changed matters. Moustafa ordered one of his men to radio ashore for a navy vessel to join their boarding party and to escort the captain and crew to headquarters for interrogation. Then he and Brad turned to go inspect the body in the hold. As they turned to leave the operation center, Brad suddenly spotted a familiar piece of paper.

"Moustafa, look at this!" Brad shouted.

There on a desk beside a computer terminal was a copy of Professor Romiel's map of the Karnak Temple area.

"This is a page from the professor's journal! This proves their involvement. And look here! A line has been drawn from Karnak Temple directly to this point on the Nile."

CHAPTER

60

LATER THAT EVENING, WHEN BRAD and Moustafa were safely back at the officers' head-quarters with crew members in custody, Brad shared the events of the boarding with Allison and Sarah as well as with Billy and Antonio, who had by now nearly recovered from their ordeal earlier in the day. Brad also knew he was overdue in reporting to Foley. After a late dinner, he retired to his room, retrieved his satellite telephone from his room, and proceeded to dial up Foley in New York.

"Foley, I wish you could have been here for the excitement. We boarded their research vessel, the *Greifen 4*, earlier tonight. We found Professor Romiel's map on board, so we have proof that they were involved in the conspiracy. They could only have obtained that map from their aborted kidnapping of Billy and Antonio."

"Whoa!" Foley interrupted. "What kidnapping? What's been going on there?"

"Well, I would have called you earlier, but I couldn't take a chance that they are intercepting these calls. I didn't want to compromise our boarding mission. Some officials from the ministry of the interior met Billy and Antonio on their arrival at the Luxor airport. They then drugged them and took them hostage. It was only because of Moustafa's quick action that they are alive and with us now. Anyway, it turns out that the body we found was that of the deputy minister of the interior, Hamid Marzouk, on board the *Greifen 4*. Billy identified him as one who was involved in the kidnapping. He had two bullet holes in his head. None of the weapons confiscated on board the *Greifen 4* were of the same caliber. Tomorrow, Moustafa and the Egyptian authorities are obtaining a court-ordered lockdown and search of the local offices of the ministry of the interior to find additional evidence or even a matching weapon."

"Great! It sounds like the bad guys are going down fast! Did you find the treasure on board the *Greifen 4*?" Foley asked.

"No. That's the greatest puzzle," Brad responded. "We thought the treasure would be located at the bottom of the Nile at the coordinates marked by Professor Romiel; but apparently we were mistaken. We even found empty compartments inside the steel buoys on deck where they had hidden some artifacts for smuggling but no real treasures."

"What do you mean? You're kidding, right?" Foley interrupted with surprise.

"No, man, I'm really not. It turns out that prior to our boarding effort, the *Greifen 4* had actually scanned the entire floor of the Nile at the designated location to a depth of about fifteen feet below the riverbed. They have some incredible river bottom scans from Luxor all the way to Karnak, and it seems clear that they found nothing but very small quantities of scattered metallic debris. Perhaps the entire existence of a buried Nile treasure is just a myth," Brad said, pausing to contain the disappointment in his voice. He continued with the sad realization, "It seems that we have been on a wild goose chase."

The disbelief and disappointment in Foley's voice was more than Brad could stand. It was clear in those rare moments when his friend was at a loss for words that the worst feelings had just taken hold. Brad tried to change the subject.

"Foley, we have a meeting tomorrow with the secretary of antiquities, who is a renowned authority on Egyptian history. Perhaps he can shed some light on this matter. Meanwhile, what's been happening with Nigel and with the police investigation of the hedge fund manager?"

"Nigel is out of intensive care but still in the hospital. He's already chafing at the bit to get back to work here in his office. He'll be happy for any news from you. As far as the police investigation goes, the FBI is being tight-lipped about their progress. Agent Lindstrom revealed that they now have phone records indicating a connection between the hedge fund manager, Dmitri Karlov; and the deputy museum curator, Daniel Gunther. The FBI cannot divulge any wiretapping activity, but I would assume they are actively recording. The fact that phone calls have been made does not really prove anything. They need substantive conversation data. My guess is that they are getting a lot more than they will say," Foley concluded.

"Funny you should mention Gunther," Brad said. "Who do you suppose showed up in Luxor this week? Our person of interest: Dr. Daniel Gunther. He told Allison and Sarah he was here on museum business. But I suspect his timing and motives go far beyond that."

"Gunther in Luxor! I'd better call Agent Lindstrom right away. He seemed concerned about Gunther's location last time we talked. I'll call him right after our conversation, and I'll go personally to share developments with Nigel at the hospital."

With that, they terminated their conversation, and Brad rejoined the others in the officer's lounge. The group manifested a general feeling of relief at all they had managed to survive to this point, mingled with a pervasive mood of disappointment that the treasure was not located where all the evidence of Professor Romiel's journal had led them to believe.

Billy expressed the greatest disappointment. "I'm sorry, guys," he said apologetically. "I was certain the obelisk measurements and

Professor Romiel's map all led to the Nile location in line with the obelisks as marked on the map. It made perfect sense that the line of bearing from the obelisks was the right navigational marker. Maybe there really is no treasure, or maybe it was already recovered centuries ago."

"I cannot believe that!" Allison objected loudly. "There's no way my father died for nothing. We must just keep looking. No doubt we've just misinterpreted the information on the map."

No one really wanted to discuss the matter any further at that point. With glum looks and complete exhaustion, it was decided that disappointing conversation was not the best fare late in the evening. They all retired with hope of a fresh perspective in the morning.

CHAPTER

61

THAT SUMMER MORNING IN LUXOR was spectacular: blue skies, cool breeze, and the music of birds singing joyfully on their migratory path along the riverbanks. It would have been easy to forget the whole matter that had brought them on this arduous journey if it had not been for the loss of Professor Romiel and for the attempts on their lives. Some members of the team were thinking that perhaps they should just join some tour group and wander around Luxor and Karnak for a few days and then fly back to New York. All they had before them was the morning meeting with the secretary of antiquities. And then there was the promise of positive results from the police probe that was ongoing at the offices of the ministry of the interior to find the weapon that had been used to murder Hamid Marzouk. The authorities had moved in, and the schemes of these international smugglers were clearly at an end.

The meeting with the secretary of antiquities was called in the conference room at the officer's headquarters at 10:00 a.m. It was a comfortable room that seated about twenty people around a large, rounded-yet-rectangular conference table with firm, leather chairs. Brad was not sure the precise direction the meeting would take, so he decided wisely to let the secretary ask the questions. Billy could address the details on treasure location, and he himself would speak to the criminal aspects of their opposition.

At precisely 10:00 a.m., the secretary general, Dr. Labib Housny, made his entry along with several officials in his entourage. Everyone in the room stood to welcome these officials. That was when the team received their first shock of the morning. There walking side by side with the secretary of antiquities was none other than Dr. Daniel Gunther, deputy curator of the American Museum of Natural History. While everyone was still standing, Moustafa politely welcomed the secretary and introduced the American team: Brad, Allison, Sarah, and Billy. Dr. Housny introduced the members of his staff that had accompanied him and then motioned for everyone to be seated.

"Ladies and gentlemen," he said soberly, "I have called this urgent meeting to get to the bottom of some serious rumors that have come to my attention. Specifically, I have been told that Professor Donald Romiel, an old friend and colleague of mine, has managed to locate a large cache of ancient Egyptian gold buried during the Akhenaten period of our long and glorious history. Furthermore, I have been told of an international conspiracy to smuggle the gold and transport it out of country. Sadly, this conspiracy has already claimed the life of my dear colleague. Deepest condolences to his daughter, Allison, who is here with us today."

He paused and nodded his head in Allison's direction before continuing, "My other concern is that we locate this buried treasure and transport it for safekeeping at the earliest possible moment. Our sincere gratitude is extended to those foreign experts with us today who have brought this matter to our attention and who are assisting us in the ongoing search. Vice Admiral El-Ezaby has graciously provided these facilities and has assembled these experts for this meeting. Admiral El-Ezaby, would you kindly introduce the American team leader who can tell us the background and current status of this matter?"

"Yes, sir," Moustafa proceeded. "Mr. Bradford Beck is a distinguished former American Coast Guard officer and a friend with whom I studied at the US Coast Guard Academy. He is also a close friend of Professor Romiel. Professor Romiel tried to contact him in New York to seek his help prior to his murder. Brad contacted me last week with some very important concerns that have led so far to the arrest of twelve people and a deeper investigation into illegal activities by a foreign corporation. He can provide more information about what has been happening. Brad."

Brad stood and, with some reservation, sensing all was not right having Dr. Gunther present at the meeting, began to speak. "Your Excellency, we became aware of this conspiracy only three weeks ago. At that time, Professor Romiel entrusted us with his research journal and details of the discovery and location of the treasure. His journal was subsequently stolen from us, except we were able to preserve a few pages of maps and details of several obelisks Professor Romiel had been studying. In his journal, we found reference to a research vessel that was carrying out suspicious activities in the Nile River in the region opposite Karnak Temple. Last night, we conducted a boarding on that same vessel. On board, we found the body of a recently murdered official of the Egyptian ministry of the interior. We also found a copy of one of the maps from Professor Romiel's journal. Although there were some ancient artifacts located, we found no cache of treasure on board the vessel. We believe the deep-water probing equipment we found was capable of treasure scanning beneath the river bottom and was far more sophisticated in nature than would ever be necessary for the installation of navigational buoys on the Nile for which the vessel had been contracted. We also discovered that some of the large buoys had false bottom compartments that were used to store and hoist artifacts ashore as part of their smuggling activity, which might have been ongoing for months.

"In the course of our work here in Egypt, there have been several attempts on the lives of members of our team. It is our belief that these international thugs will stop at nothing to confiscate this treasure. However, it is also our belief that they have been unsuccessful in locating the treasure so far. Unfortunately, our own attempts to locate the treasure have also been unsuccessful. One of our team members, Mr. William Heckman, a graduate student of ancient history at New York University, has been retracing Professor Romiel's research on ancient Egyptian obelisks. He has made substantial progress in understanding the professor's research, and this is a good time for him to share what he has learned. Billy."

"Yes. Thank you." Billy cleared his throat and began after some hesitation. "First of all, I want to say that this has been the most dangerous adventure I have ever been on in my life. Not that I'm a security freak or something, but this information really should only be shared with those who have a need to know. I am not sure that every person in this room has that need to know. Your Excellency, Secretary Housny, may I respectfully ask that everyone be dismissed from the room for this session except you, Vice Admiral El-Ezaby, and the members of our American team?"

"I can assure you, Mr. Heckman," the secretary objected, "there is no one here present who is not intimately acquainted with the historical details of Professor Romiel's research. I am confident that it is all right for you to proceed."

Brad intervened, "Yes, Billy. I think you can go ahead and share what you have learned. These details are mostly already known by the opposition, and they will soon be general knowledge. The more people who know about the treasure, the harder it will be for the thieves to steal it."

"Well, okay." Billy collected his thoughts and continued. "We found references in Professor Romiel's journal to the *keys of electrum*, and we thought this expression was the key to unlocking the secret of the location of the treasure. Electrum, we know, is an alloy of silver and gold that was used to cover the obelisks. That fact, coupled with all the measurements of obelisks in the professor's journal and reference to the Opet Festival, led us to believe that certain obelisks were used to mark the location of the treasure when it was secretly buried in the Nile River at the time of the Opet Festival during the reign of Pharaoh Akhenaten. The question then became, 'Which obelisks?' That was no doubt a question that preoccupied Professor Romiel in his research.

"We reasoned that the obelisks had to be from among those that were prominently placed in the vicinity of Karnak Temple during the reign of Pharaoh Akhenaten. That narrows the field to five obelisks: the pair that were placed there by Thutmose I; the larger pair placed by his daughter, Queen Hatchepsut; and the largest single obelisk placed by her coregent and younger ward, Thutmose III, that is now located in Rome. Some historians believe Thutmose III was the son of Hatchepsut's deceased husband, Thutmose II, by another woman. Anyway, that might explain the animosity between Hatchepsut and Thutmose III and why he later defaced many of her inscriptions at the temple and replaced them with his own when he came into power."

"Billy, Dr. Housny doesn't need a history lesson! Could you please get to the part about the location of the treasure?" Brad interrupted impatiently.

"Actually, history is very important to context," Dr. Housny replied. "You see many people don't realize that Akhenaten marked the beginning of the economic decline of Ancient Egypt. It was as if a sudden economic catastrophe had occurred—one that many scholars have simply blamed on the heretic pharaoh being extremely wasteful and foolish. But it makes much more sense for such a great amount of wealth to have been lost or stolen."

"Yes, well, we found a map of the Karnak Temple complex in Professor Romiel's journal," Billy continued. "On it, he had traced a thin line from the site of the foundation of the giant obelisk of

Thutmose III that has been removed to Rome, westward through one of the obelisks of Hatchepsut and continuing westward out into the Nile. That was also along the route of the Opet Festival. Professor Romiel's measurements suggest that he was also concerned with the height of the obelisks in relation to the temple pylons in order to establish the range of the drop site. Clearly, this became a very complex problem because the height of the horizon established by the temple pylons has changed throughout history due to successive additions to the temple. Furthermore, the depth of the Nile varied from dry season to flood stage. And the ancient priests used many nilometer structures along the Nile to record and predict river depth changes in the various seasons."

"Exactly," Brad interrupted. "And as any navigator knows, the height-of-eye measurement is a critical factor in establishing range of visibility. So, basically, we have a very good line of bearing from a range created by the obelisks in Karnak; but the distance from the temple is almost impossible to determine now that obelisks are missing or obstructed by walls that weren't there at the time of Akhenaten. Plus, even if we assumed as correctly as we could that the Opet season was during the time of the Nile flooding, we can hardly calculate how high the navigator's eye was relative to the pylons and the *akhet* that the obelisks had to clear to give him lateral fix on his line of bearing."

"Yes," Billy continued. "Unfortunately, also, we have recently learned that all the probes of the research vessel, *Greifen 4*, revealed no treasure buried anywhere in the Nile along the axis extended from the Karnak temple."

At that point, Dr. Daniel Gunther, who had been silent until then, stood up. "It turns out that I was right all along. I advised Professor Romiel repeatedly that his dream of finding buried treasure was just a childhood fantasy. I think this whole discussion has been a pointless waste of time."

The secretary of antiquities motioned to Gunther to relax and be seated. "I think we are all forgetting one important detail," he said with an unusually large smile. "I believe our Professor Romiel was absolutely correct in his theory. We can still compute a better approximation of the lateral navigational fix you need, but I suspect it won't even be necessary."

Allison could not contain her joyful surprise. "What do you mean?"

Secretary Housny turned and looked at Allison's hopeful expression, "My dear, in several digs that I have authorized over the years around Karnak, we have found some very unusual artifacts. Ah, well, let me say it like this."

Pausing briefly, the secretary's smile widened even more; and a certain air of confidence swept over the group.

"You see, my friends, over millennia, the course of the Nile River has shifted as much as three hundred meters to the west of where it was in the eighteenth dynasty during the time of Pharaoh Akhenaten. The river's path used to come much closer to the great outer walls of the Great Karnak. Subsequently, later dynasties built westward with the additional land provided. This means that if this treasure was buried in the Nile at those coordinates during Akhenaten's reign, it is now located completely under dry land, even possibly under portions of the more current structures of Karnak."

At those words, several gasps were heard and expressions of shock became visible on the faces of nearly everyone present. At this point, the secretary congratulated the team and continued, "I believe we owe a great debt of gratitude to Professor Romiel and his American friends for this discovery. I am ordering an immediate project of dry-land exploration along the coordinates identified by Professor Romiel. If all goes as I expect, we are on the verge of unearthing one of the greatest buried treasures of all time."

In sharp contrast to the smiling faces in the room, Gunther was motionless with a pained look on his face as if he had suddenly caught a terrible illness.

CHAPTER

62

ALL THAT MORNING, IN ANOTHER part of the city of Luxor, a search had been ongoing for the weapon that had been used to murder Hamid Marzouk. As requested by Vice Admiral El-Ezaby, a local magistrate had ordered the search of the offices of the ministry of the interior. Two minibuses loaded with members of the local constabulary of police had parked in front of those offices, and uniformed policemen were blocking entry and exit from the building. Other police had been dispatched to every floor of the building and were rifling through the personal effects, drawers, and files found in every room in the building. Every person was carefully searched.

They had been less than forty-five minutes into the search when one of the officers demanded the key and opened a desk drawer belonging to Director Mohsen Al-Kateeb. There, to everyone's astonishment, was a handgun matching the caliber of the weapon that had been used to murder Hamid Marzouk. It also became quickly apparent that the gun was missing exactly two rounds from a full load.

"Director Al-Kateeb, I'm afraid you must accompany us to police headquarters to explain the presence of this weapon," the officer said.

There was no such thing as Miranda rights, so the director was quickly escorted out of the building and into one of the minibuses without further adieu. The weapon was delivered to ballistics experts who had been brought in to compare it with bullets taken from the body of the murder victim. It all happened very quickly; and by early afternoon, it was established that this was indeed the murder weapon.

Director Al-Kateeb was perspiring freely in one of the soundproof police interrogation rooms. All appearances of his usual placid demeanor were now absent. What a terrible turn events had taken for him in the past twenty-four hours! He knew well that his interrogators had methods of extracting any information they wished. He knew also that, because he was a well-known official, it was unlikely that he would be executed without a trial. Beyond that, he knew that he had information that they wanted. Perhaps he could strike a deal. He had been made to sit silent and alone for more than an hour as part of the softening-up process. Occasionally, he could hear faint sounds of screams and the dull thuds of fist blows that, unknown to him, were in fact recordings that came into his room via a loud-speaker system.

When an interrogator finally appeared, Al-Kateeb begged to be taken to his commanding officer. "I have information of national importance that can only be divulged at the highest level," Al-Kateeb insisted.

As it happened, Commander Hariry had been watching and listening the whole time in an adjacent observation room. He had met the director before and might even have called him an acquaintance, but he was never very fond of him. Now he was more than eager for the director to spill his guts about the entire matter of the shooting. A few minutes later, he entered the interrogation room alone, with no one observing.

"What a shocking business this is, Mohsen! To think that a high-ranking government official like yourself would become guilty of murder! Whatever made you do such a thing?" the commander demanded.

"Look here," the director ventured forth cautiously. "Nothing has yet been established about what I have done or have not done. However, I have some important information that is for your ears only. Can you assure me that this conversation is confidential?"

"We are alone, and no one is listening," the commander said.

"The fact of the matter is this: I am in a position to be very helpful to you and to your career. What is the monthly government salary of a police commander? Five hundred Egyptian pounds (about ninety dollars US)? What if I could guarantee you a salary that is ten times as much, even twenty times? And you could continue in your present position without anyone knowing of your secondary assignment. Would you be interested?"

Of course, Director Al-Kateeb knew exactly what the salary of Commander Hariry was. He made it his business to know such things.

"That depends on what I would have to do for that salary," the commander replied.

Hariry was no fool. He knew exactly what was happening, and he had been down this path before. He also knew that Al-Kateeb was vulnerable and it might be possible to extort money from him without compromising his own position.

"The requirements would be simple," Al-Kateeb said eagerly. "All you would have to do is assist with official business from time to time. For example, I swear I have no idea how that gun came to be found in my desk drawer. But you can easily understand how this matter could become a source of embarrassment for the ministry of the interior. It is bad enough that one of our top deputies has been murdered, but it is unthinkable that accusations might be made within the ministry itself. Of course, we all want justice to be done. Our ministry could even assist you in locating the perpetrator of the crime."

"Perhaps some such arrangement could be made," the commander replied, "especially if you could provide an initial earnest deposit of the salary immediately. You understand that there are risks to such arrangements, and some sort of advance deposit would ensure that your commitment would not be forgotten easily."

"Of course! I would not have it any other way," Al-Kateeb smiled the wry smile of someone who was back on familiar ground. "Did you have a particular sum in mind?" he asked.

"Well, frankly the sum of two hundred thousand Egyptian pounds flashed through my mind just now. My car has been giving me trouble lately, and that would enable me to make some much-needed transportation improvements. It would also be an expression of good will on your part that could not be misinterpreted. Of course, we will also need to discuss subsequent salary arrangements."

Al-Kateeb blinked momentarily. His original discomfort level was beginning to return. It was clear to him that Hariry was not a person to be underestimated. He found it distasteful to enter into these discussions with no point of leverage, and he would have no leverage until after Hariry had accepted the money. No doubt Hariry would eventually have to be eliminated; but for the present, Al-Kateeb needed a way out of his dilemma.

"I like a man who knows how to take advantage of opportunities," Al-Kateeb said. "I could envision a chain of circumstances starting with my release, followed by the disappearance of the gun, and culminating in your becoming a very wealthy man. I believe I could find the required initial deposit by this time tomorrow afternoon. Of course, your continuing assistance would be needed to remove all suspicion from the ministry of interior. Then there is the matter of the release of the captain and crew of the research vessel. I could argue before my superiors that such assistance would be worth a salary of at least five thousand pounds per month."

"I can release you today with no questions asked," the commander said. "But the disappearance of evidence and the release of other prisoners is a far more difficult matter to arrange. There will be other mouths to feed, if you understand my meaning. The initial deposit would need to be doubled to four hundred thousand LE."

"I understand perfectly," Al-Kateeb replied. "Let's arrange settlement for tomorrow afternoon. We will pay half tomorrow and half when the evidence disappears."

The two men nodded and shook hands, and the director gathered up his crumpled suit coat and left the building anxiously by the front door.

For his part, the commander stroked his black moustache pensively and wondered who else was about to fall into his carefully laid trap.

CHAPTER

63

FOLLOWING THE ANNOUNCEMENT THAT the course of the Nile had shifted over time, the secretary of antiquities lost no time in ordering the best possible ground-penetrating radar scans between the temple and the present bank of the Nile along the line the professor had traced on his map. The radar skid that carried such sophisticated equipment for the probe was already present in the area and with great enthusiasm was brought quickly to the western edge of Karnak to begin the search.

Gunther's own disappointment and disgust had been evident on his face as he excused himself from the meeting. He had tried to argue vehemently that there was no treasure and that the secretary was only wasting time and resources by continuing this search. His arguments fell on deaf ears and ones far more knowledgeable than his. Now Gunther had to report the terrible developments to his sponsor. His first act, however, was to return to the offices of the ministry of the interior. Given what he had learned at the meeting that morning, he fully expected that Director Al-Kateeb would be in full panic mode.

Gunther was surprised to see that Director Al-Kateeb seemed pleased to see him.

"Did your meeting with the secretary of antiquities this morning go well?" Al-Kateeb enquired. "I was happy to get you that invitation on short notice," he reminded Gunther.

"Not well at all," Gunther replied bitterly. "I learned that they boarded our research vessel last night and that they found the body of Hamid Marzouk on board the vessel. How could you be so stupid, Mohsen? You have implicated our entire research operation in murder."

"The situation is not as dire as you imagine, Dr. Gunther," Al-Kateeb responded nervously. "While you were in the meeting, I visited police headquarters and made arrangements for them to drop the entire inquiry."

"Don't tell me you bribed another official," Gunther blurted out angrily. "How much is this one going to cost us?"

"Actually, more than one official was involved. This one will cost us four hundred thousand LE, but that is a small price to pay to keep the police from meddling in our business. However, I will need the money immediately, no later than tomorrow morning."

This was not at all what Gunther wanted to hear. How was he going to break the news to the sponsor that the treasure was slipping away? And now, on top of that, he must explain the bribery money. For a moment, he wished he was safely back within the confines of his New York museum office and that he had never consented to be party to this uncertain business. He vaguely remembered some childhood admonition that the love of money was the root of all evil.

He had not really wanted to order his security team associates from Navigational Technologies International to take the life of Professor Romiel. They had intercepted Romiel on his departure from Kennedy Airport, and the goal was just to talk with him and to convince him of the wisdom of joining their conspiracy. Because he would not listen, they had taken him to Central Park and murdered him. It was decided that his presence near the obelisk could be explained as a result of his professional interests and random death by mugging would not be unusual in that place. The simple fact was that Gunther and the museum needed the money.

Gunther sighed deeply and said, "Very well. I will have the money wired into your account overnight. But there must be nothing to connect us to any wrongdoing. As soon as the captain and crew of the *Greifen 4* are returned to the vessel, let them move downriver and resume the legitimate contracted mapping operations. I need to return to New York as soon as possible."

CHAPTER

64

THAT EVENING, BRAD COULD HARD-
ly wait to telephone Foley about the developments
of the day. The principal news was that the treasure
was likely located underground on dry land and not
beneath the Nile, as they had originally believed.
With this discovery, and given the fact that the Egyptian government was now taking full responsibility for the search, Brad saw
no reason for their continued stay in Egypt. There were still unanswered questions about Professor Romiel's murder, but he believed
those answers could just as easily be uncovered at home. And he
knew he could trust Moustafa to wrap up loose ends in Egypt.

Foley also seemed overjoyed at the prospect of the return of the
team members to New York and the opportunity for him to resume
his daily routine. The only new development regarding the police
inquiry that Foley could report was the fact that the FBI seemed
eager to invite Gunther in for questioning at the first opportunity.

That same evening, before turning in, Brad conferred with the
team members and the pilot; it was agreed that Brad and Allison
would return the following day to New York with the pilot, Antonio,
and Nigel's corporate jet. Given their archeological interests, Billy
and Sarah would stay on to follow progress in the search for the
treasure. It was decided that Kosar provided more than enough

protection for them now that the news of the treasure had become public information.

The following morning, Brad broke the news to Moustafa over breakfast.

"I hate to see you leave before we actually unearth the treasure and round up the last of the criminals," Moustafa said. "Also, I'm sure my government will want to express its gratitude to you officially. If the treasure is located in accordance with Professor Romiel's research, it will be a massive boost to our economy and to the integrity of the historical record. I can imagine also that our tourism industry will enjoy a new explosion of interest."

"We can stay in touch by telephone," Brad replied. "Billy and Sarah will be here to witness the treasure recovery. And I will be leaving our satellite telephone with Billy. You understand that just as you are arresting members of the conspiracy here in Egypt, there is work to be done in America to find those who are responsible there. Finding the treasure was only part of our objective. We wanted first of all to find and prosecute those responsible for Professor Romiel's murder. Thanks to your help, we might also have prevented an international power grab of epic proportions. I'll know more after I get back to New York and confer with Foley and with the FBI."

"The truth is, my friend," Moustafa continued, "we do not actually have proof yet that there was a conspiracy to steal the gold. We have a dead body and a map found on board the research vessel. Yesterday, we found the actual murder weapon in one of the offices of the ministry of the interior. If all goes well, we can establish that certain persons were guilty of kidnapping and murder. Conspiracy to loot a national treasure will require a confession. Of course, I do not believe that such a confession will be difficult to obtain. It will also help if we find the treasure and can establish that they knew of its existence beforehand."

With that, Moustafa smiled a knowing smile and shook Brad's hand. Brad had just enough time to accompany Allison, Sarah, and

Billy, on their own private tour of Karnak Temple and the Valley of the Kings before their flight later in the day. The minister of antiquities had insisted on guiding them personally through some of the most memorable monuments in the history of civilization. Brad, for his part, was looking forward to the tour and to the long flight back with Allison. Allison was especially eager for the tour and for Brad to share in the experience of some of her fondest childhood memories. Antonio and their pilot were busy making arrangements for their flight home.

CHAPTER 65

THAT SAME MORNING, GUNTHER boarded the first available commercial flight connecting to New York. Although his visits to Egypt were normally a source of personal inspiration and invigoration, today he was in the depths of depression. He considered his options. There was no way he could be connected to the murder of Hamid Marzouk. Furthermore, his involvement in the murder of Romiel and the conspiracy to steal Egyptian gold was beyond detection. His biggest and only worry now was the reaction of his sponsor, Dmitri Karlov, to the news that the treasure was lost.

Karlov, once angered, was capable of terrible reprisals. At the very least, Gunther could lose the significant largess of this sponsor. Economic ruin, professional humiliation, and even assassination were not out of the question. He would have to handle this communication with the utmost of sensitivity. He needed to provide himself with cover. He knew what he had to do.

It was late in the evening when his final connecting flight touched down at JFK International Airport. Gunther took a taxi directly to the museum. He had keys that would allow him to enter the building and his office. The security guards knew that it was often his practice to work late into the evening in his office. Once he was safely back in his chair behind his desk, he took out a piece of paper and began to list the key points of his conversation. Then he turned on his message recorder and dialed the personal number of Dmitri Karlov.

"Dmitri, it's Gunther. I just got back from Egypt and knew I had to contact you at the earliest possible moment to report what has happened."

"Gunther, you know I don't do business on the phone," Karlov objected.

"Yes, but because you have so much invested in the Egyptian gold recovery project, I knew that you had to know immediately," Gunther responded.

"Tell me quickly but be brief and be discreet."

"Yesterday, we learned that the course of the Nile has shifted over time so the treasure is actually located under dry land and not under water. The Egyptian government is now fully aware of the existence of the treasure. The minister of antiquities is there in Luxor today with a team of archeologists involved in unearthing the treasure. We have lost the gold. All our efforts at secrecy were futile, and your order to eliminate Professor Romiel was in vain. It only bought you a little time."

There was a long, silent pause. Gunther could hear only heavy breathing at the other end of the line. Then, suddenly, there was a clicking sound. Gunther hung up the phone and played back the recording. He was pleased that their conversation had covered all of the salient points. He removed the recording tape, inserted it into an envelope on which he had written the word *insurance*, and placed it in his office safe. Then he replaced a blank tape in his recording machine. Finally, he turned off his office light, closed the door, and headed for his apartment for a much-needed rest after his long journey.

What he did not realize was the fact that his was not the only recording that had been made of that conversation.

CHAPTER

66

BRAD AND ALLISON WAVED FARE-
well to Billy and Sarah and then climbed the ramp
into Nigel's corporate jet. They had enjoyed a memorable tour of Karnak and the Valley of the Kings, but
they were eager to return home at last. They could see
that Antonio had already fastened his seat belt and was preparing
for a long nap. Their luggage had been stowed, and the pilot had
filed their flight plan. A moment later, they were cleared for takeoff.

As they watched the Karnak Temple complex recede to the
south and the thin ribbon of the Nile unfold to the north, they
became pensive.

"It looks like your father's wishes have been fulfilled," Brad
reflected, turning to Allison beside him. "The conspirators did not
get the gold; and when they do find it, it will go to the Egyptian
people, to whom it ultimately belongs."

"Yes. He would have been pleased," Allison replied. "His
work was not in vain. And Billy and Sarah will likely get credit
for groundbreaking research in their chosen fields of history and
archeology. I can predict that their graduate research papers will
easily propel them to the top of their professions."

Brad looked back at Antonio asleep in his seat. "Even Antonio
there had quite an adventure. Billy tells me that, following their

exploits in Rome, Antonio has become a local legend among the members of his family. And the police arrested members of the local syndicate that attacked them. It turns out that they were running a fencing operation with stolen artifacts taken from Egypt. They were to become the destination for the treasure the conspirators were hoping to steal."

Both smiled a reflective smile of satisfaction; then Brad asked, "And you, Allison? What have you taken away from this experience?"

"Well, as we said, if they find the treasure where my father said it was located, there is immense satisfaction in knowing his work was not in vain. I only wish his murderers could be brought to justice. Gunther, for example. He certainly knows a lot more than he is saying. I hope the police can get to the bottom of this. To answer your question by using the analogy of Joseph as we discussed on the Nile cruise, I am just at the point where Joseph has been released from prison and has been given a revelation to save the world and has been promoted to prominence in Egypt. I still do not see the whole picture. For example, I am not at the point where his brothers were brought to justice and he was reconciled to them." She sighed. "What about you? What are you taking from this experience?"

Brad thought for a long time before responding, "For one thing, my faith has grown through what has happened. I mean, I used to believe the events of life happen to us at random. Your father's death, for example. I used to explain such things as incredibly bad luck. He just happened to be in the wrong place at the wrong time. Now I am not so sure that there is such a thing as luck. A lot of good has come from this. For me, the best thing has been the few weeks I spent with you. Do you suppose your father knew that my involvement in this case would bring us together?"

Allison shrugged then smiled. "Anything is possible," she replied coyly. Then she settled back in her seat for the long flight ahead, finally feeling completely at ease. It was an answer to prayer.

She knew she had feelings for the handsome man next to her, but now she could see Brad's faith was genuinely growing, and that was very attractive to her.

CHAPTER
67

FTER A LONG REFUELING STOP
in London, their pilot radioed ahead the time
of their early morning arrival in New York. To
their great surprise, there to greet them at the La
Guardia corporate hangar in Nigel's limousine
were Foley and Nigel. Nigel had been released from the hospital
the night before, and he was able to move around with the help of
the wheelchair they had stowed in the back of the limo. Smiles and
hugs went all around, and Brad and Allison, along with Antonio,
joined them in the limo for the return trip to Nigel's estate.

"Nigel, to see you up and about is the very best news we could
possibly receive," Brad said warmly.

Nigel responded, "You will be happy to know that we have
some even better news. Billy called early this morning to report
that they located the treasure exactly along the line of bearing
Professor Romiel said it was located. The Egyptian government
will be awarding their highest civilian award to Professor Romiel
posthumously. They have asked if Allison would return again to
Egypt at your convenience to receive the medal from their president on your father's behalf. You will also be happy to know that
the southern regional director of the ministry of the interior has
been arrested for murder and for attempting to bribe a police of-

ficer. And that's not all. A large wire transfer of money to Luxor has linked Dr. Daniel Gunther to the murder and to the conspiracy to defraud the Egyptian government. Late last night, the police arrested Gunther at his apartment. It seems he has also been implicated in the murder of your father, Allison. They have arrested him along with Dmitri Karlov, Senator Charles Lodge, and Mark Wyatt on charges of murder, attempted murder, conspiracy, and all those RICO and fraud charges."

"That's truly awesome news!" Allison responded tearfully. "My father would be so thankful that justice has been served and people like you all cared enough to risk your lives to see it through. It's only a pity, Nigel, that you have gone to so much trouble to help us and that you have not been compensated for all your expense."

"Oh. Thanks, Allison. But please don't worry about that," Nigel said somewhat sheepishly. "I actually have something to tell you, and I guess this is as good a time as any to tell you all. Before the car bombing and my trip to the hospital, I opened a massive leveraged short position on Navigational Technologies International, Karlov's front company. That position has done very well. And now, thanks to Karlov's arrest and NTI's demise, that position has skyrocketed."

"What do you mean your short position has skyrocketed?" Allison asked.

"Well, let me put it another way, Allison," Nigel replied. "I bet a lot of money on the financial decline of Nav Tech and in return have made enough to easily recover all of your travel expenses. In fact, I even managed to garner a little reward for each of you sailors who participated in this ordeal. It's too early to be precise, but I can safely say each one of you is now richer by several million US dollars."

"No way!" Foley exclaimed in disbelief.

"Nigel, you are incredible!" Allison cheered. "Can we break the news together to Billy and Sarah? I don't want to miss their reactions! This is awesome!"

"Of course," Nigel replied. Then, with a wink and a smile at Brad and Allison, he said, "At the very least, Brad can finally afford to take a certain attractive young lady on a real date."